Praise for
Somewhere a River

"Mike Brown is a wonderful storyteller. In Somewhere a River *he weaves together the complex fabric of racial hatred, Alabama football, tragic mistakes, family rivalry, and romance. The story gains momentum with the development of each character, and becomes a page turner. I did not want this book to end!"*
—Bill Curry, former Georgia Tech student/athlete, NFL veteran, and collegiate head football coach

"An extraordinary story composed by an equally extraordinary author. Michael K. Brown's Somewhere a River *takes you on a bittersweet journey of redemption—an unforgettable trek of reconciliation in the finest of Southern traditions."*
—Jedwin Smith, author of **Our Brother's Keeper**

"…beautifully flawed characters who get lost on an emotional roller coaster in a poignant tale of lost love and a struggle for redemption."
—Fred Styles, veteran movie and television filmmaker including 2014 Sedona Film Festival winner **Wish You Well**

"With a perceptive eye and sensitive heart, Michael K. Brown recreates how a man's early years evolve into a river of discovery that reveals not only an individual's character but also that of a culture."
—Nancy Compton Williams, nationally and internationally published poet

"The story quickly pulled me in and wouldn't let go. Well-crafted and relevant reminder that everyone has a river of memories somewhere."
—JD Weeks, author of **Premocar-Made in Birmingham** and **Birmingham Then & Now**

SOMEWHERE
A RIVER

SOMEWHERE A RIVER

a novel

MICHAEL K. BROWN

DEEDS PUBLISHING | ATLANTA

Published by Deeds Publishing
Marietta, GA
www.deedspublishing.com

Cover photo by Bob Dilworth

Library of Congress Cataloging-in-Publications Data is available upon request.

ISBN 978-1-941165-37-9

Books are available in quantity for promotional or premium use. For information, write Deeds Publishing, PO Box 682212, Marietta, GA 30068 or info@deedspublishing.com.

Second Edition

10 9 8 7 6 5 4 3 2 1

ACKNOWLEDGMENTS

A lot of people helped me write this book, either directly through editing and critiquing, or indirectly through their support. At the top of the list is the Atlanta Writers Club which provides a platform for over 700 members to find an avenue to express themselves through the written word. George Weinstein, Valerie Connors, and Clay Ramsey have led the group in recent years and I can't thank them enough for their leadership.

My long-time writing partners, Barbara Connor and Mary Anna Bryan, have been most responsible for any success I have had in my writing journey and becoming published. They stood by me for many years, offering invaluable encouragement and mentoring. Currently, I am also a member of The AWC Collective, a wonderful group of writers who meet monthly to support and critique members' works in progress. Thanks to all of the talented writers of the Collective for their unwavering inspiration, good coffee, and great companionship, including those of our canine friends. I also want to thank Chuck Graham for his very insightful feedback and Mary Kirkland for her excellent proofreading of the manuscript.

My appreciation is also extended to Bob Babcock and the fine people at Deeds Publishing for their faith in the book and partnership in making it become a reality.

Of course, no one deserves more recognition than my wife, Judy. Writing a novel requires a lot of solitary time, isolated from the rest of the world. And often a writer's mind is preoccupied with those imaginary characters and places that live in our head.

So we are not always the best companions. But Judy points me in the right direction when I emerge from my fanciful retreat and step into the present. I don't say it enough but I can say it now; I love her.

In loving memory of my parents, Willette and Bill Brown, who were born in Alabama, lived their entire lives there, and now lie in eternal peace not far from the Black Warrior River.

1

Bill looked through the dusty window pane at children noisily running about the trailer-park playground and their innocent joy reminded him of the promise of youth. But beyond the playground he could see a bridge, a murky river, and hear a distant splash in a still night in Alabama. Thirty years had passed and the river was now more than a thousand miles away, yet the vision remained clear, haunting him with the memory of a night when that promise was lost.

He pulled the car onto the shoulder of the road and grabbed the bag from the floorboard beside him. Stepping into the quiet darkness around the river, he headed for the bridge in a daze. No one was in sight, but he felt the presence of a thousand eyes of judgment.

Halfway across the span he leaned over the edge of the rusty iron railing and peered down at the Black Warrior River glistening in the moonlight. He moved back a step and stared at the bag as though he could see inside, then looked around to make sure he was still alone. Even with the brick inside, the bag was light but it felt like an anchor in his hands. He let out a grunt and flung it as far as he could. It felt as if he were throwing a part of himself away as well.

A muffled splash broke the silence.

Returning to the car, he quickened his pace with each step. Gravel spit from the tires as he pulled off the shoulder and made a U-turn onto the blacktop. He gunned the accelerator and shifted through the gears with a guilty rush of adrenaline. The faster he drove, the further the bridge faded behind him until it disappeared completely.

Still, the vision of the bag lying on the floorboard beside him wouldn't disappear. He couldn't throw it away.

***

Even at midday it was dark and quiet inside the trailer with no lights or hum of the air conditioner. The electricity had been cut off days earlier. The brown swivel-rocker was his last friend. He hated to let it go, but there was no place for it and no place for him either.

In his solitude, the past oftentimes flashed through his mind like a kaleidoscope, still vivid in his memory as if it were yesterday. The crowd cheering wildly as he scored a touchdown and, afterward, kissing the smiling face of the prettiest girl he had ever seen. Billy Burdette, the pride of Warrior County, lived on in a dusty time capsule.

The memories always reminded him of his life's journey—from a boy with the world at his feet to man with the world on his back.

A voice behind him shook him from his reverie.

"I don't like doin' this, but I got no choice. You're over two months behind and I've got people who want to move in."

The property manager was tall and heavyset. The rim of reddish-white hair that wrapped around the base of his bald head merged into a scraggly beard and mustache. A pearl-handled pistol was strapped to the side of his hip.

"I don't blame you," Bill replied without taking his eyes from the window. "I'll be gone in an hour." He took a bill from his wallet and handed it to the manager. "Here's twenty bucks. Sorry, that's all I got right now."

"Keep it," the manager said. "I ain't gonna take your last dollar. Just be gone by the end of the day."

"Don't worry, I'm on my way. Sorry I got behind. I'll bring the money when I can."

The manager remained stolid and Bill figured he'd heard that line so many times his heart had become as thick and wiry as the wooly beard on his face. Bill's words carried the weight of good intentions, yet he knew he was just another of the wanderers who had come and gone over the years. Until recently, he had paid his rent on time for almost two years, always in cash. There was no lease, no checks, nothing to identify him. Just Bill.

Spying a pistol lying on a corner table, the manager suddenly became tense. "Don't do nothin' stupid." He looked at Bill with a warning look in his eyes. His right hand clutched the pearl handle on his hip.

"You don't have to worry about me," Bill replied. "I won't make any trouble."

The manager nodded slightly with a smirk. "Where you headed?"

"Somewhere." Bill stuck his hand out for a shake and added, "There's always somewhere."

"Yeah, I guess there is." The manager shook his hand with a firm grip and held it for a couple of seconds as he stared directly at Bill. Then he turned to leave.

Bill's eyes squinted in the bright sunlight as the manager opened the door and stepped outside. He gathered his meager belongings and stuffed them under the topper that covered the bed of his pickup. The pistol went under the driver's seat. After making one last pass through the trailer, he stopped and looked as if taking a farewell snapshot. It was a shabby little piece of the world, but he hated to leave it.

He ambled to the truck with a blank-minded lack of purpose. As he adjusted the side mirror on the truck, he looked closely at the stubby bristles on his unshaven face, the baggy eyes that seemed to beg for a restful night, and the uneven haircut he had given himself. It was a face that implied a lack of vanity or, worse, a lack of care.

When he started the truck, the ignition yelped with a short, grinding sound and the muffler made one loud belch. At the end of the road leading from the trailer park to the highway, he stopped. The traffic was clear in both directions. His hands were frozen on the steering wheel and his mind was suspended in a vacuum as the old truck idled with a low pulse at the edge of the highway. Both directions led to nowhere. After a long pause, he slowly pulled onto the highway and headed away from town.

Soon he was surrounded by the high plains of Wyoming, alone on the highway with only rocky scrub brush and rolling hills in view. Occasionally, in the distance, a lonely cluster of thin trees appeared.

Emptiness. It was the thing he liked most about this part of the country. It took him a long time, though, to understand why a person would choose to live so far from the rest of the world. As a child he once asked his father why they lived in Alabama. Before his father could answer, he asked another question. "Why don't we live in New York City like a lot of other people?"

"Because this is where God wants us to be," his father replied.

Even to a child it seemed like a strange answer, especially from a man who never spoke of religion and viewed church as an obligatory chore for holidays. In time, Bill came to understand that people are tied to the land in the same way they are tied to a family, a way that's not of their choosing. There's a habitat for humans, he reckoned, just as there is for animals and plants.

He had trouble finding his own habitat, though, and he wasn't sure where God wanted him to be.

With long, open stretches of road ahead of him, he could drive as fast as the truck would go, but there was no hurry. The warm air felt good as it poured in from the open windows, and the blurred scenery gave him a serene feeling of being suspended in time and place. He passed a side road that ran through a stretch of desolate flatland, disappearing into the rolling hills beyond. Several miles later, he passed a long dirt road that wound its way to an isolated house. Silhouetted against the stark landscape, the fact that someone actually lived there struck him as a rugged testament of resistance to modern conveniences.

An hour later, the rolling hills gave way to a smattering of conifer trees, bushy undergrowth, and small rocky peaks. He slowed as he approached an unpaved side road that disappeared into a series of steep-pitched crags and gullies. *This will do.* He pulled onto the road and followed the rutty tracks for about a mile before coming to an open space surrounded by the banks of large, sandy hills. Tracks from dirt bikes and other off-road vehicles crisscrossed the hillsides, though there was no one in sight.

He turned off the truck's engine and was greeted by silence, broken only by the sound of some unseen creature scurrying down a nearby ravine.

Reaching under the seat, he retrieved the pistol. He walked to the side of a hill and found a spot where he could sit comfortably on a patch of sandy soil with his feet braced on a large rock. The late afternoon sun beamed low from the west and he felt a sense of calmness as the warm rays bathed his skin. For a long time he sat there with no real thoughts except about what he planned to do next.

He raised the pistol.

A sound came from the distance. It was the unmistakable roar of an all-terrain vehicle. He stood and looked in the direction of the noise as it grew louder. When the ATV appeared over the top of a knoll, he stuck the pistol in the back of his jeans. A young boy, probably in his early teens, sat astride the vehicle and stopped in front of Bill's truck.

"Howdy," the boy shouted.

Bill waved a greeting as he walked toward the intruder.

"Am I on your property?" the boy asked.

"No, you're not. I just stopped for a little target practice." Bill pulled the gun from the back of his jeans and pointed it upward, away from the boy.

The boy's eyes widened at the sudden appearance of the weapon and he backed away. "Sorry for interrupting, sir," he said. "I'll be on my way." He glanced around as if there was something he hadn't noticed before. "My Dad's not far down the road. I've got to catch up with him. Nice meeting you."

The boy spoke quickly, then made a wide turn and drove away. Leaving a plume of dust behind, he disappeared into the distance beyond the craggy outcroppings.

After the air cleared and the sound of the ATV faded, Bill remained standing beside his truck, peering mindlessly into the desolation around him. He pointed the pistol toward the bottom of a hill and, with no particular target in mind, pulled the trigger. The pistol jerked in his hand and the loud crack echoed off the surrounding hills.

One shot. Then he stepped into the truck, stuck the pistol under the seat, and headed back to the highway.

Ten miles passed before he spotted another unpaved road and turned onto it, toward the mountains. A short while later, he pulled off the side of the road and parked on a high spot where he could see for miles in all directions. He leaned back and gazed through the windshield, his thoughts as blank as the isolation around him. The air was cooling rapidly as the sun dropped behind the mountains in the distance.

All was quiet. The pistol was still loaded, but now the deadly impulse had passed.

Stirring from the stillness, he moved to the back of the truck and rummaged around until he found a can of Vienna sausage, stale crackers, and a warm beer. Leaning against the side of the truck, he had his first meal of the day. Afterwards, he squeezed his trash into a ball and walked about twenty paces away where he stuffed it into a small sandy crevice. Standing on the highest spot around, he relieved himself as he watched a large jackrabbit scamper across the dirt road. The wind blew the stream sideways and he knew he was in for a cold night. He retrieved a blanket from the back of the truck and returned to the cab on the passenger side.

Nothing to do now. He didn't want to think about anything. Certainly not the future, which seemed as empty as the landscape around him. Caught in a web of conscience, he knew that no matter how far away he had gotten from the rest of the world, he couldn't get away from himself. He didn't know what tomorrow would bring and somewhere seemed like a mirage, but it was peaceful in the truck. Dark, quiet, and calm—a comfort just the opposite of loneliness.

He pulled a wrinkled photograph from his billfold and looked at the picture of a pretty girl. It evoked images of scenes from long ago, as if the wax figures of the past had been dusted off and brought back to life again. The images would linger in the nothingness of the hour until the winds began to howl over the plains and bittersweet memories finally surrendered to the shadows of dreams in the cold darkness.

Then he heard the sharp crack of a rifle in the distance.

He sat up, only half awake, reached over and grabbed the pistol from under the driver's seat. Five bullets left. He lay the pistol in his lap and fell back asleep.

2

Most just call it the Warrior. The Black Warrior River is formed from the confluence of lesser waterways near the small town of Branford, Alabama. Named after the great Choctaw chief, Tuscaloosa—The Black Warrior—the river is a weekend playground for the residents of nearby Birmingham. In the post-World War II boom it was a place to put a house trailer or cabin for getaways from the smokestacks and furnaces of the city known as "The Pittsburgh of the South." The river defined Branford, the county seat of Warrior County, and the only place Billy Burdette had ever lived.

Branford wasn't just a place to Billy; it was as much a part of him as the blue in his eyes.

He turned seventeen years old there on a Saturday in September, 1959. That morning the birthday boy was allowed to sleep late in the house he shared with his parents and younger brother, Jackie. With his father on one of his handyman jobs and Jackie off early to help his mother at the diner, Billy had the house to himself.

A long soak in the tub eased the soreness in his body from the game the night before. Afterward he put on a pair of briefs, grabbed the dumbbells from under the bed and did several reps of curls while looking at himself in the mirror. He posed at different angles, flexing his muscles like he had seen in the Charles Atlas ads in magazines. Then he put on a white T-shirt that fit like a second layer of skin and zipped up a pair of tight jeans snugly to his waist. All set to go, he stepped out the front door on his way to the barbershop downtown.

It couldn't have been a more perfect day. The sky was clear blue, the grass dark green, and trees held their shady leaves awaiting the approach of fall. The yards were splashed with brilliant colors of blooming plants—dark pink crape myrtles and multi-colored impatiens clinging to the warm days of the deep South.

As he walked the sidewalk past rows of small, neat houses that hugged the tree-lined street, it seemed as if all eyes were on him. Neighbors called to him from porches or slow moving cars. From behind a push mower, one man yelled, "Hey, Billy, great game last night." Everyone knew Billy Burdette, the best player for the Warrior County Fighting Choctaws. Having scored two touchdowns in the first game of the year the night before, he carried himself with self-assuredness just short of cockiness.

Nearing the town square, he passed several older homes— large wood-framed structures inhabited by some of the most prominent families. The grandest of all was Doc Palmer's place, an imposing white antebellum house set far back from the street with an expansive lawn accentuated with large magnolia trees. A long, crushed-stone drive led to a circular turnaround at the foot of the symmetrically-arched dual front steps. Brick columns supported the front gate and an iron fence surrounded the property which covered several acres. One of the columns contained a commemorative slab with *Palmer 1852* etched in concrete.

A dilapidated car carrying four colored people turned into the driveway of the Palmer house. A young girl in the car looked at Billy and lifted a hand in recognition. He waved back politely. Her name escaped him, but he remembered her as the daughter of Jessie, a woman who worked for his mother at the diner. He didn't recognize any of the others, but he knew who they were: maids, cooks, yardmen. The help.

Looking at the big mansion, Billy felt a little smaller, a little less important. It reminded him who he really was—a seventeen-year-old kid who played football. Not anyone really important, like a rich person.

The barbershop was crowded by the time he got there. Through the big front window he could see several teenage boys, including three of his teammates, slouched around reading magazines, dozing off, or idly talking. Each had a flattop haircut and was obviously waiting for Chris, the best flattop barber in town, who was putting the finishing touches on a younger boy. In the other chair, Junior was shaving the nape of a fat man in overalls, while an old-timer sucked on a pipe awaiting his turn. Lud Jenkins, a prominent attorney, offered a sharp contrast to the folksy atmosphere as he hung the coat of his three-piece suit on a wall hook.

Everyone's attention turned to Billy when he walked in and sat down in line for Chris. Several greet him with spirited talk about winning the game the night before and lavish praises for his play were tossed around the room.

"You ran through them like they were store dummies," one boy said.

"Yeah, I'll bet they see that number twenty-two in their dreams," another said. "Naw, I mean their nightmares. Hah hah!"

Others joined in the laughter.

Billy responded modestly with a huge grin he couldn't suppress.

Even though it was Saturday, Lud Jenkins was dressed as if he were in the courtroom. A starched white shirt, red tie, and shiny black shoes complemented the blue vest and pants. He took a seat beside the old-timer, picked up a copy of *Field and Stream* from the pile on a table and set the magazine in his lap. When he looked up and began to speak, the room settled to a murmur. "We're going to have a good team this year aren't we, Billy?" It didn't sound like a question.

Billy looked tensely at the dapper lawyer. "Yes, sir." He felt like he was addressing a teacher in front of the whole class.

"I don't think anybody can beat us," Jenkins added. "We should be state champs." He looked at Billy as if he were addressing a jury.

"We'll try our best, sir."

"You can do it, Billy." Jenkins lifted the magazine and began reading.

The small talk started up again. Chris lowered his clippers, looked at Billy, and pointed to a newspaper lying in disarray on a nearby table. "You see what it says in the paper?" Immediately, he answered his own question. "Says you run like you been shot out of a bazooka."

Billy shrugged and smiled.

"They're right about that," the fat man said from Junior's chair. "You get past that line of scrimmage and nobody's gonna catch you. And that's no bullshit—I seen that with my own eyes."

"Yeah, like a bazooka," said Junior. "The *Branford Bazooka*!" he said loudly, with a moon-faced grin.

The room broke out in laughter again, and the spark was lit for a nickname that would follow Billy around like a friendly dog that hangs at your heels.

More than an hour later, Billy stood in front of the mirror behind Chris's barber chair and put a dab of butch wax on the bleached spot in front of his flattop. He paid his bill and stepped outside, then stopped to refocus his eyes to the sunshine before crossing the street on his way home.

Approaching the courthouse, he looked at the imposing bronze statue of Colonel Josiah Branford standing sentinel over the town square. He picked up his gait as he passed the Colonel and a few steps later, thought he heard a voice behind him.

You can do it, Billy.

***

By Monday, the word was out. The boys from the barbershop spread the story around the school, and Billy was called The Branford Bazooka so many times, especially by Jackie, that he vowed to punch anyone who said it again.

The brothers met at their lockers during the first period break.

"How's it goin', the great...." Jackie's mouth looked poised to form a B, no doubt readying to say "Branford Bazooka."

Billy looked him defiantly with his right fist clinched.

Jackie was speechless for a second and finally spit out, "... Zooka."

The brothers glared at each other with serious faces. Billy sneered, then muffled a laugh. Jackie followed and soon they both burst into laughter that turned into hysteria. They stood in the school's main corridor surrounded by baffled onlookers, shedding tears of unbridled abandonment as if they were giggly girls instead of boys seeking the stamp of masculinity. The tension washed away as tears flowed down their cheeks and they turned to go their separate ways.

When his last class ended, Billy hurried to the gym for football practice. As he undressed in the locker room, his teammates began to gather around him. A couple of players approached, clad only in jock straps and holding garbage can lids in their hands. With the lids raised like shields and their knees bent in a slight crouch, they began chanting "Zooka, Zooka," as if warriors rallying around their chief before battle. The others followed and soon the word "Zooka" bounced off the concrete block walls within the tight confines of the locker room.

Finally, Billy said, "Okay, okay", and the noise simmered down. He looked at Jackie and said, "Thanks, Peppy, you fart blossom." Jackie had earned the nickname Peppy, a morphed version of Pepe LePew, the cartoon skunk, by conspicuously passing gas in Sunday School one Easter morning.

The other players laughed before drifting away to put on their gear.

"Hey, I—," Jackie started to speak.

"Oh, shut the hell up," Billy said. Then he turned away to hide his smile.

Billy was no longer the Branford Bazooka. He was now just Zooka, a name that meant nothing to outsiders but conjured images of a powerful tribal leader to a group of young males overdosed on testosterone. As off-the-wall as it was, the name carried the weight of respect from Billy's teammates.

He wore it proudly.

***

At one practice session early in the season, it was hotter and muggier than usual. The few scattered sprigs of weedy grass that remained on the field lay parched by the sun that refused to give up summer. Sweat poured down the players' dirty faces as the coaches yelled at them to go faster, harder. When the full scrimmage began, Jackie set his cleats in the hard packed dirt as he set up behind the center with the second team on offense. At the snap, he tossed the ball to a halfback and started around end as a blocker in front of the ball carrier. It was one of the feature plays of the team and the first-stringers lined up on defense recognized it right away.

From his defensive backfield position, Billy shot forward and plowed into his little brother at full speed. The thwacking noise of the collision of helmets and shoulder pads resounded with shouts of admiration from the coaches as well as the other players. Jackie slammed backward into the ball carrier, and they both landed in a heap as Billy went flying over them. Billy jumped to his feet laughing as the other two lingered on the ground.

Coach Mills jerked his cap off and ran up to Billy, grabbing his jersey. "That's the way to hit!" he shouted red-faced. He shoved Billy back and looked at the other players. "That's what I wanna see—some fire!" he said, spit flying from his mouth.

The assistant coaches ambled over and stood around the two players on the ground. Slowly, the ball carrier stood up and staggered back to the cluster of on-looking subs. Jackie rolled over and looked up with his eyes open, but continued to stay down.

Billy stood over him and said impassively, "Get up, Peppy."

Jackie rose up groggily and started walking toward the wrong end of the field. One of the coaches grabbed him by the back of his jersey and escorted him to the sideline. For the rest of the practice session, Jackie appeared to be in a daze. He spoke incoherently to the student manager as he stood on the sidelines watching the scrimmage with no expression on his face.

After practice, Billy noticed that his brother appeared to have regained his bearings. Clad only in a jock strap, he sat down on a bench in the locker room beside Jackie. "Dang, it was hot out there. My mouth felt like it was full of cotton."

Jackie looked away.

"Look," Billy said, "you'll never be as fast as me, but you'll knock the crap out of somebody like that one day. You'll learn what it takes."

Jackie turned to look directly at his brother. "I know what it takes, asshole."

Billy laughed as he removed his jock and walked into the shower. There he positioned himself next to the big lineman, called Booger, who lathered away oblivious to his presence. Billy reached over and turned off the hot water to the faucet next to him and Booger bolted away, yelling a choice epithet.

As the season progressed and the days became cooler, the practice sessions were shorter and more up-tempo. The team was undefeated through the first half of the schedule and competition was keen among the players. Some of the second stringers were gaining more playing time, especially as the scores became one-sided.

One afternoon the team held a long scrimmage as darkness approached. The first team lined up on offense, and Jackie took his position as a linebacker with the second team on defense. When a screen pass developed, he reacted immediately. At the instant the ball floated into Billy's hands, Jackie hit him square in the sternum with his shoulder, lifting his brother off his feet and driving him into the ground.

Coach Mills looked on from the sideline wide-eyed. "Hey, Billy, what happened to your ass? I think Jackie might'a knocked it off." The coach laughed, obviously pleased with the violent contact.

As Billy got to his feet gasping for air, Jackie yelled in his face.

"Maybe now you're not so full of crap 'cause I just knocked some of it out of you."

Billy threw a punch at his brother and they went to the ground slugging and grabbing each other. The coaches let them go at it for a while, knowing they couldn't hurt each other too much in full gear.

Later in the locker room, Billy nonchalantly asked his brother for some gum.

"Here, Mr. Touchdown," Jackie said facetiously, as he tossed his brother a piece of Double Bubble.

"Nice tackle, kid," Billy said. "Must be good coaching," he added straight-faced. It was obvious whom he considered the coach.

"Thanks, and kiss my butt, Knute Rockne," Jackie said.

Billy grinned like a possum. Then, looking directly at his brother, he chewed the gum furiously before blowing a big pink bubble that covered half his face.

In a big game near the end of the season, Jackie was sent in to replace the starting quarterback, who had been injured. On a crucial play he miraculously eluded two onrushing linemen and was able to get a short pass off to Billy, who exploded past the defenders for a seventy-five yard touchdown. As Billy sped down the field with the game-winning score, the players on the sideline yelled "Go Zooka" in a wild frenzy. In the end zone Billy was surrounded by his teammates in a celebration of handshakes and shoulder slaps.

Billy took the ball and handed it to Jackie. "It's yours, Peppy," he said with a wide-eyed grin. "That was a hell of a play."

Jackie was all smiles. "Nobody but you would have scored." He tossed the ball to the official and followed his big brother as they trotted off the field to the cheers of the crowd.

After the game, Billy stripped from his uniform and sat on a bench in the locker room as his teammates engaged in horseplay around him. Jackie shook a bottle of Coke and spritzed the face of a teammate. Another player twisted his towel and snapped it against unsuspecting bare rear ends. But, the season wasn't over and Billy felt the weight of a lot of people's expectations. The state championship.

You can do it, Billy.

3

At the first light of dawn, Bill took the pistol from his lap and set it back under the driver's seat. No sign of trouble around. He got out of the truck and stretched the stiffness from his body in the cold morning air. After the peaceful night in the truck, his mood shifted from dark fatalism to a survival mode. Hungry and desperate for a shower and a cup of coffee, he grabbed a beer from the back of the truck instead, took a big swallow and let out a contented "Aaah." A rifle shot got his attention. The quick, clean burst sounded like the one he had heard during the night, only closer. Time to leave.

With the beer nestled in the cup holder on the door, he drove away from his little Walden-on-the-ridge. He hadn't gone far before he saw two men in camouflage attire outside a camper parked in a clearing just off the dirt road. The men stood beside a small fire, their rifles leaning against the camper. Near them, a dog lay on the ground gnawing on a bone of what Bill figured to be their prey. Maybe a jackrabbit like the one he had seen the day before.

He raised a friendly hand as he drove by. The men returned the greeting.

Once on the highway, he headed for a truck stop on the route to town. Thirty minutes later he pulled into a parking lot full of tractor-trailers, campers, and automobiles. He took the last swig of beer and tossed the can into a trash bin nearby.

Grabbing some clean clothes and toiletries from the truck, he headed for the restroom. Inside, the building was teeming with people eating breakfast in the restaurant, milling through the gift shop, and lined up to pay for fuel. From the tranquility of his self-imposed isolation he was now amidst a sea of strangers bustling about like ants on spilled sugar.

In the men's room, he washed off in the sink, avoiding the ten dollars for a shower, then changed clothes in the handicap stall. Refreshed but still hungry and craving caffeine, Bill made his way into the crowded restaurant and found an empty stool at the end of the counter.

A waitress approached as soon as he sat down. "Good mornin'," she said, sounding like she meant it. "What can I get you?" She was past middle age, with dyed black hair and too much make-up. But she wore a smile and looked at him directly, as if he were her only customer.

"Good morning," he replied, cordially. "I'll have coffee and a cinnamon roll." It was all he could spare from the few dollars in his pocket.

"Would you like the cinnamon roll heated?"

"No, that's okay. You can just bring it like it is."

"I'll have it right up."

She set the coffee in front of him. He thanked her and watched as she tended to other customers. She moved behind the counter with the efficiency of a professional, and he admired her attention to the menial job. Within a couple of minutes, she returned with his order.

Savoring each sugary bite, he devoured the cinnamon roll between sips of coffee, then licked the icing off the fork. The waitress refilled his coffee cup and he thanked her again.

"Thank *you,*" she replied with smile.

Watching the waitress as she went about her work, he figured she had her share of reasons to feel a little world-weary. But whatever knocks life had given her hadn't put her down. At least not that day. Her cheery countenance drew some of the funk out of him.

From the din around him, he heard a woman's voice from the side, several feet away.

"Bill, hey Bill."

He turned on his stool to see a face approaching that he recognized but couldn't put a name to.

"Bill, I'm Joan Farley," she said, making her way next to him.

"Hi." His brows arched in a questioning look.

"Remember me? You put hardwood floors in my house last year."

"Oh, yeah." In truth, he remembered her, though he couldn't recall the job.

"I was on my way back from visiting a girlfriend in Douglas, and I had to stop for gas. I can't believe I ran into you here. I called The Floor Store, but they said you didn't work there anymore. And the telephone number they gave me was out of service."

"Things are a little slow right now," he said with a slight grimace. "They didn't have much work for me."

"Yes, I know how it is. This economy is terrible. People are saving their pennies these days."

"You're right about that."

"Don't let me bother you. Go ahead and finish your breakfast."

"No, that's fine. I was just getting ready to leave."

As he spoke, the waitress placed his ticket on the counter and said, "Have a good one."

Before he could respond, Joan asked, "Can I speak to you for just a minute before you leave?"

"Sure." He felt a tug of hopeful curiosity. "Let's go somewhere that's not so crowded."

He grabbed his ticket, left a tip he couldn't afford on the counter, and paid at the register. Then he led Joan to a quiet spot among the shelves of souvenirs in the main store.

She got right to the point. "You did a great job with my floor and you were very professional. When you were there you said you did painting as well. Do you still do that?" Before he could answer, she added, "I need my house painted and I know how attentive to detail you are. And I don't want to use any of those aliens. I just don't feel safe with them. I would love for you to do the job."

He knew she was referring to Mexicans when she used the word "aliens." It was odd, as well as telling, he thought, that she would trust him just because he was Anglo, even though she hardly knew him. However, as she talked he began to remember the job he had done for her and where her home was. She had been a good customer, one of the few who'd given him a tip. She lived in a modest single-story house near the center of town, very neat and well maintained, he recalled.

Bill wondered what he had done to gain her trust. She couldn't know for sure what kind of man he was. He wouldn't hurt her or take advantage of her, but she couldn't know that.

But a job was just what he needed. At this point money was as critical to his survival as food and water. Though age had begun to seep into his bones and he wasn't the same worker he once was, he could still get things done. It might take him a little longer to finish a job but time was something he had plenty of.

"I'll take a look at it."

"Oh, great!" she said, excitedly. "When can you come?"

"Anytime." Stone-faced, he added, "I'm pretty flexible." Bill began to sense a feeling he hadn't experienced in a long time. It felt good to be wanted.

"Can you meet me there at nine in the morning? I have to be at work by ten."

"I think I can fit that in my schedule."

"Do you remember where I live?"

"Kinda."

She took a pen from her purse, wrote her address and telephone number on a scrap of paper and handed it to him. "I'm on Herring Street, just past Maple Drive. It's a white house with green trim. Call me if you need help finding it."

"I won't need to. Now, I remember exactly where you live."

She smiled and fixed her eyes on his. "Good, I'll see you at nine."

As she turned and walked away, he started to stop her and ask a question, but let it go. *How in the heck did she remember my name?*

Bill returned to his truck and leaned back in the seat, thinking about what had just happened. He didn't have any of the materials he needed to paint a house, not one brush. But this woman, Joan, was awfully friendly and nice, so he would figure that out somehow. Tomorrow might bring some promise.

It was still early, though, and there was a lot of today left. With less than half a tank of gas in the truck, he couldn't afford to keep driving around. For some reason, until that moment he hadn't totally come to grips with what he had become—homeless. It was tempting to call one of his friends and hit them up for a place to stay. He knew a couple of ladies who would take him in, but it would mean saying some things he wasn't yet desperate enough to say.

The truck stop would have to be his home for now. It was a busy twenty-four-seven operation, but that was a plus in some ways. With all the vehicles coming and going, his truck would be less noticeable.

He went into the coffee shop and found a discarded newspaper, then returned to the truck. The local daily only had a few pages and he quickly finished reading it. He looked at his watch and it was a little after ten a.m. Still twenty-three hours to kill before meeting with Joan.

He pulled the pistol from under the seat, stuffed it in his pants, covered it with his shirt and headed for a walk down the flat dirt shoulder of the highway. Walking slowly and facing the traffic, he followed the highway, just killing time and loosening his creaky joints. Cars whizzed by with an occasional wave and semis barreled past him, creating big gusts of wind in their wakes. One big rig released an unexpected blast from the air horn just as it approached and it startled the bejeezus out of him. After thirty minutes, he turned around and retraced the two miles or so back to the truck. Another hour killed, but he was cautious of burning up any more energy which would fuel his appetite and thirst.

The afternoon dragged by with trips into the truck stop to hang around, drink coffee, and scavenge odd reading material left behind by travelers. When darkness finally began to settle in, he moved the truck to the middle of the parking lot, away from the fringes where the hookers and pushers work their trades. Rummaging around his stuff in the back of the truck, he found a couple of packs of instant oatmeal. He went inside, mixed the oatmeal with water in a Styrofoam cup and returned to the truck to eat his dinner. Later, he moved things around under the topper and used a couple of blankets to make a bed where he could stretch out. One blanket covered his head with a small space on one side for breathing, shielding him from view through the windows of the topper. Feeling securely out of sight, the setup was tolerable.

He looked forward to the morning and his meeting with Joan Farley. Meeting her, or rather her finding him, was like winning the lottery. With a glimmer of hopefulness, he settled down for another long night and tried to ignore the bright lights and noise in the parking lot. Despite the swirl of activity around him, he was soon in another place.

Alone with his thoughts, he wandered the netherworld of yesterday with memories of a place far away and a pretty girl that never left his mind.

***

The first time Billy saw Olivia she was leaving the tenth grade class she shared with his brother, Jackie. With a dark complexion, silky brown hair, and a nice figure revealed by a tight sweater and skirt, she caught his eye at first sight. It was January, the middle of the school year, and Billy wondered why he had not seen this young beauty before.

"Who is that?" he asked Jackie, as they converged at their adjoining lockers between sessions.

"Some new girl."

"No kidding?" Billy asked, with a sarcastic smirk. "What's her name? Where'd she come from?"

"She just moved here from Virginia. Her name is kinda weird—Olivia or something like that."

"Okay, wise ass, Miss Penrudder called roll, didn't she? What's her whole name?"

"Why don't you ask her?"

"Because I'm asking you. I'll find out anyhow, so don't worry about that. You can give her a try if you want, but you'll have to beat me to it."

"I gotta go." Jackie slammed his locker shut and spun the dial on the lock. "Her name is Olivia Alexander."

After the last class period, Billy hung around in front of the school hoping to catch a minute with the new girl. He had already rehearsed an excuse to tell the coach for being late to basketball practice. He wasn't in a habit of being late, so he figured the coach would buy his story of an upset stomach.

When Olivia walked out the front door with a couple of other girls, Billy went into action. He walked up to her and made eye contact. "Uh, can I talk to you?"

"Me?" she replied, as the other two girls drifted a few feet away.

"Yeah. My name is Billy Burdette. I'm Jackie's brother. He's in your class."

"I know. I've heard of you. You play football and they say you're good."

"Well, we've got a good team." *Holy moly, she knows about me.* He felt a foot taller. "I'm playing basketball now and I've got to get to practice real soon. I know you're from out-of-town and I just wanted to welcome you to school."

"Thanks, that's very nice of you."

"Maybe I could show you around town. I've lived in Branford all my life."

"I've met some nice girls already who have helped me settle in. It's different than where I'm from—Roanoke, Virginia—but I'm getting used to it."

She said she'd met some nice girls. Didn't say anything about boys.

"Would you like to go to a movie Saturday night?" he blurted out.

She laughed. "You don't waste any time, do you?"

He grinned. "Well?

"Okay."

"Great. See you tomorrow." With long, bounding strides he hustled away to the gym for basketball practice. His stomach felt just fine.

***

Billy was sixteen when he met Olivia. She was six months shy of it, and the bloom of sexual awareness was just beginning to blossom. One date turned to more and soon things began to warm up for the young couple, a fact that was apparent to the watchful eyes of everyone at school.

Jackie spoke to his brother one evening as they studied in the bedroom they shared. "You're gettin' pretty tight with Olivia, aren't you?"

"Tight? Nah," Billy answered. "She's a girl. They're good for certain things."

"Yeah, I know."

"We get along pretty good. I haven't seen nothin' better. Most of the girls around here are silly-ass teenyboppers."

"You're so full of crap. She's got you by the tail."

"Just worry about your own business." Billy set his book on the nightstand. "And go to bed." Already in his shorts, he rolled back the covers and crawled into bed.

Jackie turned out the light and followed suit.

In the darkness, Billy said, "And get your own tail. Ha!"

"Shut-up."

***

It didn't take Billy long to realize there was something just as exciting as scoring a touchdown or hanging out with the guys. It was a feeling he had never known before and the intensity was overwhelming at times. It was the first time in his life he had felt that way and, though he was bursting inside, he didn't want anyone to know how vulnerable he was.

However, soon the volcano of adolescent love erupted and he was helpless to resist the urge to be with Olivia all the time. He tried to play it cool and called her Olive Oyl, the comic girlfriend of Popeye. It was in total contrast to her pretty face and curves that were well on the way to womanhood.

At Olivia's sixteenth birthday party that summer, Billy showed up wearing a sailor's cap, a blue shirt with pegged sleeves, and a corn cob pipe in his mouth. When she opened the door, he flexed the biceps in his right arm while holding a can of spinach in his left.

In the gruffest voice he could muster, he said, "Good evening, Miss Oyl. I'm Popeye, the sailor man, I yam, I yam."

She laughed, and said in a high-pitched voice, "Oh, Popeye, you're my hero."

The girls in the room laughed and the boys groaned. One of the guys shouted, "You look more like Bluto."

When the party was over, Billy stayed after the house emptied. The sailor cap and corncob pipe lay among the presents and wrapping on the floor. Moving closer to Olivia on the couch, he put his arm around her and looked into her eyes. "Will you go steady with me?"

She sighed through a huge smile. "Yes."

He said the words he had never said before. "I love you." Then he kissed her and held it a long time.

"I love you, too," she said, hugging him tightly.

The touch of her soft body and the sweetness of her feminine scent aroused in him a feeling more powerful than he had ever imagined.

When school resumed, Olivia earned a spot on the majorette

squad and on Friday nights she strutted on the field at halftime in front of the band, twirling a baton in a skimpy, sequined costume. In the stands, she joined the others as they high-kicked their tasseled white boots in chorus-line unison while the band furiously played the school fight song. Though she remained popular with her friends, hooking up with the star football player and wearing his letter sweater to class solidified her position as the envy of all the girls in the junior class.

She made him feel like *her* hero because of who he was and it was a great feeling. Not *their* hero, the football player who they cheered when he scored touchdowns. She called him Zooka in private, pretending to preserve the flimsy veil of secrecy surrounding the name. Both sets of parents approved of a match that seemed almost preordained by appearance and talents. The approvals made it easier for the young cupids to enjoy some heavy petting in Billy's car in the driveway of the Alexanders' home. Actually, the '58 Oldsmobile was his mother's car, but it was essentially his in the evening hours.

When the team won the state championship, a picture of Billy holding the big trophy dominated the front page of the local paper. A framed copy was placed in the barbershop on the wall opposite Chris's chair. Another hung in the otherwise stuffy office of Lud Jenkins.

Coming from a working class family had taught Billy that life could be a tough game but, for now, he basked in the days of no regrets.

4

Bill stayed under the blanket in the truck until full daylight glared through the windows of the topper. He got his toiletries and freshened up in the truck stop restroom before heading for the diner. There, he took a stool at the counter and ordered a cup of coffee from the same waitress as the day before. She brought the hot brew along with eggs, bacon, home fries, and toast.

"Sorry, I just ordered coffee," he said.

"Really?" Her feigned look of surprise wasn't convincing. "I guess I screwed up. Will you eat it so I don't have to throw it away?" She held the plate in her hand and cocked an eye.

He looked at her and, not wanting to feel like a beggar, considered refusing the food.

"I've been there," she said.

He nodded and said, "Thanks."

She set the food down. "You're welcome."

Digging into his first hot meal in three days, he savored each bite and washed it down with two refills of coffee. He sopped the plate with toast as the waitress poured the third cup. "How did you know?" he asked.

"I guess you could say a trained eye. That, and Frank over there." She glanced to the side, and Bill's eyes followed to a husky man in a security uniform. "He knows what goes on around here. You didn't look like trouble."

Bill looked at the waitress and saw an angel with a Travel Depot logo stitched on her blouse. "No, I'm not trouble. Try not to be anyhow."

"I know," she said.

"I think it's a good idea for me to move on, though. Quit hanging around here."

"Probably so." She picked up his empty plate and walked away.

When he finished his coffee, he grabbed a menu and checked the prices. He took his ticket for the coffee, paid at the register, and left. She would find his tip on the counter, an amount equal to the price of the food.

He drove away from the truck stop feeling better than he had in a long time. He made good time on the way to Joan Farley's house, then slowed as he approached so as not to be too early. The surrounding neighborhood was past its prime, but still desirable for those who wanted to live within a few blocks of the center of town. The area's abundance of mature trees and landscape evoked a sense of serenity. Unlike newer developments with houses of monotonous contemporary appearance, each home had its own distinctive style.

He pulled into Joan's driveway ten minutes before nine. More than a year had passed since he had installed hardwood floors there, but when he saw the house, he remembered the job as if it had been yesterday. He recalled how neat and spotlessly clean it was on the inside.

His recollection of Joan returned just as vividly. He got the impression she lived alone since he hadn't seen evidence of a man and the heading on his work order only had her name. She never said as much, and he was aware that single women living alone don't volunteer that fact to strangers. Having felt a gentleman's obligation to help her as much as he could, he took extra care to make sure the job was done perfectly. In turn, she had been very polite and friendly and expressed admiration for his craftsmanship. He looked forward to working for her again.

As he opened the door of the truck, Joan walked out of the house and started toward him. As they converged on the front walk, she offered a cheery, "Good morning." She looked to be dressed for work.

"Mornin'."

"Thanks for coming. I hope you'll be able to do this."

"Yeah, well, thanks for giving me a shot at it. I'm glad you saw me at the truck stop. That was pretty amazing."

"My lucky day," she said with a smile.

"No, mine." He looked at her and their eyes locked for a second. "Let's take a look at it." He walked to the middle of the yard.

She followed and stood beside him as they viewed the house in perspective. Although not a big house, there was a lot of neo-Victorian trim, and wood-framed windows that would require detail painting.

"I don't want anything spray painted," she said.

"I agree. They call that blow and go. It's quick, but doesn't last as long." After a thoughtful pause he added, "It needs to be pressure washed first...and there're some places that need priming."

She listened, nodding her head in agreement.

Finally, he added, "Lots of trim work, too. It'll take me at least five days, maybe more. I work by myself."

"That's fine. Take as much time as you need. When can you start?"

The question jolted him as if he had thought of the job in abstract with no consideration for the practicality of actually doing it. Everything he owned was in his truck and none of it would be of help with a painting job. He would have to rent a pressure washer and find a ladder from somewhere. And he didn't have the money to pay for anything up front.

"I can start tomorrow, but we haven't talked about the cost or the kind of paint you want." With a look of embarrassment squeezed on his face, he added, "And I'm a little tight right now, so I would appreciate something up front for supplies." He had always worked for a painting contractor and he wasn't aware of the standard terms of payment, much less the current going rate for the work.

She looked at him with a knowing expression, as if his words had stripped him bare of deception.

"Of course. I'll give you what you think is fair for the work with half in advance. You won't have to worry about supplies. I have an account at Harvey's Hardware and you can charge anything you need on it. We can go there together and pick out the paint. Is that okay?"

"Sure, absolutely."

When he offered a price for completing the job, she replied with a smile that it was much lower than a couple of other bids she had received.

"I know you'll do a good job and I want to be fair with you, so I'll give you three hundred dollars more than that. Even that's less than what the others quoted."

"I appreciate that, ma'am." Her generosity added to his feeling of blind good luck. *Why is this woman so trusting of me?*

"It's Joan," she said warmly. "So it's a deal?"

"It's a deal...Joan."

When she offered her hand, he took it firmly in his, though careful not to squeeze too hard. He dared not do anything to hurt this woman named Joan.

She went into the house and returned with her purse. She pulled her checkbook out and began to write. "It's Bill Burdette, right? B-U-R-D-E-T-T-E?"

"That'll work. My driver's license says William, but they know me at the bank."

She finished writing the check, ripped it from the book, and handed it to him. "There you go, *Mr.* Burdette."

He took the check and folded it to keep his shaky hands in motion. "Thank you, *Miz* Farley." She smiled.

"Can we meet tomorrow morning at eight to get started?" she asked.

"I'll be here."

"Good."

Well, Hell's bells, he thought, smiling to himself, as he walked to his truck. *Now I've got a few bucks in my pocket, a job, and somebody who trusts me. Maybe the butter hasn't slipped all the way off my biscuit yet.*

It was only nine-thirty in the morning with another day to kill before starting the job. But the idle time wouldn't weigh so heavily now. There was comfort in knowing what lay ahead, at least for the next week or so, and a little breathing room with the money from the advance. The first order was to get to the bank and cash the check.

At the bank he parked outside, ignoring the drive-through window. Still in the truck, he pulled the check from his billfold and stared at the signature—*Joan Farley*. A good name for a good woman. His mind wandered to the young boy on the ATV who'd interrupted him in the ravine as he raised the gun to his head. *Burdette*, he thought, *you'd better start doing your part 'cause life is hanging on to you.*

After leaving the bank, he filled his truck with gas before heading to the library to wile away the morning. He tried hard to concentrate as he waded through almost a hundred pages of *Ulysses,* but realized, even at nearly fifty, he didn't understand it any more than when he was eighteen. In the afternoon he went to a picturesque park and ate a snack lunch on a picnic bench. Afterward, he took a walk around a nearby lake and soaked in the rays of the warm afternoon sun.

As darkness approached, he decided he couldn't take another night sleeping in his cramped truck, so he drove to a motel on the outskirts of town that catered to illegals, druggies, prostitutes, and other down-and-outers like him.

Entering his room he was hit by the smell of cheap air freshener fighting a losing battle against years of mustiness. In the bathroom he flushed a cockroach from the middle of the bathtub down the drain without a second thought before enjoying his first shower in three days.

He walked across the road in front of the motel to a convenience store. There, he bought a six-pack of beer, a Styrofoam cooler and some ice, along with two large bags of chips and a couple of sandwiches. Returning to the motel, he settled onto the bed to watch television and enjoy his feast. The little TV set only received three channels, but he couldn't have felt better if he had been in a suite at the Ritz-Carlton.

Three empty beer bottles lay among the wadded wrappers and bags in the trash can when he turned off the TV after the local news. He pulled back the bed covers and wrapped himself in comfort. The pleasure of obtaining the painting job rolled around in his head before his thoughts faded to more glorious days. He could still see the scoreboard in the north end zone of Legion Field in Birmingham as he scored his last touchdown. It was the state championship game, and he knew the college scouts were watching.

Soon a deep sleep covered him with a blanket of restfulness.

***

The frost had barely melted off the grass on an overcast day in February when the black Lincoln Continental pulled into the Burdettes' driveway.

For several days everyone in town had anxiously waited for The Coach to arrive. Traffic moved slowly past the Burdette house; some vehicles even stopped nearby on the side of the road and people gathered in little clusters in neighboring yards to get a glimpse of the legendary figure.

The Coach had returned to Alabama only two years before to reclaim the luster of the glorious past for his alma mater. As a patron saint, the iconic visage of The Coach was posted in framed homage on the walls in homes and businesses throughout the state.

A state trooper's car with two uniformed officers followed the Lincoln into the driveway. The driver of the Lincoln got out first, then another man emerged from the front seat, both men wearing blue suits and red ties. The men in blue suits flanked the Lincoln as a large man unfolded himself from the back seat and stepped onto the driveway. The troopers remained in their vehicle, smoking cigarettes and blowing smoke through the open windows.

The Coach wore a black and white checked hounds-tooth hat, a plaid sport coat, and an open-neck dress shirt. He walked straight and tall with a casual shuffle as he approached the Burdette family, all of whom waited in obvious awe to greet him. Billy's father stepped forward to shake The Coach's hand, admitting later that he couldn't have been more nervous had he been greeting President Kennedy. The Coach smiled and politely introduced himself to Jim and Alice Burdette in a deep gravelly voice that sounded as if it were borrowed from a grizzly bear. Nervously, Billy extended his hand and felt the exhilarating firm grip of the man who seemed like God.

Jackie stayed in the background until the famous visitor approached with a handshake and a pat on the shoulder. "How ya doin', son?"

"Fine, sir," Jackie responded meekly.

In the living room, The Coach removed his hat and proceeded to compliment the Burdettes on their home, which made Billy and Jackie beam with pride. The boys had risen early to help their mother clean the house thoroughly, like they always did when the preacher came to visit. The Coach relaxed everyone with his down-home demeanor and warmed up the conversation with stories about growing up as a boy in Arkansas and playing football for Alabama in the Rose Bowl.

Then the Coach looked at Billy and got serious.

"Son," he said, "Coach Watkins has seen you play and he thinks you're the kind of player we're looking for at Alabama. I've looked at films of some of your games and he could be right. You're kinda small, but that doesn't bother me. I'm more interested in your heart. I can tell that your mama and daddy have raised you right, but do you think you're tough enough to beat those big old boys over on the other side of the state?"

Everyone knew beating Auburn ranked at the top of The Coach's to-do list, right after breathing.

"Yes sir," Billy said as firmly as he could. He wasn't really sure how tough he was but, like a warrior going to battle, his spirit swelled with the challenge.

The meeting was over in less than an hour. There was no need for Billy to consider any of the other offers he had received. His heart pounded with excitement as he signed the scholarship papers.

At that moment, his dream had come true. He would play for The Coach and, at the age of seventeen, his life was perfect. He would be a part of the history of the place that was, to him, the Promised Land.

Inside the Warrior County courthouse, Billy had gazed many times at the big portrait of Colonel Josiah Branford in full Confederate uniform. The bright yellow trim on the Colonel's sleeves, collar, and coattail was distinctive of the Alabama troops known as "Yellowhammers." The uniform trim and the nickname were derived from the state bird, the yellowhammer flicker.

Outside on the town square was a statue of Colonel Branford who, a hundred years earlier, had led a ragtag band of Confederate militia as they held off the Bluecoats for three days before being rooted out by superior numbers and firepower. Afterward, the Union forces moved down a road parallel to the Black Warrior River until they reached Tuscaloosa. There they proceeded to set fire to the buildings on the university campus, which served as a Confederate officer training school.

Now it was Billy's turn to follow the river down to Tuscaloosa. He would wear the crimson jersey—a red as pure as the blood of Christ, his father would say with selective reverence—and he would play for the legendary coach they called The Bear. On Saturdays the cheerleaders would lead the crowd in a raucous yell in half rhyme that would mortify Emily Dickinson:

Rammer jammer, Yellowhammer,
Give 'em hell Alabama.

Of course, being the center of attention wasn't a new experience to Billy, but having to live up to The Coach's expectations was. While it made him feel good that the whole town of Branford was proud of him, his biggest fear was letting everyone down. He couldn't forget the fate of Colonel Branford, the native son defeated by superior forces in a long-ago war. It conjured up a feeling that a lot of Southerners still harbored deep inside—an inferiority complex inherited by the vanquished.

On the night he signed his scholarship, Billy met his buddies at their usual meeting place at the river. He refused to smoke or drink, because he was afraid that somehow The Coach was watching. Predictably, his buddies teased him about it good-naturedly. Naturally, they were happy for him, and just being his teammate made them swell with importance. They talked for a couple of hours about the good times and the rough times they shared—the football games, growing up in Branford, stories of girls that "put out."

As the get-together wound down, his buddies had a surprise for him. They surrounded him and started the obscene chant they used in warm-up drills before practices. With a rhythmic beat as if performing side straddle hops, they sang:

> *He's our captain, he's got the clap,*
> *He keeps the crabs in his jock strap.*

Billy knew what was coming when they moved in on him, but there were too many to fend off. They wrestled him to the ground and, despite his fierce resistance, four guys picked him up, carried him to the river bank and tossed him in.

It was past midnight when he got home. His father was asleep, but his mother waited up for him, as usual. When he told her what had happened, she simply responded, "You boys." But he could tell that she recognized it for what it was. A celebration.

His mother prepared a fried egg sandwich for him and tossed his wet clothes in the dryer as he stripped down to his briefs.

When he entered the room he shared with his brother, he left the door ajar and the light from the kitchen half-lit the room. Jackie sat on the side of his bed in the semi-darkness, apparently roused by the voices from the kitchen.

"What did y'all do?" Jackie asked. He knew the seniors had met at the river after taking their dates home.

"We just shot the shit," Billy replied, retrieving some dry underwear from a chest-of- drawers.

"Well, they must have missed 'cause you're not bleeding." Jackie made it a habit to keep his brother's ego intact.

"Ha ha," Billy said. "Aren't you the funny little gonad? Is that what you've been doing in here—playing with yourself?"

"Kiss my ass, butt-breath." Jackie stood up and put his face close to Billy's.

"Shut up or I'll kick it!" Billy shouted.

"You and whose army?" The veins in Jackie's neck bulged and the skin on his face tightened with anger.

Their mother heard the commotion and entered the room with a stern look on her face. "What's going on? You better *not* wake up your father." She glared at them with a stare that would melt a block of ice.

"Sorry, Mom," Billy whispered. "We'll be quiet."

Jackie looked at her sheepishly and added his, "Sorry."

She turned and left. There would be no more loud noises.

Billy gave his brother a disdainful shrug and reached into a drawer to get a T-shirt. As he started out the door, Jackie's demeanor changed completely. In a serious tone he said, softly, "Hey that was cool—meeting The Coach. He's a tough S.O.B. But you can handle it."

Billy nodded, then returned to the kitchen and ate his egg sandwich alone. It was almost one o'clock in the morning.

The day of The Coach was over.

The next day there was an article in the newspaper about Billy signing the scholarship. The article included the nickname that his teammates called him and, in an embarrassment he would never live down, the accompanying picture was captioned *Billy Burdette, The Branford Bazooka.*

Billy wasn't sure who told the reporter but, despite his brother's repeated denials, he never doubted it was Jackie.

5

Bill met Joan at the hardware store an hour before she was due at work. A light drizzle was falling when they arrived and the forecast was iffy for the day. Forty percent, he heard the guy on the morning news say. He told Joan the pressure washing would probably take all day and the rain wouldn't hold him up unless it got really heavy.

"Are you sure you don't want to hold off until it clears up?" she asked.

"No, it's okay. This is a perfect day to pressure wash."

"Alright, if you say so. While we're here, let's get everything you'll need for the job. I've already decided on the paint color."

"Good. If I finish pressure washing and the weather clears, I might get a little painting done today. Let's just get a couple of gallons now and the rest as I go along. I'll be painting tomorrow morning for sure, unless it's raining again."

"Oh, I hope it isn't. I hate for you to be held up. It's bad enough you have to work in the rain today."

"It's okay—I don't mind."

Together they went through the store rounding up everything he needed, including a rental pressure washer along with some bleach, paint, brushes, and other supplies. Joan told him she'd spoken to a friendly neighbor who had a couple of ladders he could use.

"Thanks, I'll probably need them."

"Yeah, I didn't think your arms would reach that high," she said with a sly grin. He acknowledged her cleverness with a subtle smile. She gave him a key to the house and told him to feel free to use the bathroom and anything he might need in the kitchen.

Holding the key in his hand, he felt a heightened sense of connection to her. He wanted to thank her for everything, but the right words were stuck somewhere inside his head. Instead, he simply said, "You can trust me."

"I know—I just did."

He didn't feel foolish for stating the obvious. Instead, he felt a confirmation as if they had just agreed on something more than the security of her home.

After she charged everything to her account, they left the store together and stopped under an awning out of the rain.

"I'll be home about five. Here's my number at work if you need to call me for anything." She handed him a business card.

"That won't be necessary. I'll be fine."

"I'm sure you will, but it wouldn't bother me if you called. Usually I'm as bored as a house cat."

He glanced at the card and noticed she was a customer service rep at a credit union.

"Well, you look very nice, very professional. I'm sure you're great at your work."

"It's a job." Her voice carried the dull thud of resignation.

She opened a small umbrella, ran to her car, and waved at him with her fingers as she drove away.

Bill gathered all the materials at the rear door of the store. He rearranged things in the back of his truck and shoved the big pressure washer in. When he finished, his clothes stuck to his body and his hair matted with misty rain.

As he drove to Joan's house, the rain stopped, but the sky remained dark. Once there, he parked his truck and walked three houses down the street to meet Hank Stonecypher, the neighbor she'd told him about. A man stood on the front steps as if waiting for him. He was lean, looked to be in his seventies, and dressed in jeans, a plaid western style shirt, and cowboy boots. He wore a baseball cap with the figure of a jackalope stitched on front.

"Are you Mr. Stonecypher?"

"Sure am."

"Good morning, I'm Bill Burdette. Joan Farley said you might let me borrow a couple of ladders."

"Glad to meet you, partner. Just call me Hank." The man reached out and offered a firm grip. "If you're a friend of Joan's, you're a friend of mine. She told me she'd hired a hand to paint her house. You're welcomed to use my ladders."

"I appreciate that. I'm fixin' to pressure wash it now."

As soon as he said "fixin' to" he knew it was a dead giveaway. He still had the birthright Southern twang in his voice that the years in exile had never erased, but he tried to avoid phrases that made him sound like Gomer Pyle.

"I can tell you're not from around here. Mind me asking where you're from? Somewhere down south, I'm guessin'."

"Actually, I've lived in Wyoming for more than twenty-five years, but I was born and raised in Alabama. They call it the Heart of Dixie, and that's about as southern as you can get."

"Never been to Alabama," Hank said. "But I've been to Florida and Georgia, and I met a lot of boys from the South in the Navy. They're good people."

"Most are."

"What brought you way the hell out here?" Hank asked. "Or maybe that's none of my business."

"No, that's okay, but it's a long story. Once I got here, though, I didn't want to leave."

The old man nodded, as if he knew the feeling. He led Bill to the back of his house where two ladders, one short and one long, lay behind some shrubbery. Each man took a ladder and walked the short distance to Joan's house.

"Thanks a lot," Bill said. "I'll be here for several days. Let me know if you need one of the ladders—or both of them—and I'll bring them back."

"Don't worry, I won't need 'em. Be careful."

"Thanks again. Nice to meet you."

"My pleasure." Hank walked away, picking up his gait as the rain started again.

Bill unloaded the pressure washer and went about connecting it to the water hose, attaching the feed line to a bottle of bleach, and filling the machine with gas. With the motor cranked up and chortling like an idling Harley, he set the long ladder against the tallest side of the house. He stepped up several rungs with the wand in his hand and started blasting the mildew and dirt from the eaves. The spray splattered back on him and he was soon oblivious to the rain.

He worked steadily all day through fits of rain. In mid-afternoon, Hank came over.

"How's it going?" the old man shouted over the drone of the pressure washer.

"It's going fine."

"Need anything? Want something to drink?"

"No thanks. I appreciate it, but I'll pass for now," he shouted back. "Maybe later."

"Anytime. Just come down to my house whenever you're ready."

"Will do. Thanks."

Once the high parts were finished, he could stand on solid ground. He washed the front porch, the back steps and, for good measure, the walkway from the driveway. By four-thirty he was finished. There was plenty of time to put the machine in his truck and get it back to the store. Every inch of his clothing as well as every pore of his body was soaking wet. His bad ankle throbbed as if it were in a vise.

The rain stopped and the sun peered out of the clouds. After taking off his shoes and socks, he went inside, dried his feet on a door mat, and got one of the two beers he had put in the refrigerator earlier. Taking his first break of the day, he swigged it down while sitting on the back steps. He finished the beer, took a plastic cup from a kitchen cabinet and poured the other beer into it to take with him in the truck. Outside, he put back on his soggy shoes and socks.

After returning the machine to the store, he drove back to Joan's house where he found her and Hank sitting in rocking chairs on her front porch. Each had stemmed cocktail glasses in their hands, and the sounds of Jimmy Buffet floated through an open window.

"I'll bet you're soaked," Joan said. "Hank says you worked in the rain all day."

"Yeah, it's just water. You can't wash a house without getting wet."

"I guess not," she said. "Come, have a margarita." She motioned in the direction of another chair on the porch. "Pretend you just got out of the ocean. You know, the Wyoming Ocean."

She smiled at Hank and they laughed heartily at the absurdity.

"No, thanks." Bill looked at the clouds. "I was going to get started on the painting, but it looks like we might get more rain. I'd better get going."

"Aw, hang with us," Hank said.

"What's you're rush?" asked Joan. "Got a hot date?"

Middle-aged people don't talk about dating, he thought. She was probing. He had no doubt she liked him, although he couldn't figure out why. Now he felt her begin to close in.

"No hot date. I just need to dry out."

"Oh, come on—join the party," Joan insisted. "Do you have some dry clothes? You can change in the house."

She made it sound like it would be impolite to refuse, and the truth was it had been a long time since he'd enjoyed the company of people. So he fetched some dry clothes from his truck, changed in the bathroom, and joined them on the porch.

Relaxed by the tequila, Bill opened up for the first time in a long while. Joan and Hank were obviously charmed by him and he enjoyed the attention.

"So, you're from Alabama?" Joan asked. "I love that southern accent."

"Yeah, born and raised just outside of Birmingham. I guess after drinking so much sweet tea, our voices get a little syrupy."

"I like the way you talk. I think it's kind of sexy," she said with a smile.

"Oh crap, Joanie, don't scare the man off," Hank interjected.

"I'm just being nice," she countered.

"Thanks," Bill said. "I haven't been called sexy since I told Scarlett I didn't give a damn. But you know, some people think if you're from the South, you're some kind of Ku Klux Klan redneck." He paused then added, "Truth is, I haven't worn my robe in years."

That loosened them up and the conversation moved on.

"When I was in the Navy," Hank started, "I met this young kid. He was a little sumbitch, about five-four, maybe. One day we were at the urinal and when I looked down, I saw he had a tattoo on his tally-whacker that spelled *Shorty*, and I laughed. 'Don't laugh,' he said, 'when I'm ready for action it says, Shorty Washington, Seaman, United States Navy.'"

Hank laughed at his own joke and Bill followed suit.

"Hank, you lying old goat roper, don't be so crude," Joan said through a laugh.

Bill joined the other two in telling off-color jokes, as if he were being initiated into their little club.

Joan made another batch of margaritas and Bill stayed on. After a while, the tequila began to soak in and he didn't want to move, much less leave. He spoke slowly and tried to enunciate each syllable, but he knew he was slurring his words. The more he talked and the tipsier he became, the more his companions seemed to enjoy his company.

In his slightly altered state, Bill looked at Joan differently. She was in her late thirties, early forties, he guessed. She looked more attractive to him now, partly due to the alcohol, but more because she was dressed in tight jeans and a bra-clinging T-shirt.

It was if he was seeing her for the first time. She was short and slightly fleshy but had a better figure than most women her age. Her hair was auburn, tinged with streaks of red dye, and curved around her face, stopping just above her shoulders. The only makeup she wore was a modest application of rose colored lipstick, which blended nicely with her fair complexion and brown eyes.

Not a classic beauty like Olivia, he thought, but somewhere between not-too-shabby and pretty-decent-looking.

"Excuse me, I've got to hit the head," he said.

As he stood, he suddenly felt dizzy and lost his balance. He tried to catch himself on the arm of the chair, but hit the floor in a crumple.

Joan and Hank quickly rose from their chairs and bent over him.

"Oops," he said, his face planted sideways on the floor.

"Did you hurt yourself?" Joan asked.

"No." He squeezed his eyes closed, then opened them again.

"Here," she said, as she and Hank tried to help him up.

"That's okay, I can walk." He got to his feet with Joan on one arm and Hank on the other. "I just got a little dizzy. I haven't had much to eat all day and that tequila kind of messed up my gyroscope." In fact, he hadn't had *anything* to eat. Even though his words were slurred, his head was clear.

They held him on each side and walked him to the bathroom. When he came out, Joan grabbed his arm and led him to the sofa in the living room.

"Here, lie down. I'll get you something to eat."

"You don't have to do that. I can grab something when I get home." He was ravenous and there was no home to go to, but his instinct was not to impose.

"You can't go anywhere right now," Hank said. "If the cops catch you driving like this, they'll put your ass in jail."

Joan added wryly, "Besides, you might kill yourself and then you couldn't paint my house."

"Okay." He laid his head down on a velour cushion against the sofa's arm.

"How about a big ham sandwich and a glass of milk?" she asked. "Milk will help absorb some of the alcohol."

"That'll be fine. Thanks," he said as he closed his eyes.

***

When Bill awoke, he was covered with a light blanket and his shoes were on the floor. He slowly sat up, still disoriented, and felt like he was in a dream. The darkness of nighttime spread beyond the window behind him and the room was dimly lit with one table lamp. Joan sat in a chair across the room, dressed in a robe.

"Hi," she said softly.

He pulled the blanket aside and looked around. As he closed his eyes and rubbed his forehead, he asked, "What time is it?" Then he opened his eyes again.

"Almost eleven o'clock. How do you feel?"

"Rough. I'm sorry I crashed on you."

"Don't be sorry. We had a good time in Margaritaville. You were funny."

"Yeah. I think I lost my shaker of salt." It prompted a smile from her.

"Well, you sure wolfed down those sandwiches."

"Sandwiches?"

"Uh huh. Two of them and a couple glasses of milk."

"Oh, yeah. I was kinda out of it. Thanks."

"You're welcome."

"I need to get going." He rose from the sofa.

"Where to?"

"Home." It was the only thing he could think to say.

"Where's that?"

He didn't answer and he could see the doubt in her eyes.

Finally, he said, "Somewhere."

"Somewhere or nowhere?" she asked.

"It's all about the same, isn't it?"

He felt exposed, as if he were sitting naked in front of her. But it was a relief; he was tired of the charade. They stared at each other across the room, connecting in a way that was understood, but not spoken.

"You're staying here," she said.

She didn't say he was staying just for the night, but that was something he didn't need to get into now.

"I'll pay you," he said.

"No, you will not. It won't cost me a dime. That's your room." She pointed to the bedroom on the right side of the hall. "I'm going to bed. I'll see you in the morning." She rose from the chair and walked down the hall to the master bedroom, closing the door behind her. *I guess that's that.*

Still sleepy and drained of energy, he wasn't inclined to protest her hospitality. He grabbed his shoes and went into the room she had indicated, directly across from the bathroom. It was small, but spotlessly clean. A single bed, a nightstand, and a small bookcase occupied most of the space with a sliding-door closet just beyond the foot of the bed. It felt more like home than anywhere he had been in a long time.

He stripped to his shorts, turned off the light and slid his body under the covers. The pillow was soft and the sheets were cool against his skin. A few minutes later he was stirred by a faint noise at the door and opened his eyes without raising his head. Through the darkness he saw the door open slightly and the shadowy outline of a figure in the hallway. The door closed quietly and he closed his eyes again.

Soon he fell into a shroud of sleep, lost in that place called Somewhere.

6

Billy waited for his mother to stick her head in the door before he opened his eyes.

"It's six o'clock, boys. Time to get up," she announced.

He groaned sleepily, pulled the covers aside and propped himself up on his elbows.

From the other bed, Jackie jerked the sheet aside and yelled, "I got first." He jumped from bed, released a loud fart, and hustled to the bathroom.

"You skunk-ass stinkwad," Billy yelled, as the stink wave reached him. Fanning the air with his hands, he tossed on a terrycloth robe and went into the kitchen He took a seat at the breakfast table with his mother.

"Wow, oatmeal—imagine that," he said.

His mother looked at him without smiling. "You can starve, you know. Or, God forbid, make your own breakfast."

"I'm just kidding, Mom. You know I love you. But I eat so much oatmeal I think one day I might look like that guy." He nodded to the round box on the counter with a picture of a smiling Quaker.

"Jim will be on the day shift next week. If you guys are nice, I might make pancakes."

"That would be great. The pancakes, I mean. And good for Dad—it's been a long time since he's been on days." Billy thought about it for a minute. "Oh, crap, there goes the hot water."

"You can take a bath at night. It won't kill you."

"Ugh!"

"Well, I've got to get going," she said, pinning the nametag on her waitress outfit. "Don't leave a mess."

"We never do," Billy said, as she walked out the door. "Warden," he added to an empty room.

Thirty minutes later Billy stood on the front steps waiting for his buddy, Tony Pescitelli—nicknamed Toto—to pick him up.

Jackie coasted down the driveway on his bicycle, heading for his paper route. "Later, tater," he called out.

"Easy greasy," Billy replied.

As he waited on Tony, Billy's mind was somewhere else. With pre-season football practice only two weeks away, he would soon move into the athlete's dorm at the University. It was a place for a select few, a place of privilege, and he ignored the fact that it was known as the Ape Dorm by the other students. He imagined being on his own and out of the only house he had ever known. Just thinking about it made him feel grown up.

Tony pulled into the driveway in his '55 Ford and hollered through the passenger side window, "Ready for another day in paradise?"

Billy slid into the passenger seat. "Ready as a bitch in heat." Out of habit, he thumped the foam dice hanging from the rearview mirror with his forefinger. Despite his words of eagerness, he was only counting down the days working at the local produce warehouse.

That afternoon Billy's department shut down early and he had more than an hour to kill while waiting for Tony. He noticed a small colored kid, maybe thirteen or fourteen, shooting hoops at the basketball goal at the far end of the parking lot. Impulsively, he strode across the lot to join him.

As Billy approached, the kid bounced a shot off the side of the rim and the ball rolled toward him. Billy grabbed it and put up a jump shot that banked off the backboard and rattled through the chain-link net. He passed the ball to the boy, and they took turns taking shots for several minutes. The boy made most of his shots and, even in their casual playing around, Billy could tell he was a natural.

"You want to play some HORSE?" Billy asked.

The boy looked at him wide-eyed, silently nodding an enthusiastic *yes*.

As they played, Billy complimented the boy on his good shots and didn't try anything difficult when it was his turn to shoot first. The boy won the first game, while Billy played without full effort. In the second game, Billy tried his best, but the young boy won again. Finally, Billy began to get his shooting touch and won the third game. The fourth game was Billy's, too. They agreed to end it at that, tied two games apiece.

"What's your name?" Billy asked.

"I'm Zee."

"Zee? You mean like the letter Z?"

"No, Z-E-E. My real name is Zenon, but they call me Zee."

"Oh. My name's Billy. It's really William, but for some reason they call me Billy."

The boy looked at him like he recognized a hint of condescension.

"Sorry, I was just trying to be funny," Billy said.

"That's okay." The boy tossed the ball back and forth from one hand to the other. "My brother's name is Xavier. We call him Ex. You know, E-X."

The boy laughed at that, and Billy couldn't tell if he was serious. Then, to top it off, the boy said, "Our sister is Yolanda. We call her Yoyo."

As the game of HORSE wound down, the workers from the warehouse began to empty into the parking lot. Tony was one of the first ones out.

Billy gave Zee a light slap on the shoulder and said, "See ya, Zee. Good game."

The young boy bounced the ball at his side and headed toward a man waiting for him beside a battered pickup truck. From a distance the boy called back, "See ya, Zooka."

Billy was stunned that the boy knew his nickname. He stood staring into space, trying to figure out how that could be, when Tony pulled up in his car. Billy opened the door and dove into the passenger seat with the car still rolling.

"You have fun with Buckwheat?" Tony asked, as he screeched away, leaving tire marks in the asphalt and the muffler blasting away like a sonic boom.

"He could beat your ass," Billy answered. "His name is Zee."

"Zee?" Tony laughed. "What, like in Zero?"

"No, you're the friggin' zero. Toto the zero. Ha!"

"Least I don't play with niggers."

"Hey, don't be so ignorant, asshole."

Tony took his eyes from the road and looked quickly at Billy. "You can walk, you know."

"Yeah, and I can beat the snot out of you too, you know."

Tony ignored the remark and turned up the volume on the radio. The pulsating sound of *What'd I Say?* blasted from the dashboard speakers. They sang along loudly with Ray Charles, interjecting an occasional obscene word into the lyrics.

When the song stopped and the DJ started babbling, Billy gazed silently out the side window, lost in thought. He wondered if the colored boy was putting him on about the siblings with the XYZ names. But mostly he pondered another question.

How in the devil did the boy know his nickname?

***

After the visit from The Coach, Billy couldn't wait to get to the University and show that he had what it took to be a winner. Just as exciting and challenging was the prospect of getting an education and experiencing college life. Graduating from high school would mean moving on, leaving the only home he had ever known.

In the spring he used the skip-class-day awarded to seniors at Warrior County High to spend a day on the campus in Tuscaloosa. He joined up with a former teammate from Branford, Johnny

Mack Crowell. As a sophomore, Crowell had earned a spot as a starting guard for the Crimson Tide. On a beautiful spring day, Johnny Mack showed Billy around campus.

It seemed like a city within itself. Each major course of study had its own school, a special college within the structure of the university. Buildings were spread about, most identified in big block letters with their special curricula: Business, Engineering, Science, Education, Law, or whatever course of study one might want to pursue.

"I'm in Education," Johnny Mack said. "I might be a coach and teach shop, or whatever. Long as I get my degree, I'll be set."

"I think I'm gonna major in Business," Billy said.

"That's hard. You have to take accounting and statistics and stuff like that. But you can handle it. You're smart."

At the quadrangle, they studied the names of former captains of the football team whose handprints and footprints were formed in the concrete at the base of Denny Chimes.

"That's really cool," Billy said. "I'll bet you get your name here when you're a senior."

"That'd be something, wouldn't it?" said Johnny Mack. "But you gotta be a stud to make captain as a head knocker."

"You'll make it."

"Nah, you've got a better chance than me."

Billy looked dumbfounded at his buddy. "Are you crazy? I haven't even made the team yet."

"You will. You're better'n any of the guys we have now."

The comment hit Billy like a sledgehammer. Captain? The idea had never crossed his mind and it seemed impossible. He imagined his name permanently engraved at the base of Denny Chimes along with legends of the past. He tried to brush the thought aside, but it persisted to linger like a far-fetched idea that grows more plausible as it settles in one's mind.

The chimes struck eleven and soon the quadrangle came alive as hundreds of uniformed ROTC cadets gathered to assemble in formation. Neatly formed groups of student-soldiers dressed in Army green or Air Force blue soon began performing drill movements in response to sharp commands. Then they merged into a long column of squads and marched parade-style past a small crowd of dignitaries, including the President of the University and the Governor. As they passed the reviewing stand, they did an eyes-right salute to the Commanding Officer.

The Million Dollar Band played patriotic music and when the chords of *Stars and Stripes Forever* began, Billy felt his whole body tingle.

The sky was clear, the air was warm, and the campus was beautiful with dogwoods and azaleas in full bloom. The stirring anthems of John Philip Sousa blended with cadet officers barking orders, and Denny Chimes stood steadfast over the imprints of football heroes. At that moment the world seemed perfect to him.

"Boy, this is something," he said.

"It's Govenor's Day," said Johnny Mack. "It's a once-a-year thing."

"I'll have to take ROTC, won't I?" Billy asked.

"Yeah, it's a real pain in the ass."

"Why aren't you out there?"

"I'm recovering from a knee injury."

Among the crowd around the reviewing stand, Billy noticed several pretty girls dressed in female officer ROTC uniforms.

"Who are they?" Billy asked.

"They're sponsors," said Johnny Mack. "Mostly sorority girls."

"Whatta they do?"

"They look pretty. You know—keep the morale up." He laughed. "They're all spoken for," he added. "Mostly to frat boys, but a couple to ballplayers. Just the guys that score touchdowns." He looked at Billy with a grin.

Billy smiled at the hint that his football scholarship might have more benefits than tuition and board.

During the afternoon, Johnny Mack showed Billy around town and introduced him to many of the other players. In the evening, as they ate dinner at the athletic dorm, he invited Billy to a party that night.

"No thanks, I need to get home."

"Aw, come on. There's a good band and lots of girls."

"I have to go to school tomorrow, don't you?"

"Not till ten o'clock. I'm only taking twelve hours this semester so I can get my grades up. Coach don't like it when some dumbass flunks a few classes and has to sit out. He don't like that a little bit."

"Well, make sure you stay eligible. We need you next year." The word *we* came from Billy's mouth as if he was already a part of the team and, in truth, that's the way he felt.

He thanked Johnny Mack for his hospitality and the two young men parted with a handshake and a "Roll Tide."

It was beginning to get dark by the time Billy left for home. He passed through sorority row where imposing houses were adorned with large Greek letters. The sidewalks on both sides were teeming with female students heading to and from the buildings, a seemingly endless supply of girls. The number of pretty coeds on campus had not escaped Billy's attention throughout the day, and Johnny Mack had introduced him to more than one. In his eyes, none were as beautiful as Olivia, but he couldn't deny a certain attraction to variety.

As he drove home, he thought about how different his life would be in a few months. It meant making new friends, fitting in with new teammates. No one would care that they called him The Branford Bazooka or how many touchdowns he had scored for the Warrior County Choctaws. Now he would just be Billy Burdette, another hotshot freshman for the big boys to knock around.

He was not yet eighteen and all summer he thought about being on his own for the first time. Even though the University was only an hour away, it seemed like a different world. Olivia was part of his old world and though he loved her, he wasn't sure that first love should be the last love. They were both too young to close the door on youth, he thought. He decided he had to talk to her about their future, but he kept putting it off, dreading the prospect of how she might react.

Two nights before he left for college, he finally brought it up as they sat in the car outside her house. He was uncomfortable and unsure how to say what he wanted to tell her.

"We won't be able to see each other much in the next few months," he said.

"It'll go by quickly though," she said. "Absence makes the heart grow fonder, you know."

She was making it harder and he didn't know how to bring it up gently.

He made a frustrated grunt. "Maybe we should..."

"What?" She smiled and opened her eyes wide.

He knew her mind was going in another direction, thinking he was about to get really serious.

"Maybe we should...back off a little." The words didn't sound right and he couldn't have felt more awkward had he been in a straightjacket.

"What do you mean, back off?" She pulled away from his embrace. "You mean breakup?"

"No, not breakup, just...see other people. Be regular teenagers."

"Billy, I don't want to date anyone else. We don't have to be together all the time. I will be here for you. I love you and I thought you loved me."

"I do, Olivia, I swear. But I don't want you to be tied down to me. I want you to know it's okay to be with other people. It's not like we'll never see each other again. We just need to take time and make sure this is a forever thing."

"So, you're not sure? You say you love me, but now you're not sure. Maybe it's *you* that wants to be with other people."

"That's not it. Jesus, don't make it out like I'm a jerk. Well, maybe I am a jerk. You're the best looking, smartest girl in God's creation and that's a fact. And I'm the luckiest guy in the world to be with you." He kept talking as she turned her head and looked away. "But you've got your whole life in front you. If things are still the same after a while, then we'll know it's for good. I'm not leaving you."

He leaned to kiss her, but she pulled her head back.

She turned and looked at him. "Well, when you know it's for good, then you let me know. In the meantime, you have a good time enjoying other people," she said through her tears.

It was if their love was as fragile as an egg and he had just cracked the shell. "Olivia," he said as he reached for her. She pulled away and got out of the car, slamming the door behind her.

He ran to catch up with her before she could get to the front door. With his hand on the doorknob, he said, "I can't let you go feeling like this."

She had stopped crying. "You can't have it both ways, Billy. Let me in."

He took his hand from the door. She jerked it open and stalked past him into the house. The door closed hard in his face and he stood staring at it, wondering what to do next.

On the way to the car he said all of the curse words he knew and a few that he invented on the spot.

7

After the day of pressure washing, the rain clouds drifted to the east and Bill worked under clear skies for the next week. He was almost through painting the house when Hank came to visit one afternoon. He took a break and the men settled into a couple of lawn chairs under a cottonwood tree in the back yard.

Hank reached into his shirt pocket and pulled out a pack of cigarettes. "Want one?"

"Uh, why not? I haven't smoked a cigarette in years, but I'll join you." Bill took a cigarette, along with a light, from Hank. "Thanks."

"Y'welcome." Hank leaned back in his chair and stared at the back of the house. "That's a good job you've done. You work hard and do things right. If you didn't, I'd get after you 'cause Joanie's a good woman and she deserves for things to be done right. But she likes you so she wouldn't say otherwise."

"I try to do right by people," Bill said, ignoring the last comment.

"Not everybody does."

"I know. I treat this just like I would if it was my own house."

"Well, you never know."

"Hmph," Bill mumbled with a smile. It was a strong signal, but he was uncertain what might happen between him and Joan, much less what he wanted to happen.

They puffed on their cigarettes in unison.

Finally, Bill restarted the conversation. "Let me ask you something—why *does* Joan like me? She doesn't really know me."

"You'll have to ask her. But my guess is it's really more a matter of trust. You've got to trust somebody before you can like 'em, you know. And she don't trust a lot of men, especially since that sorry ass left her. You and me might be the only ones. I guess she just had that...what you call...woman's intuition about you." Hank took a drag from his cigarette. "Is she right?"

"Yeah, she's right. I may have done some things that The Man Upstairs doesn't approve of, but I'm trustworthy."

"I believe that, and don't worry about me—I won't tell nobody about that other stuff." Hank grinned as he exhaled a puff of smoke and tapped the ash from his cigarette.

"Still," Bill said, "most women who live alone wouldn't let a man they hardly knew stay in their house overnight."

Hank took the cigarette from his mouth and spit a shred of the filter from his tongue. "Well now, she does like you and she does trust you, but she wasn't alone."

Bill squinted his eyes with a questioning look.

"There's a nice easy chair in her bedroom," Hank said.

"You were there all night?"

Hank pursed his lips as if in reflection. "That chair's good for sleeping." He raised his brows and looked hard at Bill. "Trust only goes so far."

Bill smiled and dropped his cigarette butt in the empty paint can lying on the ground between them. "I don't blame you—or her."

Hank nodded.

Bill thought about something Hank had said earlier. "Who was the sorry ass that left her?" he asked.

"I figured she'd told you. Better get it from her. And don't tell her I said anything."

Hank tossed his cigarette butt in the paint can. "Are you working for somebody now? I mean besides painting houses?"

"Not full time," he hedged. "I was installing floors—carpets and such—but things got slow. I'm between jobs right now."

"Joanie tells me you've got a college degree in business or something like that. She told me you used to work at the Floor Store. I know some people there and they said you ran their warehouse for a while. You like doing that?"

"Yeah, but jobs like that are a little scarce around here." He didn't tell Hank he'd not only managed the biggest chemical warehouse in the state, but once held a position where several warehouse managers reported to him. Neither did he mention that he'd never spoken to Joan about his education. But he would hold that for later.

"You operate a forklift? Work a computer?"

"Sure."

"Good. I thought you might. They said you were pretty sharp."

"I don't know about that, but I've got a B.S. in b.s. and more sense than I've been using lately. What are you getting at?"

"I got a warehouse I need a little help with. It's not real big, but I need somebody to help out. My nephew's running it now, but he's about as sorry as a wet mule."

As the conversation progressed, Bill answered questions and made comments that seemed to convince Hank he knew what he was talking about.

After a while, Hank said, "Looks like we're pretty much on the same page. How would you feel about working for me? I can't pay you much and it might not work out for either of us, but I'm willing to give it a try if you are."

"You mean at the warehouse your nephew manages?"

"He doesn't manage much of anything. I think you could do better."

Bill's pulse picked up at the thought of a regular job, but he held his composure. "What about your nephew?"

"He's a pot-smoking bum and I'm tired of putting up with him. One man can run the place. It's not a complicated operation. I just rent warehouse space and charge a handling fee for moving things in and out. There're five or six regular customers, but I've lost some I need to get back. Rod screwed things up a few times and they got pissed off."

"So you're going to fire this guy, Rod?"

"Not right off the bat. You need to get your feet wet first. I'll take you down there Monday and get you started with him. When you tell me you've got things figured out—it shouldn't take too long—I'll fire the bastard. Just don't let on to him. I'll take care of everything so he won't blame you."

"Hank, you know that means I'll have to violate his trust. And we just talked about that."

"Well, if it's not you, it'll be somebody else. I've lost a lot of business because of his lazy carcass, and I think he has actually screwed me out of some money. So he doesn't deserve anybody's trust."

"I'll do the work and I'll do a good job," Bill said. "But whatever happens to your nephew is none of my doing."

"That's right," Hank agreed.

It was odd, Bill thought, how two men could trust each other while violating the trust of another. That thought faded away quickly though at the prospect of having a real job, no matter how lowly. The money from painting Joan's house wouldn't last long and Hank offered a modest wage he could survive on. Especially if Joan would let him continue to stay at her house in exchange for a little rent. He figured she might agree to that.

After Hank left, Bill put the finishing strokes of paint on the house. He cleaned everything up and, with childlike anticipation, waited anxiously for Joan to come home from work.

He was sitting in a rocker on the front porch when Joan arrived. She parked her car in the driveway and walked to the middle of the front yard to admire the house.

"Are you finished?" she asked.

"All done. Now you have the prettiest house in the neighborhood."

"I know. It looks so much brighter, so much fresher. I love it.

You did a great job." She walked up on the porch and planted a kiss on his cheek.

"Wow! If I had known you were going to do that, I would have worked faster."

She laughed.

"Sit down," he said. "I'll be right back."

He went into the house and returned with two glasses of wine. "I bought a little present," he said, as he handed a glass to her. "You like Zinfandel, don't you?"

"You know I do." She took a sip of the wine and moaned, "Ummmm" as she licked her lips.

He sat next to her, swirling the wine in his glass. "Looks like I got a job today."

"Really? Doing what?"

"I'm not sure exactly, but I'll be working for Hank. He's got a warehouse downtown somewhere."

"Yeah, I know where it is. That's great. When do you start?"

"Monday."

"That's good timing," she said.

He took a sip of wine and looked her in the eyes. "You put him up to it, didn't you?"

"No," she said, an indignant tone in her voice. "I know he's not happy with that nephew of his, but I can't tell Hank how to run his business."

He was pretty sure she was at least aware of the situation, especially since she had told Hank about his college degree. And he wondered how she knew, but that question could wait.

"Well, whether you did or you didn't, I'm glad I got the job. I'm not crazy about the circumstances, but it sounds like that guy Rod brought it all on himself."

"He did. He's a big jerk."

Bill nodded and casually turned the conversation. "Your yard looks good."

"Thanks. I like to work outside when the weather is nice. Hank helps me, too."

He listened dutifully as she told him the history of the trees and the flowers she had planted around the yard. Afterward, they each had another glass of wine while quietly admiring the fruits of her landscaping efforts.

Then Bill changed the subject. "Joan, you've been very nice to let me stay with you, and I appreciate it. But I feel guilty about mooching off you."

"Don't be ridiculous. I'm glad to have you around. And you've bought more than your share of food."

"So, how would you feel if I stayed on as a boarder? I'll pay you a fair rent and a share of the groceries."

"You don't have to do that. You're welcome to stay as long as you want. I know things have been a little rough for you lately."

That hit a nerve. He didn't want her to feel sorry for him, and his pride wouldn't allow him to accept her charity. "No, I can't stay unless I pay my way. Otherwise, I'll have to move on."

"Well, if you're going to be stubborn about it, okay. I don't want you to leave."

He didn't want to leave either, so it was settled.

Later that evening, over dinner, Bill decided the time was right to get a better feel for Joan's motivations.

"I need to ask you something," he said. "Well, two things really." He looked serious.

She widened her eyes. "Uh oh, what's coming now?"

"Don't worry, it's nothing shocking. I'd just like to know why you're so nice to me. You know why I like you—you've been a big help to me—but I don't know why you like me. You really don't know anything about me."

"I know more than you think."

What could she know? She couldn't know the secrets he carried around inside him.

"I talked to Betty at the Floor Store and she told me all about you."

"You mean how I can lay carpet and tile and hardwood floors and stuff?" He knew that was not what she meant.

"No, she told me what kind of person you are—intelligent and...honest and...hard working and...funny and...you have a college degree and...you don't use drugs and..."

He interrupted. "Did she tell you I'm forty-nine years old and what my social security number is?"

"What do you mean?" His question obviously jolted her.

"I mean an employment application is confidential. But I don't care—I don't have anything to hide."

"I'm sorry if I got personal. Betty just told me things she knew about you. She wasn't trying to violate your confidentiality."

"I know. I said it's okay." He paused. "So, you like me because Betty likes me?"

"Not just her. She told me that when you did a job, the customers raved about your work and told their friends to ask for you."

"I appreciate that, but I was usually in and out in a few hours. It's not like I really got to know any of them any more than I got to know you."

She paused slightly, then looked at him earnestly. "Bill, I like you because of who you are. Isn't that enough?"

Feeling guilty for pushing her, he said, "Sure, that's enough. It's the same reason I like you."

"Good, I'm glad we settled that."

They both smiled, as if acknowledging that some feelings have no reason.

"You said there were two things you wanted to ask me," she said.

"I'm not sure I have a right. It's really none of my business."

"Well, I guess if I can know what's on your employment application, I suppose you can ask me a personal question. I'll tell you I'm thirty-eight years old, almost thirty-nine, and I don't have a college degree. Just don't ask me how much I weigh."

"Don't worry about that." He paused to muster his nerve. "Hank told me about a guy who left you. A real ass, he said. Were you married to him?"

"Yes." She seemed disgusted by an old memory. "Eleven years. His name was Eric and he *was* an ass."

"What happened?"

"He had a temper. Sometimes he took it out on me."

"He beat you?"

"Yes, one time too many. I called Hank, and he came over with his shotgun and told Eric he would kill him if he ever did it again. He left the next day, and I haven't seen him since the divorce was final. Hope I never do again. At first, I wanted to have a child, but he said he wasn't ready, and I'm glad now that we didn't." With a wistful look she added, "Someday maybe, but I'm running out of time."

The air hung still for a moment before she spoke again. "So, how about you—ever been married?"

He didn't like to talk about himself. Funny how he didn't anticipate that one question might lead to another.

"Yeah, once."

"Did she beat you?" she asked with a smile.

"Not literally. I had a good job and so did she. But we partied too much. Drank too much. Ran around all the time. When I lost my job, we lost the house. After that, things just kind of fell apart. She found another man. She wasn't a bad person. It was just as much my fault as hers. We weren't good for each other. I bounced around from odd job to odd job for years, not really caring about much of anything. So, that's how I wound up with a college degree and not a thing to show for it."

He paused, holding back the impulse to tell her about his battles with depression. Finally, he added, "Probably a little more than you needed to know, eh?"

"No, I'm sorry about what happened, but I'm glad you told me. Do you have any children?"

He thought about it a long time before answering. "Not that lived."

"I'm sorry."

He acknowledged her with tight lips and a slight nod.

They finished their meal, cleaned the table, and put the dishes away. He was glad he would be staying for a while.

***

At college, Billy felt as though he had graduated into the world of adulthood. The classwork was challenging but not impossible, there were lots of new friends to hang out with, and he was holding his own on the football team. As a freshman, he wasn't eligible for the varsity, but he had earned respect from teammates for his toughness in practice sessions. He felt confident of getting some game action as a sophomore the next year. Though everything seemed to be going his way, he felt an emptiness that wouldn't go away.

He missed Olivia. He had foolishly dented their relationship and risked losing her, but after three months he realized he couldn't deny his feelings.

Finally, he kicked aside his pride and called her.

"Can I talk to you?"

"About what?"

"I need to say it in person, not over the phone."

"I don't know what we need to talk about."

"Olivia, come on, don't be that way. We're still friends aren't we?" He couldn't believe he'd said *friends. What kind of stupid talk is that?*

"Friends? I don't know—are we?"

"Olivia, just give me a chance to talk to you. I'm coming home Saturday afternoon. Can I see you for a few minutes?"

He closed his eye and gnashed his teeth as the phone went silent. Then she said, "I'll be here."

The team didn't have a game that week so right after Saturday's practice he made the short drive to Branford and went directly to Olivia's house. As he pulled into the driveway, he saw her sitting in the wooden swing that hung from the big oak tree in the side yard. She remained seated as he walked to her.

With a put-on smile, he said "Hi."

"Hi," she responded, as if greeting a stranger.

He sat beside her. "How have you been?"

"Well. And you?"

"Fine as frog hair." He had used that line many times jokingly, but now it sounded stilted.

She didn't smile.

He dug his feet in the ground and gently pushed the swing. They slowly glided in small arcs, looking straight ahead and not speaking. He felt awkward and didn't know how to start things without showing his anxiety. A veil of reserve seemed to blanket her, and he knew it was up to him to win her all over again.

"How's school?" he asked.

"It's good."

The chain squeaked as he pushed the swing a little harder.

Finally, she turned to him and asked, "How is football?"

"Pretty tough, but I'm doing okay. They try to beat the crap out of the freshmen and they've run off five or six of them." She remained silent. "I think the coaches like me," he continued, "although they won't tell anyone that. I had some good runs in practice, and I'm as fast as anybody on the team."

He was glad she asked and he didn't hesitate to show a hint of pride, but he didn't mention the three touchdowns he had scored in the four-game freshmen season. Everybody in Branford knew that.

"Good. I'm glad you're doing well."

That's all she said, and he let it settle in as she turned away.

The eek eek of the squeaking chain seemed heavy in the absence of conversation. He tried unsuccessfully not to stare at her perfectly formed body, which was well displayed in jeans that seemed to have been painted on and a tight sweater that stretched taut across her breasts. His testosterone kicked in and he fought the urge to grab her.

When he opened his mouth, the words tumbled out with no forethought. "I would be doing a lot better if you would let me kiss you."

She turned and looked at him with a blank expression. He held his breath.

"That's kind of jumping ahead, isn't it?"

"Damn it, Olivia, I love the hell out of you," he said, his voice rising in frustration. "And I've been miserable for three lousy months. So there—is that what you want to hear?"

"I didn't say I wanted to hear anything."

He didn't know what to say next, but he had gone about as far as he was going to go. They turned from each other and pushed the swing in unison.

She stopped the swing, looked at him without smiling, and said, "You can kiss me if you want to."

Slowly he moved over, put his arms around her, and kissed her. Her lips were compliant and he could feel a current of passion spread through his body.

"I love you, too," she said, pulling him tighter, with her face against his cheek. "And I've been miserable, too."

He breathed her sweet feminine smell and felt the perfection of her body next to his. He was calm in love once again.

She leaned into his chest, and he pushed the swing in motion.

"Shiver me timbers, Olive, I feel like I just ate a whole can of spinach."

"Oh, Popeye, you're so romantic," she said in her Olive Oyl voice.

It would never be better—he knew that. Most of his life was still ahead of him and he had yet to learn the wisdom of defeat, but somehow he knew this time, this place, this woman, was a piece of glorious magic to be savored for the moment.

For now, the world cheered him on, and he was the magician with the beautiful assistant by his side. One day the magician would tap his cane, but the rabbit wouldn't come out of the hat. The assistant would disappear and the audience would boo. But not this day.

This day was magic.

8

With the money from painting Joan's house and the prospect of a regular, albeit modest, wage from the job working for Hank, Bill had a little breathing room for the first time in a while.

He hadn't forgotten about the debt he owed at the trailer park, though. He doubted the manager at the trailer park expected to ever see any of it, but he hated feeling like a deadbeat.

On a gray-sky Saturday morning, he drove to the trailer village and parked in front of the office building. Inside, he found the property manager slouched in a worn stuffed chair watching television. It was the same man with the red beard who had evicted him only a couple of weeks before. The television, topped with a set of rabbit ears wrapped in aluminum foil, was tuned in splotchy color to a show about deer hunting. The familiar pearl-handled pistol lay snug in its holster on the desk beside the man.

"What brings you back?" the manager said, tilting his body forward in the chair. "I figured you'd be long gone."

"No, I'm still around," Bill said. "I came to make a payment."

"I'll be damned," the manager responded. "That's something else. Never thought I'd see that."

"I told you I'd be back."

"People say lots'a shit."

"I'm sure. Anyhow, here's a couple hundred. I'm good for the balance, but I need a few more weeks."

"That'll work. I guess I won't have to shoot you now." Without a hint of a smile, the manager rose from the chair and took the two one-hundred dollar bills. He removed a large ring of keys from his belt, unlocked a drawer in the desk, and placed the money inside.

Bill looked at the gun on the desk and had no doubt it had been used before on some ne'er-do-well. "Here's my address in case somebody tries to reach me." He handed the manager a scrap of paper with Joan's address on it and started out the door.

"Oh, hell, I almost forgot," the manager said to Bill's back. "Here—you've got some mail." He reached into a tray from the stack on the corner of the desk and pulled out an envelope. "I almost threw it away, but I figured I'd hang onto it for a few more days." He handed Bill the envelope. "See, I'm not such a son-of-a-bitch."

"No, you're not. I never thought you were. When did this come?"

"I'm not sure. One day last week."

The return address read:

Mr. and Mrs. Jack Burdette
1172 Highlands Trail
Hoover, AL 35216

"Thanks for holding on to it. It's from my brother."

"No sweat."

"I'll be back when I can give you the rest of the money."

"That'll work."

Bill went to his truck, leaned back in the driver's seat, and opened the envelope. The letter, written in beautiful cursive handwriting, wasn't from his brother. His heartbeat picked up as he read.

Dear Billy:

It's been a long time since we have heard from you and I hope you are doing well. Our life is quite hectic and I worry that Jack works too hard. All in all, though, we are doing fine.

Brooke just turned eighteen and she will be going to Vanderbilt in the fall. She will be working at Yellowstone Park for the summer and I'll be coming out with her to help her settle in. We are flying to Jackson Hole on May 14. Jack has decided he can't get away, so it will be a little mini-vacation for me.

Billy, do you think you would be able to meet us at Yellowstone? I'll be leaving on the 18th so any day before then will be fine. We miss you and would love to see you. It would be a shame to come all the way to Wyoming and not get together. Please try to make it.

Hope to hear from you soon. Stay well.

Regards,
Olivia

He read the letter a second time, savoring each word while imagining Olivia's voice and the look on her face. When he got to the part that said, "We miss you," his eyes became misty. To him, it read, "I miss you."

He was stricken with the tug of opposite emotions. On one hand, he would give anything to see her again, while on the other, he couldn't possibly face the pain of her seeing him. Even if he did meet her, it would just be for a few hours and then she would be gone again, like a vision that appears only to vanish when you try to touch it.

It was no use to fight it—he would meet with her. He would call her in the middle of a workday, when Jack wasn't around, and she would answer the phone. They would chat briefly and make arrangements for when and where to meet. Yes, that was a good plan.

May 14 was less than three weeks away.

Jeez, it will be here before you know it.

***

Billy came home one weekend late in his freshman season. The freshman schedule was over and the varsity had an away game. On Friday afternoon, he drove directly to Olivia's house. Her parents greeted him and then stepped away as the two young lovers went to the screened porch.

"God, I've missed you," he said, and kissed her for the first time in two weeks.

"I've missed you more." She pressed her body to his and they fit together like matching pieces of a jigsaw puzzle.

They stood embraced, speaking the language of lovers before she said, "I've got to get ready for the game. We can go to the Spinning Wheel after that."

"And then the park," he said with a grin.

She smiled, took his hand and led him to the front door. There he kissed her one last time and held her tightly, as if he could absorb the feel of her body and carry it with him.

"See ya later, Ms. Oyl."

"See ya, Popeye." She eased away from his reluctant arms and headed to her room for the ritual of putting on her majorette costume and make-up.

That night he went to the Warrior County game to watch his old team and bask in the glow of celebrity. People of all ages hovered around him, vying for his attention before the game, and he soaked it up as if he were a war hero returning home. However, when the game started, all of the attention turned to Jackie, now the star quarterback.

Billy was proud of his younger brother, who had outgrown him physically but remained a notch below him in talent. The difference separating them was understood but unspoken. Jackie was a good player, while Billy was a dominant player with sprinter's speed and a relentless competitive spirit.

Intensity. It was the missing ingredient that Billy knew would keep his brother from reaching his level of competition. He knew there would only be one crimson jersey in the Burdette home.

But Jackie was the star that night. When he completed his

second touchdown pass, the rout was on and the band played *Dixie* over the roar of the crowd. The Warrior County fans were already on their feet, and even the visitors stood and sang along to the words to the southern anthem.

From the stands it was easy to see the other team was overmatched, and Billy relished the memory of playing in games like that. It wasn't like the competition he faced in practice each day, where everyone was a high school hotshot and every drill, every play in scrimmage, was another test of worthiness.

Now he felt like he was an adult watching children play.

Between quarters, Billy made his way to the concession stand and noticed a small group of colored kids hanging around outside the stadium. From a grassy hill just beyond the chain link fence surrounding the field, the outsiders had a clear view of the game. He stopped in his tracks when he saw a familiar face on the other side of the fence. It was the young boy named Zee with whom he had tossed a basketball in the warehouse parking lot the previous summer. Their eyes connected and they waved at each other.

Billy imagined the kid in the same spot a year earlier as he headed for the end zone with shouts of "Go Zooka" from his teammates on the sideline. Obviously, the boy had picked up on the nickname and remembered it when they played their game of HORSE.

He was glad Zee had seen him play, but it bothered him that the fence separated them in a way that didn't seem right. It was like the invisible fence that ran through the town—the fence of segregation. Even as a young man, he could see that the fence was used not only to keep the coloreds out, but to keep the whites in as well.

At halftime Olivia tossed her baton twirling into the air, caught it in stride, and strutted around as the band played their repertoire. When the school fight song began, she marched off the field, leading the band with her baton thrust high as the cheering fans rose from their seats. Billy looked on as his ego swelled with the knowledge that every red blooded young man in the county would give his eyeteeth for a date with his girl.

After the game Billy met Jackie, along with some of his old teammates, in the locker room and congratulated them on a good game. The players greeted him with handshakes, accompanied by respectful admiration laced with obscenities. He stood by as the coach praised Jackie for leading the team to victory and the players began a shout:

He's our quarterback, he calls the huts,
We say, not until you kiss our butts.

"All right," Coach Mills shouted over the din, "good game tonight, guys. But next week we've got Robert E. Lee, and it'll be a lot tougher. I promise you they'll knock your butt clean out of the county if you're not ready. And you better start getting ready at practice on Monday or I'll be on you like stink on a pig. So, don't listen to those knucklehead jock sniffers out there who tell you how great you are."

After the coach left the locker room, a big fullback called Moley let out a whoop. Then, jumping up on a bench, he pulled off his jock and held it in front of his face, pretending to smell it.

"Hey, you knucklehead jock sniffers," Moley said. "You know what this jock smells like? It smells like eight-and-oh, baby. Eight-and-oh!"

The rest of the players picked up the cue, raised their jocks to their faces, and yelled, "Eight-and-oh," in homage to their, so far, undefeated season.

The excitement in the locker room reminded Billy of seasons past, but things had changed. Even though he still had strong friendships on the team, he felt apart, as if he were a stranger looking at them through a glass window. It was Jackie's team now. The mantle had been passed to his brother. He tried not to admit it to himself, but it peeved him a little that the Branford Bazooka had been silenced.

Knowing that Olivia was waiting for him in the parking lot eased the thought.

***

The next day Billy and his brother joined a group of their buddies to go swimming in the strip-mine quarries on the outskirts of town. He and Jackie, in their mom's car, were joined by two other carloads of guys. It was mid-November, but the weather had turned into the eighties and the craziness of going swimming that time of year was part of the fun.

The road to the quarries led them past the local high school for coloreds. The bright blue lettering of *J. W. Nash High School* arched across the front doors in sharp contrast to the peeling white paint on the rest of the facade. The building's shabby condition and the scruffy grounds surrounding it seemed a world removed from that of Warrior County High School. Behind the main building was a football field, where a game was in progress.

"Look—they play their games on Saturday," Jackie said.

"They don't have lights, dumbass," countered Billy.

He stopped the car on the side of the road where they had a distant view of the action and could faintly hear the stadium announcer describe the play in an excited voice. On one side of the field a large bank of concrete tiers overflowed with the home crowd, while on the other side a smaller set of wooden bleachers was scattered with visiting fans.

Near the main gate leading to the stadium a small Nash Rambler with lots of dents and scratches and a streaky blue paint job was parked on a slab of bricks. A banner draped on the side of the car read *Go Wildcats*.

As the game progressed, the players and coaches on the sidelines moved up and down the perimeter of the field following the line of scrimmage. A small group of fans followed in unison. Behind them, the cheerleaders waved their pompoms with gusto, and the fans wildly cheered the action.

On one play a runner scored a touchdown on a long punt return and, after tossing the ball to the official, simply laid down in the end zone to catch his breath.

It was obvious from the ragged uniforms and the dirt-swept field that the facilities were at a different level than what the white boys of Warrior County were accustomed. However, it didn't seem to dampen the spirits of the players or fans and the intensity of the game was apparent even at a distance.

At a break in the action, Jackie said to his brother, "We could beat the snot out of them. They can't pass worth a crap, and they run the same plays all the time."

"They need some coaching, but they're fast. They've got some big guys, too, but they're not in shape," Billy responded.

One of their friends in another car yelled out a mock cheer, in an affected Stepin Fetchit voice. "Yea white, yea blue, Yea Nash, we's fo' you."

The other boys in the car laughed and derisively hollered, "Go Nash."

A few of the colored fans nearby heard the words and shouted back at the three carloads of white boys.

"Don't be such jerks," Billy hollered to his buddies through an open window. He started the car's engine, floored the gas pedal and, as the Oldsmobile surged through the automatic transmission, headed onto the road leading to the quarry with the other cars close behind.

Even on a warm fall day, the water in the quarry was bound to be cold. The quarries around Branford were big open craters left from the days of strip-mining coal, leaving the landscape looking as if it had been ravaged by bombing raids. Underground streams fed some of the pits with water fifteen feet or more in depth that supported schools of small crappie. At the biggest quarry, one side rose high above the water, making an ideal platform for jumping and diving.

When they arrived, the boys stripped to their bathing suits and began jumping off the high point into the chilly water. Some tried to make the biggest splash with cannonball tucks, while others flipped backward or splayed out in a swan dive. After an hour of diving, swimming, and horseplay, they put on T-shirts and gathered around a large rock to smoke Tampa Nugget cigars and trade sips of white lightning from a Mason jar.

Afterward, they had a self-judged contest from the high spot to see who could make the biggest pee stream into the water. The one named Jewboy declared himself the winner over the protests of the others, who then pushed him off the edge into the urine-tainted water below. Afterward, they jumped into the far end of the quarry, giddy from the alcohol, and played a made-up game with a rubber football. Four of the boys, including Billy, grabbed Jackie and pulled off his bathing suit. They tossed it to another boy on the bank, who ran with it down a path into the bushes.

Jackie searched the bushes, covering his private parts from the briars, but he never found his bathing suit.

On the way home, Billy smiled and said, "You need a new one anyhow. That thing looks like something Dad would wear."

"Eat me," Jackie said. "It looks better than that crotch hugger you wear that shows your nut sack."

"You're just jealous."

When they arrived home Billy walked to the back of the car and raised the trunk lid. He pulled out Jackie's still wet bathing suit and tossed it to him.

"I guess that's why they call them trunks," he said with a laugh.

"Yeah," Jackie replied, as he snatched the suit out of mid-air. "I guess that's why they call you turdhead."

Later, at dinner, Billy mentioned to his parents the game between the colored high schools.

"It was funny," Jackie said. "Some of their uniforms didn't match, and the stadium is a piece of crap, and—get this—the players and fans walked up and down the sideline with the play. It was hilarious."

Billy didn't say anything, but he felt a twinge of guilt. It was guilt born of the knowledge that some things weren't fair, and somehow he felt a party to the unfairness.

He watched Alabama on television that night as the Tide won a close, low scoring game in the last few minutes. The whole family—including his mother, father, and brother—and Olivia, gathered in front of the television and watched intently, screaming in excitement or groaning in frustration with each play, as if the fate of their lives hung in the balance. Watching the game, he imagined what it would be like the next year. The thought of playing on national television and his name being announced in homes all around the country was a tantalizing feeling. He couldn't wait until his family was cheering not for just Alabama, but for him as well.

On Sunday morning Billy fetched the newspaper from the driveway and opened it to the sports page before he reached the front door. Inside, he meticulously poured over the articles and pictures of the game the night before. He read every word in the sports section until he came upon a small article on the last page, headlined *Nash Smashes B. T. Washington.*

The final paragraph grabbed his attention: *In the fourth quarter sophomore halfback Zee (Zippy) Willingham took a handoff and burst around the right side for 57 yards on his way to his second touchdown of the day. That closed the scoring on a 42-13 Wildcat rout.*

He put the paper aside and a familiar face appeared in his mind. He knew there could only be one Zee.

***

That night Billy took Olivia to the drive-in movie in Birmingham to see *Casablanca*. It was the third time they had seen it, and it always stirred irresistible romantic feelings that made them feel like grownups. They knew many of the lines by heart and mimicked the characters in some scenes.

Olivia used her most melodramatic voice as Ilsa. "But what about us?" she said in sync with Ingrid Bergman.

As Humphrey Bogart spoke the famous line—*We'll always have Paris*—Billy pursed his lip to the side and spoke through his teeth in a poor Bogey impression, "We'll always have Branford."

They felt as if they were in their own movie. Branford was as far away as you could get from Morocco but, in their young hearts, the world was a movie set and they were the stars. Unlike the Hollywood version, though, in their script the two lovers would never part.

As the movie ended, Olivia said of Ingrid Bergman, "Isn't she the most beautiful thing you've ever seen?"

"No, you are. Here's looking at you, kid." He held her tightly and kissed her, tasting her tongue with his.

He really did think Ingrid Bergman was beautiful, but to him, she was a movie star, not a real person. Yes, he wasn't lying— Olivia was the most beautiful person he had ever seen in the flesh. She wasn't just an image on a screen, but someone next to him that he could touch and smell and taste.

After the movie, he drove to the little park on the other side of Branford, where no one would recognize his mother's car. There, they embraced in total privacy and surrendered to feelings more powerful than they could understand.

***

The letter from Olivia stirred feelings in Bill, as if the picture in his billfold was speaking to him. The thought of seeing her in the flesh again, after years of trying to forget about their past, was unsettling. Conflicting emotions swirled in his head, the embers of passion still glowing amidst the ashes of old wounds.

He thought about what to say, even rehearsed to himself. Still, he felt a nervous tingle as he began to punch the numbers on the phone. Before he hit the last digit, he quickly hung up.

"Calm down, Burdette," he said aloud to himself. He took a deep breath and slowly punched the numbers again.

When she answered the phone, he deepened his voice to mask his anxiety.

"Hello, may I speak to Miss Olive Oyl, please."

"Oh, my gosh," she gushed. "Billy—it's you. I can't believe it!"

The excitement in her voice was infectious, and a smile broke out on his face.

"Yeah, it's been a while, hasn't it?"

"Too long," she said. There was a brief pause and he heard a sniffle, or maybe imagined he did.

She resumed in a voice that seemed to be struggling to stay calm. "I'm so glad you called. When I didn't hear from you, I was afraid you didn't get my letter. We don't have your phone number, and I couldn't find a listing for you anywhere."

"I know. I just got your letter yesterday, and I didn't have a phone for a while."

The conversation was brief. Olivia would be staying at the Lake Yellowstone Hotel for a couple of days, helping her daughter get settled into the dormitory provided for the summer staff. Bill agreed to meet her at the hotel.

"I'm so glad you can come." Her voice turned softer as she added, "I can't wait to see you again."

"Me, too." It didn't seem like enough, but that was all he could think to say.

"So—I'll see you in Yellowstone," she said.

He couldn't let it go at that. "Olivia," he said, speaking her name for the first time in so long he could almost taste it.

"Yes, Billy?"

"We'll always have Branford, won't we?'

"Oh," she sighed. "Yes. We'll always have Branford."

The sound of her voice touched him, and the thought of seeing her again lifted his spirit for a moment. Thirty years of bad memories seemed to fade away, and for the first time in a long while, he was, once again, Billy Burdette, the Branford Bazooka.

Still, there was a feeling of guilt he couldn't shake. Did Jack know about this rendezvous? Bill could never betray his brother, but there was no denying his feelings for the woman who was now his sister-in-law. He had never gotten used to that, or the darkness in their past that she seemed to have flicked away, like a pesky bug on her sleeve.

He wasn't sure it was wise to meet with her, because he was afraid Olivia was something more than just the girl in the picture he carried in his billfold.

But he knew he had to do it.

9

Bill was the first to arrive at Hank's warehouse on Monday morning, ready to start his new job. He looked at the building, a modest-sized metal structure in a small industrial park, and thought how it paled in comparison to the huge automated warehouses he had once managed. As he waited in his truck, he reflected on the decline of his career and his life. Not that he wanted to, but the past stuck in his mind and he couldn't brush it aside as if sweeping the dirt off a porch. He would soon be fifty and he had nothing. A college degree was pissed away. The love of his life was lost long ago. Alone, with no future, the only thing he had now was the thing that kept him going. Trust in himself.

His reverie was interrupted when Hank drove up in his well-preserved older model Cadillac. "Good morning," he said, through the open driver's window. "The bastard is late."

Hank got out of his car with a frown on his face and shook his head in obvious annoyance. Bill exchanged small talk with him as they waited for Hank's nephew to arrive.

Twenty minutes later, a dusty Jeep pulled up and Rod Reynolds stepped out. A large man with a body settled at the middle, symmetrically rounded above and below the wide leather belt that encircled his belly, he resembled a real life Humpty Dumpty. Dark hair hung over his ears and curled behind the collar of his denim shirt. Horned rimmed glasses, ankle-high work boots, and a gaudy silver belt buckle completed the picture of a man who appeared to be out of tune.

"Rod, this is Bill Burdette," Hank said, as the three men came together. "He's the fella I told you about."

The men quickly exchanged greetings before Rod unlocked the warehouse door and led the other two inside. The spacious office contained two desks, an upright file cabinet, and a large table. Bill was struck by the amount of clutter. Stacks of file folders lay on the floor, papers were strewn on both desks, and an assortment of food, magazines, dead plants, and all sorts of odd items were scattered about the room. Rod offered seats to the other two and they positioned themselves in front of his desk. He plopped his big frame into a low-back desk chair and leaned back.

"This is a lot to handle on your own," Hank said. "Bill can free you up from the everyday stuff, so you can build the business. Like we've talked about, we need some more customers."

"Yeah, maybe I can pull some out of thin air," Rod said. The smile on his face quickly disappeared.

Hank looked as if smoke might start coming out of his ears. "I don't care if you pull 'em out of your ass. We've got to have more revenue."

The air in the room was thick with tension and Bill sat uncomfortably still.

"I've got some ideas," Rod said. He looked at Bill.

"Good," said Hank. "I'll let you men get to know each other." He stood and walked to the door. Turning back, he said to Rod, "You know what I'm looking for."

Rod remained seated in his chair. "Yeah, I know Hank."

As soon as Hank left, Bill began to ask Rod questions about the warehouse operation. Rod appeared suspicious and answered Bill's questions tersely.

When they went into the warehouse, Rod flipped on the light switches and several of the fixtures didn't come on. The drab lighting added to the shabbiness of the warehouse that drew Bill's attention as they walked through the aisles of merchandise.

After the meeting with Hank and a couple of hours alone with Rod, Bill doubted their working arrangement would last long. However, he knew he had to establish some level of rapport with his lame duck boss in order to learn about the operation as quickly as possible.

For the rest of the week, Bill engaged Rod with casual conversation as they worked closely together. Once they warmed to each other, he found Rod to be personable and fairly bright, but with a lackadaisical approach to running the warehouse. He quickly picked up on some things that needed to be changed, but he was cautious to offer suggestions to avoid the appearance of a threat.

Clearly, organization was not one of Rod's assets. The merchandise in the warehouse was scattered about haphazardly and paperwork in the office was stacked in piles before being placed in file drawers with no apparent system.

Bill concentrated on keeping the warehouse going and he encouraged Rod to spend his time developing new customers. It wasn't a task that Rod felt comfortable with and he made phone calls to local businesses with little success. Overhearing some of the calls, Bill quickly surmised that Rod wasn't much of a salesman.

"This is a waste of time," Rod said. "The only ones that'll talk to me are the ones that want something for nothing. Or they want me to buy some of their crap."

"Talking to people on the phone is tough," said Bill. "Maybe you'd have better luck if you saw them in person."

"I know that, but I can't leave until I'm sure you know what you're doing."

"I've got it handled." Bill knew it was just an excuse for Rod to keep from making personal calls.

"I'm going to start tomorrow," Rod said.

For the next several days, Rod left the warehouse at noon and never returned. Bill didn't get any feedback on the sales calls and he seriously doubted many had been made.

On several occasions, a customer came to pick up their

merchandise and Bill was forced to sort through a stack of pallets with the forklift to get to it. As he apologized for the delays and reassured the customers that improvements were being made, he tried to establish a relationship with each one, knowing they would be his customers at some point.

On Friday of the second week, Rod was late, even more so than usual. When Bill greeted him, he detected the unmistakable sweet smell of marijuana. Hank's suspicions were confirmed.

Rod stayed at the warehouse all day. "Nobody wants to see a salesman on Friday afternoon," he said.

Later, as the day wound down, the two men relaxed in the office.

"So, whatta ya think?" Rod asked. "How's it going?"

"I think I'm getting it," Bill replied. "I've done this kind of work before."

"I can tell."

"Yeah, I think I need to straighten up the warehouse. Get it better organized."

"That's a good idea. The place has gotten a little messy." Rod spoke as if the warehouse had a life of its own, rather than a victim of his own negligence. "You can start on that Monday. I'd help you, but my back's been bothering me."

"No problem, I can handle it. Also, I think we might consider setting up a customer-based system for filing the receipts and shipments."

"I guess you're right. I know how to get my hands on everything, but what if I get run over by a beer truck? That could happen any day, couldn't it?" He stared at Bill steely-eyed.

The look on Rod's face and the tone of his voice gave him away. Bill realized Rod knew what was going on and he was throwing out a piece of cheese in a mental game of cat-and-mouse.

"It could happen to any of us but, more likely, you could get sick or have an emergency," Bill responded.

"Yeah, I could get sick—sick of this damn place. Sick of that overbearing old fart of an uncle."

Bill remained quiet.

"He's going to fire my ass, isn't he? I know that's why he sent you here."

"That's between you and Hank."

"Yeah, it is. But I'm asking you what you think."

"I think he believes this place would make more money if you were a little more aggressive."

"Aggressive, eh? Well, you know what I think?"

Bill raised his eyebrows and didn't respond.

"I think I've done okay running this chicken-shit operation for two years, and if Hank doesn't like it he can kiss my ass. I don't have anything against you, but we wouldn't get along. We've got different ways. And even if we could, there's not enough revenue coming in to justify two people in this place."

"I think we could get along—I'm pretty easygoing—but I don't know how much the business can grow." Bill hedged his feelings, knowing that he and Rod would never be compatible.

"Well...it don't matter 'cause I'm gone. Here—tell the old hemorrhoid to mail my check. And tell him I said go to hell." Rod tossed a set of keys on the desk, rose from his chair and stomped out of the office, slamming the door behind him.

Bill watched through a window as Rod drove away, then picked up the phone and called Hank. "Rod's gone. He just quit."

"Good," Hank said.

"Yeah, I don't think you're losing anything. It'll take me a little while to get everything organized, but I'll get it."

"I know you will. What did he say?"

"He said he hated to leave, but he had an offer from Donald Trump he couldn't refuse. And he said to tell you thanks for your support."

"I'll bet. Ha! Bill, you're so full of it, it's coming out your ears. But screw it, he's gone. That's the main thing. Welcome aboard, sailor."

"Aye, aye, captain. But just to let you know, I get seasick in the bathtub."

"That's all right. We're a thousand miles from the nearest port, but I still have a little salt water in my piss."

"I'll keep that in mind as I get this place shipshape."

"There you go. I'll see you in a while."

As soon as he hung up, Bill put the keys in a desk drawer, pulled out a legal pad, and began to make a to-do list. On Monday he would be on his own, just the way he liked it. He would get this place straightened out, and he would make Hank glad he had hired him. It was a good reason to stay on at Joan's place, too. It had become a comfortable arrangement, maybe too comfortable. He felt they were growing on each other and he couldn't decide how he felt about that.

After he finished the list, he locked the warehouse doors and turned into the bright daylight as he headed for his truck. *Damn, it feels good to have something to look forward to.*

***

At dinner that night, Bill told Joan about Rod's departure.

"Wow, that was quick," she said. "But I'm not surprised."

"Yeah, y'all's plan worked better than you thought."

"What do you mean *our* plan?"

"I know how tight you and Hank are. But don't worry—it's okay. I'm not mad at you. I just don't want you to pull strings for me or feel sorry for me."

"Bill, I don't feel sorry for you one bit, so get that out of your mind. You can take care of yourself. This is the best thing that could happen for Hank. Maybe it's him I feel sorry for. But that's not it. It's not that I feel sorry for you or for Hank. I just want the best for both of you."

She paused and Bill looked back at her sheepishly, like a scolded child. "Besides," she continued, her voice becoming more animated, "you made this happen, not me. I simply hired you to paint my house. You're the one that gained Hank's confidence. He's not going to hire somebody he doesn't trust or doesn't think can do the job. And, believe me, if you can't do the job, he'll get rid of you, too."

"Okay, okay—I said I'm not mad at you. I'm happy with the way things worked out, and I think I'll like working for Hank. And don't worry—he won't have to get rid of me."

They dropped the subject and finished their meal with small talk. He poured himself a beer and handed her a glass of wine before they went to the front porch. There they settled into rocking chairs that had become, more or less, their personal domains.

Daylight had faded into a faint glow and the air was warm and dry.

"I love this time of year," Joan said.

"Yeah, the long days are nice."

They nursed their drinks without speaking, lulled by the sound of the rocking chairs on the wooden floor of the front porch and the smell of blooming plants. The colorful flowers he had helped her plant near a stand of river birches—bright yellow daisies, red salvia, and lavender violets—glowed with the vibrancy of a Thomas Kincaid painting. Occasionally, a car slowly passed by and, rather than disturb the serenity, seemed to blend in as if it were part of a movie set.

Bill hesitated to break the mood but, after a few minutes, he cleared his throat to speak. "You know, we've left this living arrangement kind of open-ended. Maybe I should look for another place. Give you a little space. At least give you your bathroom back." He laughed. "Don't misunderstand—I like your company. But people might get the wrong idea."

"You mean like we're living together? Of course, we are. But it's strictly a business arrangement, right?"

He looked at her in feigned disgust. "No, it's not strictly a business arrangement," he said in a sarcastic tone. "We're friends." After a pause, he added with emphasis, "I think."

"Yes, we are. So what's the problem?"

"Nothing, really. I just don't want to give the impression...I mean, for people to think...I mean for you—"

"Bill, I don't care what other people think, and don't worry about me. I'm almost forty years old, and I can have anyone in my house that I want. We know what our relationship is, and that's all that matters."

"And you don't mind when I leave the lid up?" A huge grin grew on his face.

"No, I wouldn't mind if you would just wipe the pee off." She returned his grin.

"I don't do that," he said, indignantly.

She looked directly into his eyes with a pleading look, extending her glass toward him. "Would you, please?" she said.

He took her glass and went inside to refill it. When he returned, they didn't speak about their living arrangement again.

As darkness began to close in, they saw Hank walking on the sidewalk toward them with an attractive white-haired lady at his side. The elderly lady was neatly dressed in tailored slacks and a blouse. She walked with a spry step and Hank strode beside her at a pace which was a notch higher than his usual gait.

"That's Lois McElvey, Hank's lady friend," Joan said.

When the couple reached the porch, introductions were shared before Joan invited them into the living room, where everyone settled into polite conversation.

Bill noticed that Hank assumed a slightly different demeanor with Lois, a little less casual. He doubted Hank tried his crude Navy stories on her.

Lois looked at Bill. "I understand you will be running Hank's warehouse."

"I guess so. I'll give it my best."

"He'll be a big improvement over Rod," Hank said.

"That's nice of you," Lois continued. "I'm sure Hank appreciates your help."

"It's me that owes the appreciation. Jobs aren't easy to come by around here these days. And I've had my fill of muckin' stables."

"Yes, I'm sure," Lois responded. "I can only imagine what that's like. Wyoming is a long way from the big cities." She paused before adding, "Hank tells me you're from Alabama."

"Yes, I was born and raised there, but I've been out here for more than twenty-five years."

"What brought you to Wyoming?" she asked.

"I guess you might say the wide open spaces. There's a certain attraction to living out here. Kind of hard to put my finger on it. Maybe it's a feeling that there are still places not totally ruined by man."

"So, I take it you're an outdoorsman."

"Not really. I used to fish and water ski when I was a kid, and I like to hike the trails. But I'm not much of a hunter and I haven't been camping in years. I guess I'm basically a city guy, but I hate the incivility that seems to come with civilization."

Joan and Hank silently observed the conversation.

"That's interesting," Lois said. "I find this part of the world to be refreshing also. I grew up in Chicago, and everyone was always in a hurry. I prefer a more relaxed lifestyle. Since I've been here, I find myself to be more in tune with living and not worried about rushing toward death."

Bill seized on her words. "I know what you mean."

That's just the way he felt lately—in tune with living rather than rushing toward death. It was a feeling that had sneaked up on him, and now this woman he had only known for a few minutes expressed it in a way that struck a chord with him.

Joan offered everyone drinks and the conversation drifted from local politics to social issues. Then Lois turned again to Bill's background.

"When I think of Alabama, I think of football," she said. "I'm a Notre Dame fan and we love our football, but I know that people in Alabama are crazy about their team, too."

"Yes, they are," Bill agreed. He almost mentioned something about his football days but, not wanting to relive the pain, he caught himself.

"When I was a child, my family went through Alabama on the way to Florida," Lois continued. "I don't remember much about it. The South seemed...different...to me. I'll never forget the first time

I saw signs on the restrooms for white men, white women, and colored. As a child, that was so odd to me. Odd enough that the restrooms were separate, even odder that the blacks only had one."

Hank cleared his throat. "Ahem. Let's not drag that out..."

Bill interrupted. "No, that's okay. I grew up in the days of segregation and it seemed—as you say—odd, even to me."

Lois looked at Bill, as if slightly embarrassed. "I'm sorry. I didn't mean any offense. I know it's not like that in the South now."

"No offense taken," Bill said. There was a pregnant pause in the room. Then he began speaking as if he were narrating a documentary. "Once, I was at a place where they served your food through a window, like an old Dairy Queen or someplace like that. Anyhow, a black man was in front of me and when he placed his order, the girl inside told him to go around to the side window. That was the window for colored people. The girl inside was a teenager and the black guy was a full-grown man, but he went to the side window where he placed his order. After she took my order, the girl got the black guy's food from the same place mine was being prepared and shoved it to him through his window. The whole thing was ridiculous and I was embarrassed just standing there. I can't imagine how the black guy felt." He hesitated, wondering to himself why he had blurted out the story, and the others remained silent, maybe wondering the same thing.

"That's the way things were," he continued. "I've never forgotten that incident. I wish I had said something or done something—I don't know what. Maybe order the man's food for him. But I didn't. Like I said, that's just the way things were."

"If it bothered you, then your heart was in the right place," Joan said.

"Maybe, but I'm no saint. In truth, I liked going to segregated schools and I've told my share of—let's just say—racial jokes."

"Ah, that ain't nothing," said Hank. "We're not judging you. Hell, I've done a lot worse than that myself."

"I know you're not judging me," said Bill. "No more than I would judge people around here whose ancestors hated Indians.

You know, the government's treatment of the Indians was worse than slavery in some ways. Everybody knows about the lynchings in the South, but the U.S. Cavalry killed and mutilated more than a hundred unarmed Indians at Sand Creek, mostly women and children. The majority of the settlers hated the Indians. Considered them less than human."

"That was a horrible thing," said Joan.

"A bunch of drunk militia cowboys," Hank added.

"They say John Evans planned it," Lois said, picking up on the story of the well-documented massacre. "He was the Governor of Colorado." She looked at Bill and added, "He was from Chicago. Evanston was named for him. A good man mostly, but he died with blood on his hands."

Bill was stung by the comment, thinking it might be his own epitaph, but he maintained his composure. "Man's inhumanity to man," he said. "It seems to know no boundaries."

"Let's not be so morbid," Joan said. She stood and assumed a broad smile. "Would anyone like to play bridge?" The air in the room turned lighter.

"I would love to if everyone else does," Lois replied.

"I'm game," said Hank.

"I'm not very good, but I'll give it a try," Bill said.

Joan retrieved the cards from the desk and everyone moved to the kitchen table. They played bridge for almost two hours, and the women beat the men handily.

"The next time we're playing at my house," Hank said.

"Is that an invitation?" asked Joan.

"You know it," Hank said. He looked at his lady friend quizzically and said, "Lois?"

"Hank," Joan said, "you don't ask a woman for a date in front of others."

"It's just a game of cards," Hank said.

"It's okay," said Lois. "It would be my pleasure."

"So—next Friday night at my house?" Hank asked.

Everyone agreed and the date was set.

After the elderly couple left, Bill and Joan began clearing the table. As he leaned over to gather the score sheet, she rose up with a handful of cards and they came face to face, their bodies touching. They looked at each other with frozen expressions. She leaned her head into his chest and he placed his arm on her back. The room went quiet as they stood pressed together.

"Aren't they a fun couple?" she finally said, her head still in his chest.

"Yes, they are."

"Are we a fun couple?"

"I think we are," he replied.

"That's good."

"But I need to talk to you about something." His tone was serious.

"I know—I don't mean to push you." She looked up at him.

"It's not that. There's something you need to know. It's not about you or about us. It's about someone else. And about a letter I got the other day."

It was time for him to tell her about his trip to Yellowstone. He wanted her to know it meant more to him than meeting with his sister-in-law. He needed to tell someone, because he felt weak and vulnerable at the prospect of seeing Olivia again.

Although Joan was leaning on him, he felt as if he were the one that needed support. He couldn't keep it to himself any longer. Before he could be honest with anyone, especially to Joan—the person to whom he owed the most—he had to face his feelings for Olivia.

"I'll be going to Yellowstone in a couple of weeks to meet an old friend from Alabama."

"That's great."

"Well, it's not exactly an old friend. It's kind of hard to explain but, among other things, this woman is my brother's wife."

"Your brother's wife is an old friend...among other things? It sounds very personal. You don't have to tell me more. It's your business."

"That's why I brought it up. I want you to know. I need to get a few things off my chest."He took a deep breath and sighed. "Her name is Olivia. She's married to my brother, but we were high school sweethearts."

"And you still love her," she said, sounding more like a statement than a question.

He could feel her body go limp.

"That's not it—not exactly. Honestly, I don't know how I feel." He stumbled for words. "Here, look at this," he said as he retrieved the picture of Olivia from his billfold.

"She's beautiful."

"Yeah, but that was a long time ago. I haven't seen her in...I can't remember how many years."

"How long has she been married to your brother?"

"Over twenty-five years."

"Is that why you left Alabama?"

"No. I have nothing against her or my brother. I love them both...I mean, I love them like family...uh, you know what I mean."

"No, I really don't, and I'm not sure you do either."

"I don't guess it matters how I feel. It won't change anything."

"Yes, it does matter. It matters that you face up to the fact that you're still in love with this woman. As soon as you showed me her picture, I knew that. You can't keep love bottled up."

"Joan, I'm sorry to bother you with this, but it eats me up and I need someone to talk to."

She moved back a step, put both of her hands in his, and looked at him with sympathetic eyes. "You can talk to me," she said.

"It's not that I want to. It's that I feel like I have to tell somebody." With that, he released her hands and put one of his on her back. "Let's sit down."

He gently led her to the living room where they settled at each end of the sofa. Then he told her about Olivia. He started from the time when they were in high school, to their break-up in college, and her marriage to his brother.

But he didn't tell her about a bridge, a river, and a night that haunted him or what really caused them to fall apart. He had never told anyone about that.

10

In the summer before his sophomore year, Billy returned to work at the produce warehouse in Branford. One afternoon as he headed to his car after work, he saw Zee shooting hoops in the parking lot, just as he had the year before. The boy was still thin, but he had grown several inches.

Billy joined him, and they casually took turns shooting baskets. No game of HORSE this time.

"Do you remember me?" Billy asked. He tossed one up from the make-shift free throw line. The ball caromed around the rim, then fell in.

"Sure, you're Billy Burdette. You play for Alabama." Zee retrieved the ball and passed it back to Billy.

"I will this year. I remember you, too. You're Zee Willingham and you play for Nash. I've read about you in the paper, and you're pretty doggone good, Zippy." Billy looked at the boy and returned his wide smile for the mention of his nickname. He dribbled a couple of times and let fly another free throw.

"Not as good as you. Maybe someday. I don't think they'll let me play at Alabama, though." The smile faded from Zee's face as the ball barely grazed the rim before nestling in the chain net.

The boy's voice was matter-of-fact, as if resignation trumped hope. Billy didn't have an answer for that. He retrieved his own shot and passed the ball to Zee. They continued to quietly shoot baskets before Billy spoke again.

"Maybe you can't go to Alabama, but there are other schools like State and A&M, or some place up north."

"I know."

Billy felt strange talking to the boy about what he could and couldn't do, but the rules were clear. That's just the way it was and there was nothing either of them could do about it.

Zee threw a bounce pass to Billy. "I better get goin'"

"Are you waiting on somebody?" Billy asked.

"Not today. I don't live far from here. I walked. Really, I dribbled the whole way. I play basketball, too."

"I bet you're good."

"I'm okay. We've got a good team. I play guard, and I think I'll be a starter this year."

"That's great. I played basketball. I was better on defense than offense. We had a couple of guys better'n me, including my brother. Y'all could probably beat us." Billy's voice had the ring of polite deference.

"I don't know. I've never seen you play. It ain't like playing HORSE."

"You're right," Billy agreed. With no forethought, he added, "Want a ride home?"

"Nah, I don't want to start no trouble."

"It'll be okay." Billy wasn't so sure about that, but he felt an urge.

By that time, the parking lot had cleared out. Billy waved his hand, ushering the boy to follow him. Zee slowly moved forward, then joined Billy for the walk across the parking lot to Billy's car. Clutching the basketball in his lap, he sat stone silent and wide-eyed as if he were uncomfortable. Billy suspected Zee had never been in a car alone with a white person before. It was a similar experience for Billy, but instead of discomfort he felt a slight stirring of something that was difficult to pinpoint. It didn't feel like courage as much as it felt oddly like righteousness. He would look back on it later, after the turmoil of the protests and violence that was to come, as an act that meant nothing to anyone else, but everything to the two of them.

Billy followed Zee's directions to his house. It was broad daylight and, during the short drive, they passed a lot of eyes glaring at them from faces of different colors. He had passed through the neighborhood many times before, but as he let Zee out, he took a closer look at the surroundings. He felt a sudden surge of sadness. It looked like a place where hard times lived.

He headed home and soon was clear of Chalkville. Niggertown, a lot of whites called it. He was glad he didn't have to live there, and was sorry anyone else did.

***

It was almost six o'clock when Bill left the warehouse on Friday night. At the house he found Joan in the kitchen, standing over the stove.

"I made you some soup," she said. "I've got to get ready. I have a date tonight."

"All right!" he said. "Do your thing, girl. But you didn't have to worry about me. I'm not helpless, you know."

"It's called being thoughtful."

"Yeah, it is, and I appreciate it. I'll make you dinner some night. How would you like some beanie weenies and cheese toast?"

"Sounds delicious." She left the kitchen and headed for her bedroom.

A few minutes later she returned wearing jeans, a western shirt and boots, all in black with accents of white and red. The jeans stretched tight against her shapely rear end and the shirt tugged at her breasts. Bright red lipstick glowed against her fair complexion. He had never seen her look so young and fresh.

"Damn woman, you're one foxy looking cowgirl."

"Thanks. I only have one outfit like this. We're going to Sidewinders."

"One outfit like that is enough. I hope you have a whip, 'cause you'll need one to fight off the ranch hands."

"I don't think so." She smiled. "But look at this." She went back into her bedroom and returned wearing a black cowboy hat.

"Wow, now that's a look," he said. "And I can't say exactly what I'm thinking. I'll just say that's sexy as hell."

"You're so funny," she said, giggling.

"I'm serious. I'm not much of a cowboy myself. I bought some boots one year for Frontier Days, but they weren't comfortable. I didn't like the pointy toes. I had a big belt buckle, too. But I can't wear a hat, and I'm no good at horse talk."

"I'm not a cowgirl either, but sometimes it's fun."

The doorbell rang and she went to the door where she greeted a tall man dressed in western garb. He stood at least six-two and had a thick, blond mustache and light complexion. Long blond hair flowed from beneath his white Stetson. He looked young, maybe less than thirty.

"Bill, this is Ben," Joan said.

Bill stepped forward and shook hands with the young man. "Hi, I'm Bill Burdette. Glad to meet you."

"Same here. Ben Hawkins." His words belied the solemn look on his face.

"Ben plays the bass," Joan said. "His group is playing tonight."

"What's your group called?" asked Bill.

"The High Plainsmen."

"Um." Bill pursed his lip and nodded his head in approval. "Y'all play any bluegrass? That's my favorite kind of music."

"Not much. Mostly western swing and country."

"Well, we'll be off," Joan said briskly. "I'll be late coming home."

"Okay, have a good time." Bill looked at the bass player. "Nice meeting you."

"My pleasure," Ben said, without a trace of expression.

The two men faced each other, silently stone-faced for an instant, as if waiting for the bell to start a twelve-round bout. Joan latched onto Ben's arm and they walked out the door. Bill watched from the front porch as they drove away in an extended cab pick-up truck.

He returned to the kitchen and ate a bowl of Joan's soup. Afterward, he reclined on the sofa to watch television. Four hours later, he fell asleep with the *Tonight Show* still on.

In a while, he roused himself and turned off the television. Sluggishly, he trudged into the bathroom to take a leak when he heard the front door open. Quickly, he closed the door and finished his business. Leaving the bathroom, he looked into Joan's bedroom where she sat on the side of the bed taking her boots off.

"How was the boot scootin' boogie?" The drowsiness had begun to wear off and his blood was stirring again.

"Shitty!" she snapped.

"Oh." It was uncharacteristic language for her and it mildly shocked him. He stood in the doorway waiting to hear more.

"He's a real ass."

"What happened?"

"A twenty-something-year-old happened. That's what happened. Hell, she may have been younger than that. That's what I get for going out with this … boy!"

"Sorry to hear that."

"Well, it won't happen again. I poured a beer right on his crotch and told him to go to hell."

"Sounds like the *bass* player didn't get to first *base* with you."

She looked at him with angry, squinted, eyes.

"I guess *Ben's* a *has* been." There was a sly look on his face.

The hint of a grin formed on her face. "He sure as hell is. And if I had a knife, he'd be a gelding."

"Whoa! I get shrinkage just thinking about that."

"I'm glad you think it's so damn funny." She smiled through a fake frown.

"Did he bring you home?"

"No. I left him with the little … groupie. He tried to make up to me, but I told him to stick it in his ear. One of my girlfriends brought me home."

"You should've called me. I would've picked you up."

"There was no need. I had friends there."

Her boots were off, and she had pulled her shirt out of her jeans. When he started out of the room, she said, "You want a drink? I can't sleep right now."

"Sure."

As she started for the kitchen, he said, "I'll get it."

She went to the living room and he to the kitchen to pour their drinks. He returned with a glass of wine for her and some scotch for himself.

She put the glass to her lips and swirled the wine in her mouth before swallowing. "Thanks." Her anger seemed to have calmed and she spoke softly, staring straight ahead. "There are three men to every woman in this town." Bill sensed the pensiveness in her mood. Then her voice became stronger and she looked directly at him. "But every one of them is either dumb as a rock, sorry as hell, or ugly as a pig in slop."

"That's great. So where does that put me?"

"I don't mean you. I mean every other man I've met."

"Finding a woman is the same way, you know. Like you say, the odds are against a man in this town. But that doesn't bother me—I'm not looking. That's the best way to be. You can't make something happen. If it's going to, it'll just happen. At least that's what I think." He looked at her and there was no reaction.

"Of course," he continued, "you might not want to listen to me 'cause my track record hasn't been too good about anything lately."

"I do listen to you. I'm glad you were here when I got home tonight."

"I'm glad, too. Maybe you won't go to bed all upset."

"No. No, I won't do that. Thanks," she said.

As the night wore on, she told him about growing up in Kansas before meeting her ex-husband, an Air Force lieutenant, at a singles' bar in Wichita.

"Eric was good looking and outgoing. He was also a little arrogant, but that seemed attractive to me at the time. We only dated for four months before we got married. I was in love with him or, at least, thought I was. But, more than that, I was tired of the single life and ready to settle down."

"So he got transferred to Warren?" Bill asked, referring to the big Air Force base nearby.

"Not really transferred. He left the service and went to work for a company that had contracts with the Air Force. He said he could make a lot more money as a contractor. It didn't turn out that way."

She paused and sipped her wine before continuing.

"His company sent him to Cheyenne to work at Warren. I had been to Yellowstone and Jackson Hole, and they were nice. But I hadn't been anywhere else in Wyoming. Kansas was the only place I had ever lived, and I was looking forward to a change."

"A change is good, sometimes." Bill realized that his words clashed with his own ill-fated move to Wyoming.

"It was a good life at first," Joan said. "But before long, the glow began to wear off. Eric started drinking too much. Some nights he went out with friends after work. We argued a lot, but we always made up. I really wanted things to work out, and I was in denial for a long time." She sighed and looked down, running a finger around the rim of her glass.

"Then," she added, "we made friends with Hank and his wife, who was alive at the time. Hank liked Eric at first, but soon they were at odds. Hank didn't trust Eric."

"Hank's pretty sharp. A lot sharper than he makes out," Bill said.

"Yes, he is. Anyway, Hank stayed friendly with me, but I could tell he didn't care for Eric. So, when Eric put his hands on me the first time, I didn't tell Hank. It bothered me, but I kept it to myself."

"What do you mean, *put his hands on you?*"

"He grabbed my arm real tight, and shook me. Then he pushed

me away, and shoved me hard against the wall. He was angry, and it scared me. Later, he apologized and tried to make up, saying that he would never do it again. And he didn't for a long time.

"But the next time, it was worse. He slapped me. Not real hard, but it hurt and I slapped him back as hard as I could. Then we screamed at each other and said every nasty thing we could think of."

"Did you call the police or threaten to leave him?"

"No, but I told Hank about it. It made Hank furious, and he told me to call him if it ever happened again. It was almost a year later when Eric lost his job. He was mad at the whole world, and he stayed drunk for two days. Finally, I came home one evening..." she tightened her jaws, "...and told him I wanted a divorce. He went into a rage, and punched me hard in the shoulder with his fist. It really hurt. I went into the kitchen and got a big knife. I told him that if he came near me I would kill him. And I meant it. But I knew he was too strong for me. He was well over two hundred pounds. He stayed in the living room and threw his beer can and broke the mirror on the wall. 'Kill me, bitch,' he said. I called Hank from the phone in the kitchen and told him to come quick."

"I guess that's when Hank brought his shotgun."

"Yeah. Now you know all about my wonderful marriage. Wasn't that uplifting?"

"Well, the uplifting part is that guy Eric isn't around anymore. And neither is that bass-playing cowboy. You've still got me and Hank on your side."

"And I'm so glad for that. More than you know. When I divorced, I changed back to my maiden name. I was Joan Patterson for twelve bad years. But when I went back to being Joan Farley, I vowed never to be a victim again."

"I don't blame you. My marriage wasn't so great either, but I would never hit a woman."

"Tell me how you got here from Alabama. I assume it was connected to your marriage somehow."

"No, I was single when I moved out here, and I was desperate for a change in scenery."He told her about a church bombing in Birmingham and about a University campus under martial law. And he told her about meeting a black boy named Zee and realizing how screwed up things were. How his whole outlook on life changed after an accident at a quarry, and when the only woman he ever loved married his brother.

Joan listened intently as he told her things he had never shared with anyone else. Still, he didn't tell her everything about himself and Olivia.

It was almost two o'clock in the morning when they finally decided to call it a night.

"You know what?" he asked as they headed to their rooms.

"What?"

"If I had been in that jerk Ben's place, and I saw you in that outfit, I would have jumped your bones before we got off the front porch."

"I wish you had been in his place," she said in a serious tone.

He just laughed and said, "Good night."

As he undressed in his room, he thought to himself, *she did look pretty damn good tonight.*

11

Billy got out of the driver's seat with the keys of his first car in his hand. His father stepped from the "shotgun" seat and Jackie uncoiled from behind and crawled out the passenger door of the coupe. The trio gathered to one side and admired the red and white '56 Chevy.

"Don't forget, son," said Jim Burdette, "this is your birthday present. Don't expect anything more'n a card and a cake in September."

"I know, Dad, thanks."

"Don't forget to keep the oil filled and air in the tires. And, you gotta' buy your own gas. It's only got twenty thousand miles on it. Orta' be good for another twenty thousand."

"I will and, don't worry—I'll take good care of it." Billy knew that $1,200 was a real strain on the family budget, a fact his father had made amply clear.

Jackie walked full circle around the car, then tapped Billy on the shoulder with a smile. "You earned it."

That eased Billy's concern that his brother might harbor some jealousy.

Billy's mother emerged from the house and stood on the side stoop. "It's pretty."

"Not *pretty*, Mom," Billy said. "It's sharp."

"It's cool," said Jackie.

Billy's father looked at him. "Just don't act no Elvis Presley fool."

Alice rolled her eyes and turned to go back inside. "Oh, good Lord, Jim."

The brothers laughed, and their father grinned like he knew who the joke was on.

***

With preseason football practices only a couple of weeks away, Billy was counting the days to get back with the team and play in his first varsity game. Each morning, he lifted weights and ran a couple of miles. He was in tip-top shape and full of energy, like a young colt ready to burst out of the gate.

On a blazingly hot afternoon, he drove Jackie and a couple of their friends to their favorite quarry for a swim. He parked the Chevy at the end of the dirt road and the four boys began walking up the hill leading to the quarry. They were met by a larger group coming down the hill.

"Don't go there," said one of the boys in the other group. "Go to another quarry."

"Why?" Billy asked.

"There's a bunch of niggers up there—they might find a surprise."

"What'd you mean—a surprise?" asked Jackie.

"Just don't go up there."

The larger group continued down the hill. Jackie and the other two started to follow. "Hey, screw you," Billy shouted to the others. Turning to his brother and the two buddies, he swept his hand forward. "Come on, let's go swimming. Don't listen to those chicken shits."

"There's niggers up there," one of his friends said.

"I don't give a crap. I'm tired of this stupid bullshit. I'm going swimming, and you can go with me or you can walk home."

His two buddies looked at each other, then turned to follow the larger group.

"I'll go with you, you hard-headed fool," said Jackie. "But we could get in trouble, you know. Especially with Dad."

"Come on, chicken liver," Billy replied.

Reaching the quarry, they saw several colored kids shedding their clothes, getting ready to swim. Billy recognized Zee among them and waved to him.

"You know him?" Jackie asked.

"Yeah, a little bit. He's a good kid."

After stripping to their bathing suits, Billy and Jackie walked around the edge of the open pit to the highest point. Billy got a running start and jumped out over the emerald green water.

In mid-air, he looked down and saw a large dark spot, just beneath the surface. "Oh hell!" he yelled as he headed for what was sure to be a painful collision.

He hit the object hard with his legs and his left ankle turned sharply to the side. With excruciating pain surging through his body, he struggled to get his head above water. "Jack," he screamed out, before sinking below the surface. He felt for the bottom with his good foot and bent his right knee to get a good push.

From the high point above, Jackie shouted, "Billy, what happened? Can you hear me?"

There was no answer.

Jackie scurried down the bank, jumped into the shallow water, and began swimming toward Billy. The colored kids, watching from the other side of the quarry, raced over to see what was happening.

Billy's head emerged from the depths, blowing out a lungful of air. Jackie grabbed him and started pulling him to shore. Zee waded out to shoulder depth and grabbed the other side of Billy, who was now gasping in agony with his eyes closed. When they finally got him to the edge of the water, they laid him on a towel one of the colored kids had spread out.

"There's a car in the water. I think I broke my ankle." Billy spoke in gasps with his face contorted in grimacing pain.

"We'll get a doctor," Jackie said, with his voice racing. Then he looked at Zee. "Can you drive a stick?"

"Yeah, but I don't have a license," Zee replied.

"I don't care," Jackie snapped. He hurriedly reached for Billy's jeans nearby and nervously fumbled through the pockets for the car keys, then tossed them to Zee.

"You know where the police station is?"

"Yeah."

"Get there as fast as you can and tell 'em Billy's hurt. Tell 'em to send an ambulance as soon as possible."

"*You* better go," Zee stammered. "I'll stay here with him. The po-lice won't believe me."

"You've got to go, dammit. I'm not leaving him—he might go into shock. Get your *ass* to the police station."

Jackie kept his eyes on the young colored kid he had never met as Zee hustled to Billy's car and sped away. The car bounced over the rutty road and lurched forward in spurts as it jerked through the gears.

Jackie turned back to his brother. Billy lay on the towel, writhing in pain and cursing through the rivulet of tears streaming down his cheeks. He grabbed Jack's hand with a vise-like grip. "My car," he said.

***

"I don't remember exactly what happened after I hit the water," Bill said, reliving the moment to Joan at breakfast. "Jack told me about it. I just know that he and Zee did what they had to do, even though we found out later that Zee couldn't swim. And I was right—I broke my ankle. Jammed my hip, too. They put some pins in my ankle, and my left foot was in a cast for two months. It was sore to walk on for a good while after that, and it never really healed."

"What did you hit?" she asked.

"It was a car that the black school used as a kind of mascot. It was a little Nash Rambler—Nash was the name of their school— and it was painted blue. Their school colors were blue and white. Some sorry-ass white guys had stolen it and dumped it in the quarry. What happened to me was supposed to happen to a black kid." He flashed a smile. "Funny, though, Jack said I was as worried about my car as my ankle at the time. But Zee handled it just fine and the police figured he was telling the truth, seeing the Alabama decal on the back window."

The smile disappeared and Bill stared blankly as if he were turning back the clock thirty years. He felt Joan's eyes fixed upon him as she held a croissant in one hand, resting it on a plate. He took a sip of coffee and spoke again.

"The next day they pulled the car out of the water, posted *NO TRESPASSING* signs, and blocked the road to the quarry."

"Did they catch the people who put the car in the water?"

"No. The kids at school knew who did it. It was grownups— some of the mean bastards that were always causing trouble and getting away with it. But no one was ever arrested."

Joan took a bite of the croissant and remained silent as Bill gathered his thoughts. "Coach gave me a jersey and let me stand on the sidelines, but I couldn't run for a long time. And once I could, I'd lost a lot of speed. The next year they gave my number to another guy. I never played a down."

"That's terrible." She spoke with a doleful frown.

"That's the way life is sometimes. You know what they say—the Lord giveth and the Lord taketh away. Well, he giveth to me and then he taketh away, so I guess I can't complain. Most guys never had what I had been giveth."

He muffled a laugh at his biblical parable before turning serious again.

"I can't say that Jackie or Zee saved my life, because I think I could have somehow gotten out of the water by myself. And I don't think anyone has ever died of a broken ankle. But what they did was what I needed for them to do, and I'll never forget that."

"Maybe they saved you in a different way."

The comment struck him as profound, although he couldn't quite put his finger on why. "I never looked at it that way, but you may be right." He finished off his croissant and washed it down with a gulp of coffee.

Then he realized what she meant. It was a lesson in basic humanity as much as it was in physical survival. Maybe he wasn't meant to live the life of a narcissistic football hero. And maybe he would have been a better person after that, had it not been for another story—the one about him and Olivia.

The story that haunted him like a nightmare that never ended.

***

It was a banner season for the boys in crimson, and Billy found himself standing on the sideline aching to be a part of the action. Guys that were behind him on the depth chart the year before were now getting plenty of playing time. Although he gathered with teammates in the locker room after the games, joining the celebration if they won and sharing the disappointment if they lost, he was no longer a contributing part of the team. It was a humbling ordeal, humiliating for one accustomed to being the center of attention.

Instead, he was nothing more than a fan, like the prominent alumni and boosters who hung around the team to bask in the vicarious glory of association.

He went through grueling rehab sessions in an unsuccessful attempt to regain normal use of his ankle. By the time the season was over, he came to the painful realization he might never play again. But it was hard to let go of the dream. Slowly he drifted away until he was content to simply sit in the stands and watch the spring game. Olivia and Jackie, both now freshman at the University, sat on either side of him.

"Look at Matheny—he's pitiful!" Billy put his head in his hands and muttered in disgust, as one of his former back-ups missed a block. He looked up wistfully at Olivia and she put her arm in his.

"They look ragged," said Jackie.

"It's just a spring game," replied Billy. "They'll be ready by September—you can bet your life on that. Coach will make sure of it."

"Will you be ready?" asked Jackie.

Billy gazed straight ahead. After a long silence, he spoke softly. "No."

Olivia and Jackie stared at him as the thought sank in.

"I can't do it anymore," Billy said. He looked at Olivia. "No sense kidding myself. And I sure can't fool Coach or the other guys." Turning to his brother, he added, "Or you."

Until then, Billy didn't know how or when he was going to admit what was obvious to everyone else. Once he said it aloud, he felt relieved. There would always be the regret of "what might have been," but now he viewed things with a new perspective. In one way it felt like a sad ending and in another, it felt like a new beginning.

After the game the trio went to a greasy-spoon diner and indulged in burgers and fries.

"I know you're disappointed," Olivia said to Billy. "But you still have your future ahead of you. You'll be great at whatever you do."

"I hope so. I just don't know what that is. I thought about coaching, but I've decided against it."

"Why not?" asked Jackie. "Everybody knows what a great player you were. You'd be a good coach."

"No, I've got to move on. I've had my day in the sun. It's time to get serious about something besides a stupid game. Once I get my degree, I'm going to find a job in the real world."

The words implied a newly found sense of maturity, but letting go was harder than just saying it. He sensed that he hadn't totally convinced the other two.

"Yeah," Jackie said. "You don't want to be stuck in some dead-end job like Dad, working your ass off your whole life. I sure as heck know I don't."

"Billy, I've never looked at you as just a football player," Olivia said. "You're smart and caring and … sweet.…"

"Oh, crap," Jackie said. "Pardon me while I throw up."

"Hey, y'all," Billy said. "Let's not talk about me anymore. I appreciate your concern but, really, I'm okay. Don't feel sorry for me. By the way—I realize that both of you have your own futures ahead of you, so I'll be here for you like you've been for me." He leaned over and gave Olivia a hug and a kiss.

"Well, aren't we the flippin' Three Musketeers," Jackie said. "But if you kiss me, I'll punch that sweet face of yours."

After they left the diner, Billy walked Olivia back to her dorm.

"Thanks for sticking with me," he said. He kissed her good night, but it wasn't a passionate kiss. Rather, it was one of duty, as if there were other things on his mind.

"I always will," she said.

Without football, Billy was a different person and, almost immediately, his whole perspective changed. Now life seemed a lot bigger than the one-hundred yards between goal lines. The tantalizing fog of young love had lifted, and his relationship with Olivia had grown into familiarity. He was no longer a giddy kid, ever ready for a session of heavy petting and teasing foreplay. Now, intimacy meant going the limit, a physical exercise in carnal desire. The sex gave him a sense of maturity as if it had brought him into manhood. With it came a sense of responsibility he wasn't accustomed to. No longer were there teammates, coaches, or parents to fall back on. He was on his own. The responsibility sometimes felt like freedom, and other times felt like a straight-jacket.

Half way through the spring semester, things became more confusing. Billy sensed a change in Olivia. He knew her well enough to know when something wasn't right, but she said she was just worried about her studies.

They went to a movie on Saturday night and afterward parked near the river downtown.

"Why do you worry so much?" he asked. "You made the Dean's List last semester. It's not like you're flunking out."

She looked away and didn't reply.

"Olivia, what's wrong? Have I done something?"

"Billy, do you still love me?" There was a serious tone in her voice, unlike the rhetorical way a woman usually asks.

"You know I do."

"Then there's something we need to talk about."

He knew what was coming. It was about getting married. They had discussed the subject and had agreed to wait until they finished school. They also agreed they didn't want to announce a formal engagement that far in advance.

"What?" He acted as if he were clueless.

"I'm pregnant," she said with a solemn tone.

He was temporarily numbed as the words hit him like a bolt of lightning.

Their eyes met without expression, and he stared at her as if he could see the thoughts running through her mind. What she had said was *I'm pregnant,* but what he heard was *we're pregnant.*

"Are you sure?"

She leaned toward him. "Don't ask me that," she said slowly with anger hovering in her voice. Then she began to cry. "This is not some trick to get you to marry me. Of course, I'm sure."

He pulled her to him and hugged her tightly. "I'm sorry, that's not what I meant. You know I'll marry you. It's my fault—I should have been more careful."

Her voice returned to normal. "No, it's as much my fault as yours. I couldn't wait for the times when we made love."

He relaxed his embrace. "Jeez," is all he could say.

She wiped her eyes on his shirt sleeve. "We need to think about what to do. My parents will be furious, and I think yours will be, too."

She was only eighteen; he was nineteen. They were still minors legally, not old enough to vote or drink. But now they were suddenly thrust into the reality of adulthood.

"Our parents have always supported us," Billy said. "My parents think the world of you, and I think your parents like me, too."

"Of course they do. But they want us to finish our educations. I have three more years to go, and you have two more. I don't know how we can raise a child and go to school. And we can't ask our parents for any more help."

"I'll just have to get a job and wait a little longer to get a degree," he said.

"I'll have to quit for a while anyhow." She leaned her head into his chest.

He buried his face in her hair and tightened the embrace. "We'll make it."

They closed their eyes and lingered in silence before Olivia lifted her head. "There's another way."

He knew what she meant. The same thought had crossed his mind, but he didn't want to bring it up.

"You mean, not have the baby?"

"We can have another one later."

"I don't know how to do what you're talking about."

"A girl at the dorm knows a man. He's a retired doctor in Peavy."

She obviously had considered the option. Neither spoke for a minute as the darkness of the idea began to fade.

Olivia finally continued. "We've got to have some money."

"How much?"

"Five-hundred dollars."

That's how they decided. Five hundred dollars would make their problem go away. But that was more money than they had, so the challenge became how to get it—and get it quick.

Billy hit up a few friends for loans, promising to repay them by the end of the year. Olivia asked her roommate to pass the word around the dorm that she was collecting money for a "sick friend", a recognized code among the girls. She collected almost two hundred dollars in a couple of weeks, but Billy was reluctant to "go begging" and his efforts were not as successful.

The semester was nearing an end before they had scraped together the money. They talked in his car at a park off-campus.

"Are you sure you want to do this?" he asked.

"Don't think about it anymore, Billy. We have to do it."

"I know."

"You have the money, don't you?"

"Sure."

"We have to do it soon, before school's out. I'm beginning to gain weight."

"I've set it up. We're going Saturday night."

"To Peavy?"

"Yeah. The doctor said it wouldn't take long. I got us a room at a motel."

Billy spoke as if it was simply a business arrangement and he tried to ignore the sad resignation on her face. It was too late for that.

Having acquiesced to the darkness of his conscience, he would fix the problem he had caused. Everything was set up. In three days, he would take her to a little town not far away. There, he would give their money to a man he had never met for a procedure he didn't understand.

He tried to convince himself it was the best thing to do. It would save both families embarrassment and avoid interrupting his and Olivia's education.

But it didn't feel like the right thing.

12

As they neared their destination, Billy began to feel a pall of dread, as if he were driving into a dark tunnel of uncertainty. Olivia had not spoken for several minutes and a choking tension filled the car. He had to stay strong.

Peavy was a small community just south of Branford, on the other side of the Black Warrior River. Not really a town, it was simply a collection of mostly abandoned stores, a filling station, and a saw mill on its last legs. A low, L-shaped brick building occupied one corner of the four-way stop, where two county roads crossed.

They arrived there in the stillness of a warm night. Billy parked behind the brick building near the only other car.

He turned to Olivia with a look of assurance and put his hand on her knee.

"I'm scared," she said.

"It'll be okay." He leaned to hug her tightly. "I'll be right here with you."

He kissed her and the sweet taste of her lips couldn't hide the tenseness he felt in her body.

They went to the door and found it locked. Billy knocked and waited nervously until a man opened the door. "Dr. Harris?"

"Yes," the man replied. He eyed the young couple with a

serious look. "Come in." He led them inside to a dimly lit room containing only a desk and chair.

The doctor was an elderly man of short, trim stature with a full head of close-cropped white hair. He wore wire-rim glasses and a white lab coat. Before the young couple could introduce themselves, he asked, "Do you have the money?"

"Yes," Billy said. Reaching into his pocket, he pulled out five one-hundred dollar bills and counted them out to the doctor.

"Good," the doctor said. "Come this way. It won't take long."

He led them into an adjoining room with a bright fluorescent light and cooled by a window air-conditioning unit. A surgical table with foot stirrups and green sheets was positioned with the head of the table against the back wall. Next to the table were a sink and a side table with a stack of towels and a metal basin on top.

"Young lady, you may leave your top on, but remove everything below your waist," the doctor said. "You can cover yourself with the sheet."

Olivia complied with his instructions, reclined on the table and placed her feet in the stirrups. Billy sat on the edge of the table, holding her hand as the doctor grabbed a syringe from a small side table and pulled back the sheet. He noticed some medical tools on the table and, terrified at the thought of their use, was glad Olivia couldn't see them.

Olivia began shaking and fighting tears as Billy hugged her and tried to comfort her. Within a few minutes, she became calmer as the sedative took effect.

"I'll be back in a few minutes," the doctor said, leaving the room.

"Billy, Billy," Olivia repeated groggily.

"I'm right here," Billy responded. "I'm with you." He put his cheek to hers and whispered words of assurance as she held his neck tightly with her teary eyes closed.

Time seemed to stand still until the doctor finally returned. He bent over between Olivia's legs and silently went about his business.

Billy pressed firmly against Olivia and closed his eyes. He didn't know what was happening; he just wanted it to be over. Above the drone of the air conditioner, he could hear the chilling sound of metal cutting flesh, much like the sound of his mother's pinking shears when she worked at her sewing table. He opened his eyes and looked at Olivia as she moaned lowly with her eyes glazed. At last, she tightened her face and whimpered, "Aah!"

The doctor stepped away and pulled the sheet back over Olivia.

A phone rang from the other room and the doctor left to answer it.

Left alone with Olivia, Billy felt helpless. He stood down from the table, listening to the faint sounds of the doctor speaking on the phone in the next room. Then the voice stopped.

Not knowing what he was supposed to do, Billy went into the other room, looking for the doctor.

"Billy, don't leave." Olivia cried.

"I'll be right back."

The other room was empty. Billy opened the back door and saw the doctor getting into his car.

"Where are you going?" he shouted. "Come back." He raised his fist and hollered vainly at the doctor's car as it headed away, "Come back, you bastard—you're not through!"

He ran back into the building and into the room where Olivia lay still on the bed. She was crying with her eyes closed, a bloody sheet beneath her. Looking at the small mass on the table near her feet, a feeling of horror and crushing guilt struck him. For a brief moment he focused on the unborn flesh, a being of his making and of his destruction. Tears welled in his eyes as he realized, for the first time, the depth of his inhumanity.

He noticed a lined paper bag on a shelf and quickly placed the fetus in the bag with trembling hands. After grabbing some towels from the side table, he soaked them in the sink, and used them to wipe the blood from his hands and Olivia's body. Between the two rooms was a bathroom where he dumped the bloody towels into the toilet. Returning to Olivia, he placed a warm towel on her face and a dry one to wipe her clean. Then he helped her off the table and put her skirt on her.

"Can you walk?" he asked.

"Yes," she said through the tears.

Slowly he led her through the building and into the car. Then he ran back inside, retrieved the bag and put it in the trunk of the car.

"Where are we going?" she asked.

"Back to the motel."

Billy pulled out of the parking lot and drove away as fast as he could, almost hitting the side of the building as he made a hard right turn onto the highway. Keeping his foot heavy on the accelerator, the road was a shimmery blur through his watery eyes. He kept whispering to himself through clinched teeth, "*Damn it!*"

He drove to the cheap motel near the river where earlier that evening he had registered as Mr. and Mrs. Rick Blaine. Once in the room, Billy covered the bed with the extra blankets from the closet before laying Olivia down. He kissed her and held her until she fell asleep.

Ripping a sheet of paper from the small pad on the bedside table, he left a note in big letters next to the lamp: *I'll be back in a few minutes.*

With a guilty feeling of abandonment, he turned off the lights and quietly closed the door. On the way to his car, he noticed a brick lying in the parking lot and impulsively picked it up. Retrieving the bag from the trunk, he gently placed the brick inside the bag and set it on the passenger-side floorboard.

Then he headed for the river.

Twenty minutes later, the deed was done and he was back at the motel. When he entered the room, he was relieved to find Olivia still asleep. He went into the bathroom and washed his hands and face, but he couldn't wash away the feeling in his heart. Looking in the mirror he saw a monster looking back at him and he knew he would never be the same again.

***

The next day on the way back to school, they didn't speak for a long time. It was like awakening from a nightmare and trying to forget it.

Finally, Olivia spoke. "What … I mean … where ….?"

"It's gone."

Billy said *it*, as if the bag he tossed into the river contained nothing more animate than the brick. His voice dripped with sarcasm, but it was steel-hardened from having lived through the nightmare.

It seemed to satisfy her. He didn't want her to know any ghastly details that would haunt her. Just the blankness of something that no longer existed was all she apparently needed. But when she spoke, he realized she couldn't simply dismiss her feeling of guilt.

"What have we done?" she said.

"We've done what we came to do."

"I feel dirty." She began to cry.

"It's over. We have to go on," he said.

Billy tried to be strong, knowing that's what Olivia needed from him. It was different from the way he felt, but he didn't know what else to do. Maybe helping her through this was the only thing he had left.

She stopped crying and wiped her face with a tissue, then leaned against the car door to gaze out the window.

"Was it murder?" she asked, sniffling into the tissue.

He didn't answer at first. Finally, he said, "God will decide."

She composed herself and asked ruefully, "It was, wasn't it?"

Billy simply stared into the windshield. His heart filled with shame as he looked at the shiny hood of the car. Once his pride and joy, he now saw the Chevy as an undeserved gift.

They drove home in silence. Billy couldn't clear his mind of thoughts about the night before. He wondered if Olivia shared his overwhelming sense of regret.

It didn't change anything.

***

Joan was spellbound as Bill told the story.

It was the first time he had ever told anyone and, while painful to relive the memory, there was a sense of relief in exposing his inner demon.

"That's so sad," she said.

"Yes, but it's not sad for me or Olivia or that sorry doctor. We've lived our lives. Maybe we've lived in purgatory, but we've lived." His eyes glazed as he let out a long breath.

"What happened to the doctor?" she asked. "Why did he leave?"

"I don't know who he was talking to on the phone, but it must have been a tip-off that he was being busted. I heard later that he was arrested for practicing without a license. I'm not even sure he was a real doctor."

Joan closed her eyes and sighed. "That's horrible."

"Sorry to unload on you," Bill said. He rose from the sofa and began to walk away.

She stood from her chair. "Bill, are you alright?"

He nodded. "Yeah, I'm okay." He went to his bedroom to put the memory to sleep.

They never spoke about it again.

***

After the trauma at Peavy, Billy no longer felt like a lover boy. Instead, he felt fully grown and hardened to the consequences of making decisions. His relationship with Olivia also changed. Harboring a deep shame, he felt unworthy of anyone's love. A couple of weeks went by before he spoke of it.

"How are you feeling?" he asked.

"Billy, I'm okay now," she said.

"You mean physically?" he asked.

"Yes."

"How about in your head?"

"I'm not sure," she replied. "How do you feel?"

"I don't know either. It's hard to explain. I just feel different."

"Do you still love me?"

"Yes, it's not that. It's just that I'm not sure you should love me," he said.

"That's crazy—don't say that. You're the only one I ever have or ever will love. We can't let this destroy us."

She said the right words, but he knew her well enough to sense the doubt in her mind. He knew she felt differently than before, just as he did. It was hard for him to admit to himself that his love for her was no longer white-hot. The flame had not burned itself out, but it had flickered, and he felt the heat beginning to wane. He thought she felt the same way, and he didn't blame her. But it bothered him that she seemed more concerned about something destroying them than vice versa.

One night, after studying at the library, they walked to Billy's car on the back side of the campus. In the car, she put her hand on his leg.

"Are you still attracted to me?" she asked.

"Of course I am," he answered half-heartedly.

"So...I'm not damaged goods?"

"Olivia, what in the world are you talking about? Damaged goods? What kind of question is that?"

"You're not as passionate as you were before."

That hit a nerve and he lashed out in anger. "Before? You mean before we destroyed a life?"

"Don't say that. Is that all you think about? Can't you think about me—about us?"

"Yeah, I think about you and I think about us. Maybe we should think about something besides ourselves the next time we make a decision."

"We thought it was the best thing to do. No—not we—it was my idea. I made you do it."

His anger quickly turned to guilt. "No, it's my fault. I took you there. I gave the man the money. I made you stay when you were afraid and I held you down when you were helpless."

"I needed you." She began to cry. "Don't relive that night... please." Through her tears, she said, "I still need you."

Suddenly he felt remorse for piling his guilt on her. "I'm sorry," he said, softly.

He kissed her, then hugged her and said, "I love you."

It was something he *had* to say, something she needed to hear. Something he desperately wanted to believe.

She kissed him with the same lack of passion she had accused him of.

Yet, as they clung to each other, he felt her drifting away. He sensed a strange degree of separation he didn't understand and couldn't shake.

The passion that wrapped them so tightly together was beginning to tear them apart.

13

Bill left Saturday morning for the seven-hour drive across the state to Yellowstone Park. As he made his way, he wondered if he had done the right thing in telling Joan about Peavy. It didn't serve any purpose, and it might have made her feel differently about him, maybe even lose respect for him, but it was something he couldn't help. It wasn't from weakness as much as it was from necessity. If he didn't exhale the guilt at some point, he would suffocate.

Before he reached the entrance to the park, he stopped at a roadside station to freshen up in the men's room. He splashed his face with water and added a couple of blasts of deodorant under his arms. Although it didn't alter his appearance, he felt revitalized. Looking at his cleanly shaven face in the mirror, he wondered if he really looked younger than his years like he was often told. Others had not seen the transformation that Olivia was bound to see. Hopefully, the fresh haircut didn't highlight the few white hairs or make his ears stick out too much.

He admired the new blue shirt with the prominent Polo logo which he had splurged on especially for the occasion. A sharp look with the tan khakis, he thought. Since meeting Joan, he had given more attention to his appearance, and he thought he looked decent, but he wondered how closely he resembled the man Olivia remembered. A few extra pounds had been added over the years but when he tucked his shirt in, the belt buckled snugly with little bulge to his belly. The anxiety over his own appearance was compounded by the question in his mind of how closely Olivia would look like the girl in his wallet.

He followed a slow caravan of traffic through the park, past a field of geysers until coming to a complete stop as a herd of bison wound slowly across the road. The afternoon was clear and mild when he finally pulled in front of the hotel nestled among the trees on the shore of Lake Yellowstone. He was a few minutes early, so he walked around outside the building to work off the tension as if he were outside the locker room before a championship game. The big hotel, constructed of wood plank siding and painted bright yellow, looked pleasantly well aged, but less upscale than the lavish facilities of some tourist venues.

Large pine trees surrounded the area, reaching into the sky higher than the four-story building. In the background the huge lake glistened calmly without a trace of noisy water craft. The hotel seemed in harmony with the simplicity of the surroundings, exuding an aura evoking the tranquility of yesteryear.

When Bill entered the hotel, he looked around and felt as if he had walked into the 1920's. He could envision Teddy Roosevelt relaxing there in the luxurious manner of the day. The unpretentious surroundings settled him a bit, but he couldn't shake his nerves altogether. Ignoring the chairs in the lobby, he stood anxiously awaiting Olivia. When she appeared from the hallway, he was stunned. Attired in navy blue slacks, a white blouse, and a hot-pink cardigan sweater, she seemed to brighten the surroundings as she approached. A large smile erupted on his face, and she smiled back.

"Billy!" she said, with a ring of excitement in her voice.

Without a response, he simply met her with a long embrace.

"You're as beautiful as ever," he said.

It was true. She had matured from a pretty girl to a beautiful woman, a transformation that deepens a woman's appeal beyond the surface.

"You look great yourself." She pulled slightly from his arms. "Oh, it's so good to see you. How long has it been? Oh my God, fifteen years."

"I lose track of time. You know me—live today, screw tomorrow." He cleaned it up a little for her.

"You haven't changed a bit," she said. "I'm glad."

Of course, he had changed more than a bit. In fact, he was a different person altogether, and he knew she realized it. She was the one who hadn't changed, he thought. They lived in two different worlds now, and he felt like he didn't belong in hers. But here in this place, surrounded by a setting of simple serenity and a reverence for nature, they were free from the boundaries that separated them. His anxiety of how she might feel about him faded in the euphoria of seeing her.

"Would you like to go for a walk?" he asked.

"That would be nice, but not just yet. Brooke should be here any minute. Her schedule is real tight right now, but she really wants to see you. You know, she was only three years old the last time you were home."

"Hmm, time flies, doesn't it?" Bill smiled meekly.

"Yes, it does. I wish Jack could have come. He's been in China for two weeks trying to make some kind of deal for his company. I don't really understand it all. He promised he would make some time and we would come back later this year." She paused, then added, "He said you wouldn't show up."

Bill pursed his lips and wondered how he and his brother had travelled such different paths. "I don't blame him for that. I've not been very good at staying in touch. But, it would be great to see him again. He's done well. I'm proud of him." The thought of Jack's absence gave him pause. "He's okay with us getting together, isn't he?"

"*Of course.*" She looked at him sternly. "Billy, we're family—remember?"

"Yeah." He tilted his head with a pretend smile. How in the hell could he forget that?

As he stood speaking to the woman whose memory he carried around in his billfold, Bill felt a dreamlike disconnect from reality. Olivia looked different, but the same. The last time he had seen her was fifteen years earlier when he had met Jack and her at the Atlanta airport when he was working for a chemical company. That day, she could have passed for a college coed. Even now, her body held its shape in all the right places, but the firmness of youth was replaced with the soft ripeness of maturity. Yet, her flawless dark skin, gray eyes, high cheek bones, and silky brown hair recalled the vision of an eighteen year-old beauty. The vision brought back fond memories and he felt younger, as if seeing her made the years of separation disappear.

Soon, a white passenger van pulled into the parking lot with Yellowstone Park written on the side. The driver and another passenger stayed in the vehicle while a slender girl got out.

"There's Brooke," Olivia said

The young girl walked quickly to them.

Olivia beamed with a bright smile. "Brooke, this is your Uncle Bill."

"Hello, young lady," Bill said. He stepped to Brooke and gave her a big hug. "The last time I saw you, you were in diapers."

"Finally, I get to meet you," Brooke said. "I've heard so much about you. Dad thinks the sun rises and sets with you."

Bill laughed. "Jack was always full of it."

Brooke, casually dressed in jeans, a sweatshirt, and sneakers, was cute, but not the spitting image of her mother. She was taller and leaner, lighter skinned, and blond like her father. But, like Olivia, she exuded an unmistakable radiance at first blush and her youthful energy was infectious. Bill felt his spirits lifted by her mere presence.

"I'm sorry," Brooke said, scrunching her face. "I can't stay."

"She's in training," Olivia offered. "I told her it was okay if she would just stop by for a few minutes to see you."

"Oh, sure," Bill agreed.

Brooke spoke directly to Bill with a breathless urgency. "This place is awesome! My girlfriend and I are staying in a dormitory and we'll be working at the General Store. I hate that I have to leave now, but I'll be here all summer. Maybe you can come back or, when I get some time off, we can meet somewhere." She looked at Bill and Olivia. They both wore a "we'll see" look. "I don't have a car, but some of the guys do. Here's a number where you can leave me a message. Please tell me we can get together again." She handed Bill a business card for the Mammoth General Store with a number circled.

"Well, I'm five hundred miles away, but we'll work something out," Bill said. "You go with your friends and don't worry about us. Your mom and I will be fine."

"I know you will." Brooke hugged Bill again, then Olivia. "Bye," she said, then turned to run to the van. "Don't forget to call," she said as she got in. The sound of girls' voices singing at the top of their lungs to *Hotel California* roared from the open windows, then faded as the van drove away.

"Oh me, she's so excited to be here."

Bill nodded. "She's something else. I know you guys are proud of her."

"Yes, we love her to death. We spoil her, too. She's an only child, just like I was, and she gets all the attention, just like I did."

"I think I remember all that attention you used to get." Bill grinned.

Olivia looked at him in mock scorn. "You got plenty of attention, yourself, Mr. *Branford Bazooka*."

Bill faked a grimace. "C'mon, let's take that walk now." He put his hand gently on her back.

Olivia smiled and began walking with him toward the wooded area around the hotel. "I love this place," she said. "Like you told me, it's not fancy, but it's so peaceful."

"Yeah, it's kind of like going back in time. "

As he said it, he realized the irony. Here he was, walking with Olivia and sharing feelings with her in a place that evoked nostalgia. It *was* almost like old times. Other people might mistake them for a married couple, or mature lovers, but he knew he had to guard against those sentiments. Before he left Alabama years earlier, they had shared their feelings, and the pain that had torn them apart gradually faded away. Although they had agreed to be friends, he had never really accepted that condition. It was a relationship he felt to be better served if completely severed. But his brother had made that a tough proposition.

"Let's forget about everything in the past for a while and just enjoy this," he said. He spread his hands out to indicate "this" to mean the natural surroundings.

"Let's do that," she said. "I feel like clearing my mind of clutter and just relaxing. I won't talk about anything except the moment. In fact, I don't have to talk at all. We can just walk."

"No, I can't ask you not to talk. That's like asking a woman not to breathe," he said with a grin.

"Oh, you sexist!" she said in feigned disgust. "Okay, I'll talk—just not too much."

They shared a laugh and the pact was on.

They walked around the area surrounding the hotel, winding through the village of cabins and along the shore of the lake. It felt strange to be with her, pretending they were simply in-laws, but he couldn't divorce his thoughts from the past. He was sure she felt the same way. There was no way to erase old memories, no matter how hard he tried, especially as he walked beside a living reminder.

"This is so beautiful," Olivia said, staring up at the tall pines. "I'm really glad you were able to meet me. It makes the experience all the more special."

"Yeah, me, too. It would be a shame for you to come this far and us not hook-up."

"Is that what we're doing—hooking-up?" she said.

"Well, I guess that was a poor choice of words. I don't think you're supposed to *hook-up* with your sister-in-law. Maybe we could just call it a little trip down memory lane."

Olivia looked at him with a sober expression.

"Sorry," he said. "I haven't gotten any smarter over the years.

I still suffer from foot-in-mouth disease. Besides, I violated our covenant of silence, didn't I?"

She responded with a slight smile and put her arm in his. It made him feel uncomfortable in the way a man should feel when he's in the grasp of another man's wife. Especially when that other man is his brother.

The afternoon drifted by, and the evening began to settle in. They went inside the hotel for cocktails in a casual area beside the dining room. As they looked through the large windows overlooking the lake and watched the sun disappear, a man in a tuxedo played familiar tunes on a piano nearby.

When Olivia excused herself to go to the ladies room, Bill approached the piano player and put a five-dollar bill in the tip tray. "Do you know *Stars Fell on Alabama*? I'd like you to play it in honor of my lady friend."

The piano player squinted his eyes as if trying to remember the song. Bill hummed a few bars and the piano player nodded in recognition.

"Wait 'til she comes back."

When Olivia returned to their table, her face perked up as she recognized the song. "Listen," she said. "That's *Stars Fell on Alabama*."

"Yeah, it sure is. How about that?" he said, straight-faced.

She pursed her lips, recognizing the ruse. "You're still the charmer. That was nice."

They listened to several more songs and nursed their cocktails. Then Olivia's mood changed, and she began to wipe the tears from her eyes.

"I'm sorry," she said.

"This is pretty awkward, isn't it?" he said.

"It's just me," she sniffled.

"No, I feel the same way. I don't know what to say either. But here we are, so we need to get it off our chests. I think it's time to talk about the past."

"I know, Billy, I know," she said as she put a tissue to her nose. "I'm sorry—it's Bill now, isn't it."

"Whatever. I'm the same son-of-a-bitch, no matter what you call me. You know, my dad always said that you can't take the stink out of a polecat."

"Don't put yourself down like that. You're such a good person. I know that."

"I'm not the person I used to be."

"I'm not, either. None of us are."

The piano player finished a song and they clapped politely. The room was beginning to fill with patrons, but they ignored the bustle around them and connected with their eyes as they nursed their cocktails.

"Why did you run away?" she asked.

"I didn't run away," he said indignantly. "I left a place that was no good for me. I needed a new start."

"Do you hate me?" she asked.

"Why in the world would I hate you?"

"Because of what I made you do."

"You didn't make me do anything. We've talked about this a million times. It was my fault. I should have been a man, been a father."

"It was my idea."

"I caused the problem. I should have been more careful." He took a sip of scotch and braced himself to ask the question he wasn't sure he wanted answered. "Does Jack know?"

"Of course not. There's no need for him to know—it would only hurt him. Have you ever told anyone?"

"No."

He didn't intentionally lie. He just considered Joan so far removed from anyone Olivia knew that it didn't matter.

"I've made my peace with God," she said. "He's forgiving, you know. He forgives me, and he'll forgive you if you ask. If you truly repent."

"I don't know about God, but I can't forgive myself. I think God knows that, and that's part of his punishment."

"God doesn't punish you."

"I hurt my leg and couldn't play ball. That's a hell of a punishment."

"That's crazy. That was before what happened with us."

"God knew what would happen. He knows what is going to happen before it does, doesn't he?"

"Bill, don't keep punishing yourself for the rest of your life. You can't change the past, but you can use it to be a better person. We were young and we made a mistake—a horrible mistake. I've tried to learn from that."

"I wish I could say the same. That's the right way to look at it, but I haven't learned a damn thing. It has just about eaten me alive. And do you know what the worst thing about it is?"

"What?"

"I carry a reminder around with me, even though it almost kills me." He pulled out his wallet. "Look at this," he said, as he removed the picture and showed it to her.

"Oh, my gosh—look at that hair."

"Miss Queen of the Prom—that was you."

"Why do you carry that with you?"

"I don't know. I wish I knew." He looked at her, knowing that she knew even if he pretended not to. He regretted showing it to her, but as he put the picture back in his wallet, he said once again, "I really don't know."

Over dinner, she told him all about Brooke's ambition to be a teacher and her own plans to run for the local city council. Then she told him what little she knew about Jack's business.

"It's something about trade. He works all the time. He travels a lot and pushes himself too hard. I worry about him because sometimes he looks so tired. He's gained weight and drinks more than he should. He's so much different than you."

"Yeah, like he's successful, and I'm a bum."

"No, that's not true. I remember you have a mind that looks at things beyond the surface. Not material things, but people things. I don't feel I have to impress you or that you're trying to impress me."

She exhaled a deep sigh and added, "Oh heck, I can't explain it. I just feel comfortable with you."

Those words made him forget everything for a moment—the broken football dream, the shameful act they shared, the emptiness of looking for himself in the vast loneliness of the West.

"I'm glad," he said.

The piano man, now joined by a drummer and bass player, played softly in a corner of the room away from them. They moved to a closer table to listen and ordered more drinks. The alcohol loosened them up, and the grieving they had shared just a few minutes earlier dissolved in the swirl of their swizzle sticks.

"Here's looking at you, kid," he said in his best Bogart voice.

"Oh, Rick, you're saying this just to make me go." She picked up on his cue and started quoting lines from *Casablanca* that they had memorized as teenagers.

She asked the man on the piano, "Can you play *As Time Goes By?*"

Without answering, the trio started playing the song.

"This could be the start of a beautiful friendship," Bill said.

"You're not supposed to say that to me."

"I know. It's the only thing I could remember."

"Well, think a little harder." She looked at him in a serious way. "But what about us?"

"We'll always have Branford," he answered.

Branford was their Paris. It was the line he had used when he left to go to college. They laughed at their silliness.

"Hey, do you remember The Canebreak in Birmingham?" he asked, referring to a popular nightclub in their younger days. "You know, with Bob Cain and the Canebreakers?"

"Oh, I loved that place."

He turned to no one in particular in the trio and said, "Will you play *Just a Closer Walk with Thee?*"

The trio tried a few cords to get the tune, then began to play the hymn. Bill started singing *Just a Bowl of Butterbeans* with the secular words to the sacred tune.

Just a bowl of butter beans,
I don't want no collard greens.
A foursome at a nearby table looked on in polite amusement as he motioned Olivia to sing the next line. Softly she sang,
Pass the cornbread if you please.
Bill joined her for the last line in a loud voice with his arms outstretched like an opera tenor.
All I want is a bowl of butter beans.
The nearby foursome clapped in good-natured approval.

With his inhibitions dulled by the alcohol, Bill stood up and spoke to the small audience in the room. "One more time—join in," he said, waving his hand in encouragement.

The trio began playing the tune again, and Bill led the room in a sing-along. He recited the words before each line and the audience picked up on the spirit and sang the words he recited:

Just a little piece of country ham
Pass the butter and the jam
Pass the biscuits if you please
And some more of the good ol' butter beans
When they lay my bones to rest
Place a rose upon my chest
Plant those blooming evergreens
But all I want is a bowl of butter beans.

When the song was over, all sophistication was deflated from the room. The trio picked up the tempo and people left their tables and started dancing as the room broke out in smiles.

"Well, I guess they don't mind a couple of rednecks picking up the party," Bill said.

"Billy—I mean, Bill—that was so much fun. What a great night this has been."

"Better than cheese grits?" he joked.

"Better than cheese grits."

"Damn, that's about as good as it gets."

They listened to the music for a while before moving onto the dance floor, swaying in two-step to a slow song.

When they returned to their table, Olivia said, "I've got to go to bed. It's past my bedtime in Alabama."

"I know. And I've got a good little drive just to get to my motel in Jackson Hole. This place is booked up way in advance."

She looked him straight in the eye and said, "Don't go."

He kept her gaze, but didn't say anything.

She signed the tab over his weak objection, then led him to her room on the third floor.

As he closed the door, she came to him and they embraced. They stood silently, her head resting on his chest for a long time. Then she lay down on the bed, and he lay beside her. They remained fully clothed, facing each other with their eyes open.

"I'm so sleepy," she said. "I'm not used to drinking this much."

"You've had a long day. Just get some rest."

"Um." She closed her eyes and rolled over with her back to him.

Bill switched off the light but kept his eyes open, his mind racing as the woman of his dreams lay next to him. A few minutes later, she rose and kissed him with passion, arousing him in a way he hadn't felt in many years. With her figure outlined in the faint light, she moved to the edge of the bed on the opposite side and began to take off her blouse. Moving to her side, he began unbuttoning his shirt.

He stood and looked at her with her open blouse draped around her bra. She looked up and, even in the darkness, he could sense her vulnerability. He wanted her so badly, he was shaking, but he could see his brother clearly in his mind. His heart could take no more guilt.

"We can't do this," he said.

"No," she agreed, and then began to cry. "I'm sorry."

He kneeled in front of her. "It's all right," he whispered. He kissed a tear from her cheek. "It's all right," he repeated.

She pulled her blouse together and he sat beside her. He pulled her to him and they rolled back onto the bed, still fully clothed. He wiped the tears from her eyes with the sheet and pressed her face to his chest. She sniffled and two hearts found rhythm in the quiet darkness.

Soon they were both in a deep sleep.

***

At mid-morning, Olivia awoke as he stood over the bedside table, scribbling on a small notepad.

"Time to get up and get your clothes *off*," he said to his own amusement.

"What time is it?" she yawned.

"Almost eleven."

"Oh, gosh," she said, rolling over and rubbing her eyes. "I have to meet Brooke at noon."

"I'm on my way. Here is my address and phone number. A woman named Joan might answer."

"You're living with a woman?"

"Yeah, she's eighty-something years old. She uses a walker and sits with her cat in a big stuffed chair, talking to the television all day."

"Sounds like a real charmer."

"The place is clean and the rent's cheap."

He leaned over to kiss her on the cheek. "Here's looking at you, kid," he said in his Bogey voice. "Don't forget—we'll always have Branford."

"Thanks for...uh...last night," she said. "Thanks for everything."

As Bill closed the door, he turned and said, "Thanks to you, too. It *was* a good night. Tell Jack I said hello."

Yeah, it was a good night, he said to himself, as he walked down the hall.

On the drive home, he had a lot of time to think about his reunion with Olivia. It wasn't what he had expected. She had acted boldly. He should have held back more, too, and not encouraged the temptation.

But it was no use. No use to deny the longing he still carried around with him in his wallet. He felt guilty to have that longing, and strangely it bothered him that she had no more resistance than he did. It was as if they were destined to compound their youthful shame with the sin of adultery.

Yet, in the end, they had both resisted temptation, and that made him feel a lot better on the long ride back to the comfort of Joan's house.

14

On the Monday after Rod's departure, Bill walked through the warehouse with Hank. Standing in the main aisle, he pointed to the third level of a rack. "See those boxes on that pallet up there?"

"Yeah," Hank replied.

"When I asked Rod about them, he kinda blew me off. I pulled them down with the fork lift this morning to see what they were. They're covered in dust and they've got shipping labels on them from a company in California. They belong to a mechanical contractor in Hillsdale. I called the guy and he said he filed a claim for lost merchandise two years ago. We paid him over twelve hundred dollars."

Hank shook his head. "Damn."

"They've got electrical panel boxes in them and I told the guy he could have them for half price if they were still of any use. He's coming Monday." Bill swept his eyes around the warehouse. "I think there was other merchandise on top of these boxes at one time and Rod just couldn't find them. There are a lot of pallets with mixed merchandise and I'll have to sort them out."

"It don't surprise me," Hank said. "But it's more screwed up than I realized."

"Let me show you something else." Bill led Hank to a corner of the warehouse. "This is our *miscellaneous* stuff." In front of them, a large area of the warehouse was occupied with cardboard crates, machines covered in stretch wrap, metal pails, and odd merchandise piled in a seemingly random fashion. "I can't get to most of this stuff without moving a lot of other things around. Some of it needs to be palletized and put in the racks. I've got some big tags and I'm going to mark each piece so that I don't have to search all over for the shipping label."

"I told you it was a mess," Hank said.

"Rod's inventory records aren't very good either, so matching everything to the customer files will be a chore."

"That's why you're here. You know what you're doing."

"Besides," Bill continued, "it's dirty as hell. Look at these floors—they need sweeping. And the walls..."

"Bill," Hank interrupted. "You see how things are. Do you still want the job?"

He narrowed his eyes at Hank. "You're damn right, I do." Then he grinned. "It's a piece of cake. It'll just take a little time to get things organized and cleaned up."

"I can see that, but the fact of the matter is—I wanna' make some money with this place. Otherwise, this other stuff won't make any difference, will it?"

"No." Bill instantly realized the challenge he faced. "I've seen the expense report and believe me, I know how business works. We obviously need more revenue. I think if we get the place organized and looking decent, we can attract more customers."

"I hope so. And I'm glad you said *we*, 'cause we're in this together. Look, I'm not going to bullshit you—this place has been more trouble than it's worth lately. I'm tired of hearing from pissed-off customers and having to give them money back." Hank began walking slowly toward the office and Bill followed along. "I could sell this building and land for a lot more than I'm getting out of it, but I'd take a big hit on taxes and I don't want to do that right now. I think it'll continue to appreciate in value."

Hank kept talking as they entered the office. "Besides, if you've looked over the books, you know that I write some things off."

Bill nodded. He had seen the bills for some of Hank's personal expenses, including his car and insurance. "It's your business."

"So," Hank continued, "for now, all I want to do is at least break even. A little profit would be nice. You think we can do that?"

"Honestly, I'm not sure, but I'm going to give it my best shot. And I know if we don't do some of the things I've talked about, it'll be real tough. I think I can deal with the customers better than Rod did, but we have to gain their confidence back. We need to show them that we run a clean, well-organized operation. I'll have to spend a little money on paint and cleaning supplies, but mostly it needs a lot of elbow grease."

"Okay, you're probably right. I'm not going to be a tight-fisted old codger. I can see some things need to be done. Go ahead and get what you need. We can hire a couple of amigos to do the dirty work."

"We don't need to. I can do it myself."

"That's your call, but that's not what I hired you for. I don't want you to wear yourself out on grunt work."

"I know. I just need some time."

"I realize that. I can hang on another year unless things fall apart."

Bill was relieved to hear Hank say that. With a little breathing room, he felt like he had a chance to turn things around. As soon as Hank left, he began the task of completely reorganizing the warehouse. Tackling the hardest job first, he started in the miscellaneous area he had just shown Hank. He dug through the jumbled array of merchandise, sorting everything by customer, and marking each item with large tags.

The next day he set up a numbering system for small bins and pallet locations along with a spreadsheet indicating where everything was located. He knew it would take a lot of time to move everything in the warehouse while continuing normal operations, but it became a challenge to him. For the next three days he worked late a couple of hours and hardly made a dent in the project.

On Friday afternoon he unloaded one customer's delivery and loaded another, finishing a little after four o'clock. On sheer impulse he decided to make an all-out attack on the reorganization effort. After calling Joan and telling her he would be late, he put the radio on the window sill outside the office and turned the volume up high. He got on the forklift with a beer in a makeshift cup holder and a cigar in his mouth. The roar of the propane engine blended with the rock music blasting from the radio as he restacked pallets, moved merchandise around the warehouse, and labeled the bins while violating every safety rule in the book. As the day turned to night, he continued to work in a timeless fog, fueled by adrenaline and beer.

It was almost one o'clock in the morning when he stopped. The radio had long since been quiet and when he killed the engine to the forklift, the total silence seemed spooky. Dead tired and beer woozy, he was tempted to crash on the office floor. Instead, he forced himself through the ritual of turning out the lights, setting the alarm, and locking up. Even in his zombie-like haze, he felt the satisfying warm glow of accomplishment.

When he arrived home, he found the light on in the kitchen. There on the table was a plate with two ham sandwiches and a note:

My specialty, remember?
Get some milk from the fridge.
See you in the morning.

The note brought a smile to his face, and for a moment he forgot his tiredness as he recalled the sandwiches she made for him the first night he crashed at her house. He ate one of the sandwiches, washing it down with milk. After taking a bite from the other sandwich, exhaustion began to settle in and he laid it back on the plate. He took a pen from his pocket and wrote on the note:
Thanks!
He trudged down the hall past the closed door of Joan's

bedroom. In his room, he collapsed on the bed without bothering to remove his clothes.

***

Bill rose a little after seven the next morning. He ambled toward the bathroom to take a shower and stopped when he saw Joan in the living room. She was sitting on the sofa in her robe, drinking coffee.

"What time did you come in?" she said.

"About one, I think."

"Why did you get up so early? It's Saturday."

"I've got to go back."

"Why?"

"I can get more done without any customers or truck drivers around. There's still a lot of work to do. The place is a pigsty."

"I can help. I'll go with you."

"No, I don't want you to come. I don't want you to even see the place 'til I get it in shape. I told Hank the same thing."

"Bill, Hank doesn't expect miracles overnight."

He knew she didn't understand. No one did. He felt like the whole world was watching and mocking him for getting so wound up about a crummy two-bit job. He looked at her, tired and frustrated, and set his jaws tight. "I know what the hell I need to do." His temper welled up, then quickly spewed out like a burst steam pipe. He raised his voice and shouted, "This isn't about Hank, damn it!" His face turned red and he bent forward, like a cobra ready to strike, as he spit his words. "This is about doing things right, something a lot of people wouldn't know anything about."

Joan's eyes widened and she stared at him as if she was looking at a different person.

Bill kept his eyes fixed to hers. "I'm doing what needs to be done!"

Her look turned resolute and she raised her voice to match his. "Don't raise your voice to me in my house!"

He breathed heavily and held his words, knowing he couldn't control them. Then he straightened up and the red blush left his face as he regained his composure. "I have to do this."

She sighed, then said calmly, "I understand."

He exhaled a deep breath and his whole body seemed to deflate. "I'm sorry," he said.

"It's okay. The coffee's ready. What do you want for breakfast?"

He rubbed the whiskers on his unshaven face. "I'll grab something at Seven-Eleven on the way." He paused, then said again, "I'm sorry."

"I know. Have a good day." She kept her eyes on him as she raised her cup to her mouth.

He headed to the bathroom to take a shower.

***

For another week Bill worked long hours to get things cleaned up and organized. By the end of the week, he had made good progress and could see the end in sight. On Saturday afternoon, he picked-up the debris around the outside of the warehouse and filled the dumpster with assorted trash, including bottles, cardboard, broken pallets, tires, and an old sign. Then he called Joan and said he was ready for a little break.

"I'll be home about four," he said. "I'm pretty dirty. You might have to hose me down before I come in. But, after I clean up, would you like to go to that Chinese restaurant downtown? I'm buying."

"Yes, that sounds great."

At dinner, Bill was relaxed and more upbeat than he had been since he took the job at the warehouse. "Sorry I've been such an S.O.B. lately. You don't deserve that."

"You haven't been. I know you've been working hard."

"That's no excuse. I appreciate your putting up with me, though."

"I didn't know I had a choice." She smiled.

He returned the smile and took a sip of hot tea. "It's coming along. I bought a long extension pole and tomorrow I'm going to clean all the cobwebs off the walls."

She drew her brows into a questioning look. "Why?"

"For the same reason you keep your house clean." He poured some tea into her cup, then his. "That doesn't make sense to you, does it?"

"It doesn't have to. If it makes sense to you, that's all that matters." She took a bite from her spring roll.

"A lot of things matter, but right now, I need to do this."

She took a sip of tea. "I know you do. I'm glad it's going well."

"I'm crazy, aren't I?"

She shook her head. "No." Then she laughed. "Have fun with the cobwebs tomorrow. I'm going to church."

He grinned. "Say a halleluiah for me. I'll be home early."

When they finished their meal he told her he was almost ready for her and Hank to visit the warehouse.

"He'll be here Tuesday at five o'clock. Can you come?"

"Of course. I might get there a little after that, but I'll come straight from work."

***

When Hank arrived at the warehouse, Bill was waiting at the front door.

"Okay, I'm ready for the grand tour," Hank said.

As he walked through the warehouse, Hank remarked how clean and neat it looked. "Well, I'll be hot damn," he said, gazing around. "This doesn't look like the same place. Did you do all this yourself?"

"Yeah. Maybe with a little help from cigars and beer."

"Whatever it takes," Hank said, matter-of-factly.

When they went into the office the changes were even more dramatic. It was clean, brightly painted, and neatly organized. Bill opened the file cabinet and showed Hank the customer records he had setup. Afterward, he displayed his inventory spreadsheet on the computer as Hank looked over his shoulder.

"That looks real neat," Hank said. He appeared fascinated as Bill explained how he had laid out the warehouse by aisle, row, and pallet position. "Hey, that's something. I *like* that."

Finally, Hank went into the bathroom and his eyes opened wide.

"Man, a clean crapper! I don't think even Joan would mind using this johnny hole."

"Well, that's the way it should be. I just have to keep after these truck drivers so they don't piss on everything."

When Joan arrived, she walked through the building with Bill and Hank. Having seen it when Rod was in charge, she reacted with enthusiastic approval—especially with the bathroom. "Even I wouldn't mind using this toilet."

Bill and Hank looked at each other and laughed.

"All right, so women are a little more...particular...about where we'll sit," she said.

"I know," Bill said. "We're not making fun of you. It just means that if it meets your satisfaction, that's the highest compliment."

"Bill, you've done a hell of a job with this place," Hank said.

"Yes, it's amazing," Joan agreed. "I know how hard you've worked. Now you can relax and not try to kill yourself."

"It's just a start," he said, looking at Hank. "I've got to develop some new revenue. I'm going to really put a full-court press on that. Now that the warehouse looks decent, I don't mind inviting customers and showing them around. I know some people around town that I'm going to call on and see if I can get some business out of them. We can lower our rates a little if we get more volume."

"I'm going to let you make that call," Hank said. "You can set your own prices. I'll tell you what I think, but I trust your judgment." He grinned at Bill. "Until you screw up. Ha!"

It was Bill's operation now and that was a good feeling. It wasn't a lot—a small operation teetering on being shut down—but it beat the hell out of roaming the hills looking for a place to put a bullet in his head.

***

With the job at Hank's warehouse, Bill felt his life had meaning for the first time in a long while. At the same time, he found in Joan someone who cared. He felt comfortable in her house. It was beginning to feel like that place where God wanted him to be.

He sat in "his" recliner and she sat on "her" sofa as they spoke one evening.

"I think the warehouse is in pretty good shape now," Bill said. "I'm spending a lot of my time lately trying to get more customers. In the afternoons, I've been going around town talking to just about anybody that might be a customer."

"I'm sure you're good at that," Joan said. "You make a good impression. People like you, especially with that laid back southern way."

"I like meeting people." He deflected her compliment. "You hit a lot of dead-ends, but I just have to keep working at it."

"I think you enjoy this job."

"Yeah, it's good for me. I've been kind of out of it for a while, mostly of my own making, but now I feel like I'm back in the world."

"Hank told me you've already done more than he ever expected." She smiled. "That's funny. Seeing you bust your fanny has rubbed off on me in the way I approach my job."

"Good, I'm glad to hear that." Then Bill's mind wandered away and he looked at the blank screen on the television. As if talking to himself, he said, "I've wasted a lot of years."

She looked at him sadly as he turned back to her. "I've wasted a lot, too. Living here by myself in the middle of nowhere with all these cowboys and horse...." She clinched her teeth and finally spit out, "...manure."

Suddenly he felt her mood turn somber as if a switch had been turned away from hope and toward regret. He moved to her and gave her a hug. "Don't let that part of me rub off on you. I didn't mean to get us on the bus to Pity City."

"I'm sorry," she said, snuggling into his chest.

He took her hand and led her to the sofa. They sat quietly for a while before he said, "Let's have a drink. How about some margaritas? You know—for old time's sake."

"Let's eat first," she said. "I know how you are with margaritas on an empty stomach."

"Yeah, I guess that's a good idea. I don't want to crash on you again."

"That wasn't all bad," she said, as a grin crept upon her face.

He knew what she meant, but he ignored the thought. "Maybe not for you, but I felt like a whipped mule the next day."

Dinner was followed by margaritas and the late news on television. As they retired, he answered her "goodnight" with his and, on the way to his bed he stopped in the doorway of her room.

"Did I ever tell you how pretty you are?"

"Only when I was a cowgirl," she replied. "But you make me feel pretty."

"Sorry about the oversight. But I'm glad if I make you feel good. You make me feel good, too."

He walked over and stood beside her, next to the bed.

"You can tell me now," she said.

"You're one fine-looking woman," he said. And he meant it. Then he kissed her on the cheek.

"Thanks, I needed that."

"Me, too," he said, before turning away. From the mirror on the dresser, he saw her behind him with a large smile on her face.

In his room, Bill peeled to his shorts and sat on the side of the bed for a minute. Then he lay back and stared at the ceiling in the dark, fighting the urge to go back into Joan's room.

He knew if he did, there would be no turning back.

15

Olivia turned sideways to study her profile in the dresser mirror. The bathing suit clung snugly to the round contour of her rear-end and held firm to her flat stomach. The cups in the one-piece pushed her breasts up with a peek of cleavage. Her naturally dark skin, tanned to golden bronze by the summer sun, blended brilliantly with the bright yellow fabric. She turned around as Mary Sue Harrison came out of the bathroom.

Mary Sue, wrapped in a towel, vigorously combed her hair with a brush. "You all ready?"

"Yeah," Olivia said. "Let's get going. It's almost ten."

A cute blond with a Sandra Dee hairdo, Mary Sue had been Olivia's best friend since their days at Warrior County High. Now, on vacation with Mary Sue's parents, they shared a room at the Seahorse Inn. In a month they would be starting their second year as roommates at Alabama.

Mary Sue dropped the towel and grabbed her bathing suit from a suitcase on the floor. She quickly put on the suit, then studied herself in the mirror. There were slight tan lines on her arms and legs, but in other places the black two-piece contrasted sharply to her milky white skin. She snatched a comb from the dresser and began stroking her hair again.

"Quit worrying about your hair," Olivia said. "We're just going to the beach."

"Bed head," Mary Sue said. She put down the comb, then turned and looked at Olivia with a sigh. "I'll look like an albino next to you."

"You look fine. C'mon."

"Okay, let me call Mom." Mary Sue picked up the phone from the bedside table and called her mother in the room next door. "We're going to the beach. See you later."

They put oversized T-shirts over their bathing suits, grabbed their towels, and walked out into the blazing morning sun. Weaving their way through a steady line of traffic, they crossed the road beyond the Little Birmingham tavern and onto the blinding white sands of Panama City Beach. The beach was teeming with people on a July weekend. Middle-aged couples, kids and the elderly mixed with high school and college students who strolled the beach in packs, as if on display.

The girls walked for several minutes before they found a spot that was not crowded. Shedding the T-shirts, they spread their beach towels in the soft sand above the high tide line.

"Do you want to go into the water?" Mary Sue asked.

"Not yet," said Olivia. "Let's wait a little while." She knelt down on the towel and flattened onto her stomach.

Mary Sue sat down and rubbed suntan lotion over every exposed pore. "Can you get my back?"

Olivia sat up and rubbed the lotion on her friend's back, then lay back down with her head on her rolled-up robe.

"Thanks." Mary Sue rolled over onto her stomach.

They had barely settled down to soak up the sun when Mary Sue spoke without raising her head from her towel. "Do you wish Billy was here?"

It irritated Olivia. "I told you we are through. Don't keep talking about him."

"I didn't know you meant forever."

"Well, I do."

Olivia wasn't too sure about forever, though. Maybe she and Billy would get back together. If not, what would happen then?

She closed her eyes and tried to clear her mind of thoughts. The morning sun was already hot and the beach buzzed with people moving about and talking loudly. Her mind wouldn't go to sleep. *Forever?*

Within a few minutes, Olivia was sweating and restless. She rolled over to lie on her back. The sun felt good as it beat down on her face, but she couldn't clear her mind. It seemed as if she were trapped in a timeless void where nothing existed except her thoughts. Finally, she said, "I'm going in."

"Me, too," said Mary Sue. "It's *so* hot."

They made their way through the throng of beachgoers to the water's edge and walked ankle deep into the foamy surf. The water was warm and aquamarine clear.

Mary Sue reached down and splashed water on herself. "Ooh, this feels so good."

Olivia bent her knees and got wet to her waist. "I love the ocean."

The water barely got deeper as they waded further out, past young children and pot-bellied old men frolicking in small waves no more than a couple of feet high. A hundred yards beyond the breakers, the water still came only to their shoulders.

Olivia looked back at the shore. "Look how far we've drifted." The current had taken them away from where they started and there were fewer people around. She continued to deeper water and stood on her tiptoes as briny ripples lapped up to her chin and into her mouth. In front of her all she could see was the vast expanse of the Gulf of Mexico and a lonely fishing boat in the distance. A few more steps and she was in over her head. She began to slowly paddle her arms to stay afloat. The noise from the beach became a low murmur as the water filled her ears and the world seemed to calm. The churning in her head was washed away and she was at peace as she gently floated in the warm depth.

"Here goes the hair," Mary Sue said, then dipped beneath the surface.

Olivia followed suit and closed her eyes as the sting of salt water hit. She rose out of the water and her skin glistened like polished marble in the bright sunlight. She felt clean and pure like a goddess arising from the sea with new life.

It had only been three months since she had gone through the ordeal in Peavy and suffered the fickleness of love. Not all was lost, though.

She was still beautiful.

***

When his bachelor uncle died, Jackie inherited a white '50 Chevy convertible. "Take it," his father said. "It'll get you to Tuscaloosa and I've got no use for it." But Jackie had plenty of use for it, including driving to Panama City and cruising the strip.

Owning that car was a big ego boost for Jackie, even when he wasn't driving it. He felt especially cool that evening as he parked the car on the back side of the amusement park and put the top up. Then he and his best buddy, Kenny Jordan, walked past the ferris wheel, the tilt-a-whirl, the merry-go-round, and the throng of people screaming over the noisy arcade sounds. As they approached the Hangout they could hear the music and see the place was rocking.

"Alright!" said Kenny. "Here we come."

Jackie just smiled and kept walking.

The Hangout was an open-air beachside dance pavilion and one of the most popular places in town. The dance floor was always full, especially at night, and the jukebox seldom stopped. When the boys arrived the sun was an orange glow just above the horizon and a cool breeze blew from the gulf. They stationed themselves on the outside of the crowd and watched as couples bopped to the music blasting from the speakers.

They moved around the edge of the mostly young crowd, sizing things up and looking to see if they recognized anyone. Kenny went to the concession stand and bought each of them a Coke. Jackie swigged his Coke and continued to scan the crowd, assuming a casual expression as if he were the second coming of James Dean.

They stood and watched as two more songs played. A slow tune seemed to charge the air with sexual attraction as couples filled the dance floor, clinging to each other like mating insects.

"Looks like some decent pickins," Kenny said, looking around.

"Not bad," said Jackie.

When another fast song began, Jackie approached a young girl who was milling around in a group of several others.

"Wanna' dance?" The girl didn't answer, but reached a hand out. Jackie took her hand and led her to the dance floor. Over the sound of the loud music, he said, "What's your name?"

"Sandra. What's yours?"

"Jackie. Where you from?"

"Ohio."

"Alabama," he said, without her asking.

The song ended and Jackie said, "Thanks, Ohio," as he led the girl back to her friends. He didn't remember her name.

"Thanks, Alabama," she said, looking back with a huge smile.

Jackie rejoined Kenny on the sideline. "She's a little young, but not too bad."

"There's more to choose from," Kenny said. "They're still coming in."

A few minutes later, the sound of *Big Girls Don't Cry* blared from the jukebox and, just as Frankie Valli reached a crescendo, Kenny hollered over the din to Jackie, "Hey, look who's here!"

Jackie followed Kenny's eyes and saw a couple of familiar faces. Olivia and Mary Sue had apparently just arrived. Even at a distance, Olivia's tan skin seemed to radiate with vitality and her well-developed figure was on full display in white short shorts and a snug fitting royal blue top. And, were it not for her, Mary Sue would have been the prettiest girl in the crowd.

Mary Sue spotted the boys and waved at them. Olivia looked in that direction, smiled and pantomimed an excited "hi".

Jackie started toward the girls and Kenny followed.

"I didn't know y'all were in town," Jackie said, as he approached.

"We just got here last night," Olivia replied.

"This is funny running into y'all here," Mary Sue said.

"Well, they call it Little Birmingham," said Kenny. "I guess we can call it Little Branford. Ha."

They chatted for a few minutes, then a fast song started and the crowd came alive.

"Let's do it," Kenny said. He reached out, grabbed Mary Sue's hand, and led her to the middle of the dance floor.

Jackie lifted his hand and Olivia stepped to him and offered hers. They found a spot where they could move without bumping into other couples. At first they danced apart, connected only by one hand each. Then he put a hand on her back and she did a spin. When the song ended, they stood looking at each other and neither made a move from the floor. They danced to two more songs before the tempo cranked up with *Twist and Shout* and they gyrated furiously to the pulsating beat of the Beatles. Then a slow song started and the floor began to fill with couples in amorous embraces.

Jackie moved to Olivia and put his arm around her for the slow dance. They were sweating and breathing heavily from the fast dances and their inhibitions seemed to melt away. The smell of perfume mixed with her sweat only added to her allure. He had never felt her body next to his and it didn't seem right, but she moved closer to him and nudged her tousled hair against his chest as they swayed to the music.

"I love this place," she said. "I can't believe we ran into each other tonight."

"Yeah, that's wild." They danced a few more steps singing along to *Donna* with Richie Valens. Then he finally brought up the awkward subject they had both avoided. "Billy's coming down next week. He's helping Dad paint a house this week."

"Good for him," she said.

"Dad's a hard worker. He doesn't put up with any goofing off."

"He seems very nice, though."

"Yeah." He had to probe further, but he didn't know how to say it. Clumsily, he blurted out, "Billy said y'all quit going together." It was a dumb way of stating the obvious and he felt foolish.

"Yeah, we did."

"That's too bad."

"It's for the best."

The music stopped playing and there was a break before the next song. They stayed on the dance floor along with a few other couples, just talking. Jackie grabbed the front of his shirt and pulled it out from his body to cool off. "Thanks for dancing with me." Then, as if to cover his uneasiness, he said, "I didn't know you would be here."

She took his hand and smiled at him. "I'm glad I am."

Her words caught him by surprise and his ego swelled up. He didn't want to feel the way he did, but he couldn't help it. *Maybe this won't be our last dance.*

It wasn't.

Two hours later, they sat on a bench at the edge of the beach, along with Mary Sue and Kenny. The foursome peered out at the moonlit gulf as the music from the Hangout blared behind them.

"We have to go," Olivia said. "We told your folks we'd be in by eleven-thirty."

"I know," Mary Sue sighed. "I think Daddy's more worried about his car than he is about me. And I promise you he'll check my breath. Ha!"

"You said you're at the Seahorse, didn't you?" asked Jackie, as they began to walk.

"Yes," said Olivia. "Why don't y'all come down and go swimming with us tomorrow."

Jackie looked at Kenny who grinned back. "What time?"

"Not before ten," Mary Sue said.

They walked to Mary Sue's car and the girls drove away with a good-bye wave.

"That's some nice stuff there," Kenny said. "Both of 'em. And, hey, I'd take Billy's leftovers any day."

Jackie grabbed Kenny by the shirt and snarled, "Don't you ever say that again."

They stared at each other intently. Then Kenny grimaced and said, "Just kiddin' Jacko. Calm down."

Jackie released his grip and exhaled deeply as the anger left his face.

They walked to the convertible, back through the amusement park that was beginning to clear out. On the ride to their motel, Jackie's thoughts wandered ahead. Tomorrow he would put the top down when they went to meet the girls.

She'll think that's really cool.

***

When school started in September, Billy and Olivia sometimes passed each other on campus. They spoke in friendly voices without really saying anything. There was no bitterness or sadness as much as there was a loss of the idealism of youth. The experience at Peavy brought them into adulthood with a strong dose of reality. Billy was aware that Jackie and Olivia had dated a few times, a fact that he acknowledged with mixed feelings.

The brothers spoke about it just after finishing a game of pool at the student center.

"You know I've been out with Olivia," Jackie said. "I don't want to cause a problem, but I figured it was okay since you two have broken up."

"Yeah, I know y'all have dated. I'm okay with that. Olivia and I are still friends, but we're not together anymore. It was a mutual decision. You can go with her if you want to."

"I'm not asking for your permission. I just want you to know we're not hot to trot or anything like that. But, you know, she's a good looking woman, and we seem to get along pretty well."

"Look, Jackie, I'll be honest with you. I was in love with Olivia for a long time—you know that—and I feel bad about the way we drifted apart. We didn't exactly break-up; we just changed how we feel about each other. It was probably my fault more than hers. So I don't have the right to tell you or her who you can go with." Inside, Billy seethed with the thought of anyone dating Olivia, especially his brother.

"You say you're okay with it, but I'm not so sure about that."

"You don't have to be sure about it. I'm the only one that has to be sure."

"Not just you—Olivia, too."

"Well, she must have already decided that."

"Billy, I'm not doing this to make you jealous or make you mad."

"Jeez, how many times do I have to say it?" In a raised voice and deliberate tone, he added, "I don't care."

Billy had always played the role of the dominant big brother, but now it was hard for him to convince himself he was not jealous of Jackie. It would have been a lot easier to distance himself from Olivia had she been attracted to a stranger. But now she was back in his life in a way that he couldn't ignore. He couldn't help but wonder if she had feelings for him still mixed up in her head.

Was she haunted by the memory of their trip to Peavy? Was the guilt of that memory seared into her heart like it was into his? It didn't make sense that they could be separated by a tragedy for which they shared complicity. Nor did it make sense that she could befriend the brother of someone with whom she shared such a dark secret.

A lot of things didn't make sense to Billy right then and some never would.

"See you later," Jackie said.

Billy had said what he knew his brother wanted to hear. But he had hedged his feelings and he knew that things would become more complicated.

Damn that Olivia!

16

Within a few months, Bill's sales efforts began to pay off and business was picking up at the warehouse. One morning, as he was moving pallets with the forklift, Hank paid a visit.

"How's it going?" Hank asked.

"Like a clock," Bill said, stepping down from the lift.

"Got a few minutes?"

"Sure. Want some coffee?"

They went into the office where Bill poured two cups from the pot on the warmer. Bill sat behind the desk and Hank settled into a chair in front. The office was not as neat as it had been after Bill's initial housecleaning. Papers lay scattered in small heaps on the desk and the cover to the overhead light fixture was off, revealing a missing bulb.

Bill looked up at the light fixture, slightly embarrassed. "I tried a new bulb, but the ballast is out. I'm going to get a new one this afternoon."

Hank never looked at the light. "Bill, you're doing a real good job and I appreciate what you've done with this place. But I've been talking to Joan and I know how many hours you've been putting in."

Bill took a drink of coffee. "Hank, I like this job. I appreciate the fact that you give me free rein and trust me to do the right things. When I was in corporate life, I hated the bureaucracy and all the assholes with bullshit egos. Here, it's up to me and the results speak for themselves." He noted Hank's nod of understanding, then added, "Besides you're not an asshole."

"I can be," Hank replied in a serious tone. "Rod thought I was. But I don't need to be with you. Here's the thing though—I don't want you tied down to a forklift or fixing the damn lights. You need to hire somebody to work in the warehouse and do all this grunt work. It takes too much of your time."

"I can do it," Bill said. "I like staying active. It keeps me in shape."

"I know you can do it—that's not the question. The question is, why waste your time on stuff that can be done by some young buck? We can afford to spend a little money now. I'm not about to sell this place. That is unless you ever get a notion to buy it. I would make you an offer you couldn't refuse." He took a swill from his cup. "You know—long term financing, of course. Ha!"

"That's real funny. You know I couldn't buy the pencils in my desk right now. Besides, if I did have any money, I'd move out of Joan's place and give her house back to her."

"What the dickens are you talking about, man? You're the best thing that's ever happened to that woman. If you had any sense, you'd just make it a permanent arrangement. You don't even have to tie the knot these days. You can't beat that deal with a stick."

"Hank, there's no *deal* between Joan and me. I know y'all are good friends and you need to understand that."

"Whatever you say." Hank set down his coffee cup and stared directly at Bill with a serious look. "Don't screw with Joan's feelings. She took a chance on taking you in after that crap with her ex-husband."

"Took me in?" Bill's head recoiled and he winced at the thought of being an object of charity.

Hank spread his arms and opened his hands in an apologetic gesture. "You know what I mean."

Bill gritted his teeth, pursed his lips, then moved on. "Her ex-husband beat her, didn't he? She said you helped run him off."

Hank looked away for a moment, then back again. "She didn't tell you anything else?"

Bill looked puzzled. "No."

"It's not my place to tell you and don't let her know I said anything, but there's more. I know she likes you though and she trusts you. She'll tell you when she's ready. But I know it's none of my business, so I'll get my nose out." He took a sip of coffee, made a face as if it were cold and set the cup down. "Anyway, we were talking about getting you some help."

Bill hesitated, thinking of Hank's comment about Joan, then spoke as if he were in a trance. "Okay," he said. "I'll see if I can find a part-time guy."

"No. You never know when you need somebody and I don't want you tied down doing all this dirty work. It's more important for you to keep working these customers. You're good at that, and that's where the payback is."

Bill's mind drifted back to the subject at hand. "All right, I'll look for somebody. I can train about anybody to do the basic stuff around here if they really want to work. I'll find a good guy."

"I know you will."

Hank left the office and Bill went to the counter to warm his coffee cup with a refill. He looked into the dark liquid and tried to imagine what it was he needed to know about Joan.

***

One of the applicants that answered the newspaper ad was a young man named Toby Chambers. His resume indicated he had graduated from high school two years before and was captain of the football team. His experience consisted of a few entry-level jobs, including Wal-Mart, from which he had recently been laid off.

Bill walked around the warehouse with Toby and briefly

explained the basic operation. "You unloaded trucks at Wal-Mart, eh? And you operated a forklift?"

"Yes sir, I have my license right here." Toby reached for his billfold in a back pocket.

"That's fine. I don't need to see it."

Bill moved briskly in the cold November air of the barely heated warehouse as he explained the duties of the job. Toby listened patiently with his hands buried in the pockets of his jacket.

"I saw on your resume that you played football in high school. What position?"

"Center and linebacker, sir."

"That's good. You look to be in good shape. I played football when I was your age, but I wasn't as big as you. Bet I could outrun you, though."

Toby shifted his weight and said with a look of embarrassment, "Yeah, I'm not fast."

"I don't mean now," Bill said. "Thirty years ago."

Toby smiled.

By the time they moved into the office, Bill felt confident that Toby could do the physical work and he had formed a favorable impression of the young man.

"What makes you a good employee?" he asked.

"I'm a hard worker, Mr. Burdette. I'll do anything you need me to."

"Toby, just call me Bill."

"Yes, sir."

He solemnly looked at the young man, letting the last words linger in the air.

Toby looked puzzled before taking the cue. Finally, he said, "I mean, Bill."

Bill nodded with a grin and continued. "It's good to be a hard worker and I expect that of everyone, including myself. It's more important, though, to do things right than just to stay busy. This is a lot different from Wal-Mart. Things aren't all bright and shiny with lots of people telling you what to do. You'll be on your own mostly, and it'll be as cold as a well digger's ass sometimes. You know how cold it gets around here. And it can get as hot as Hades in the summertime."

"Sir, I've worked on a farm and a ranch, too. I'm used to working in bad weather."

"Good." He tried again to test the boy's commitment. "So, don't plan on calling in sick or taking a day off either, 'cause there's no back-up."

"Yes, sir—you can count on me. I don't get sick, Mr. …. uh … Bill."

"I don't either." Bill paused and interjected, "Toby, don't worry about what you call me—it's not important." Then, he asked, "If I ran a background check on you, what would I find?" He knew Wal-Mart had run a drug screen and a criminal background check, which was good enough for him, but he wanted to see if the boy would reveal anything.

"Sir, it would say that I'm a good Christian. I don't smoke or drink. And I made pretty good grades in school and.… "

"Okay, that's enough." *Boy, this kid is raw.*

He went over more of the job duties with Toby. The youngster responded with a lot of "yes sirs."

"Okay, then, I only have three rules. Number one—be here on time. Number two—be polite to everyone, even if they're not polite to you." As an aside, he said, "I don't think you'll have a problem with that one." He continued, "Number three—don't hurt yourself or anybody else. Do you think you can follow those rules?"

"Yes, sir."

"I thought you might say that." Then he added, "Oh yeah, one more thing—have fun. You can call that rule Three-A."

The young man grinned and said, "Yes, sir."

Apparently, it would take a little while for "sir" to become "Bill". Still, it was refreshing to find a youngster with good manners and it impressed Bill. He called Toby the next day and told him he was hired. "I'll see you at seven-thirty on Monday."

"Yes, sir!"

***

Bill didn't forget Hank's comments about his relationship with Joan. He was curious about the missing link in Joan's past, but more bothersome was Hank's reference that he had been "taken in" by her. It made him feel like something less than a boarder who reliably paid his rent and contributed his share of the food. He procrastinated for a couple of weeks, trying to decide on the best way to bring it up. Finally, as they finished dinner one evening, he opened the subject.

"You know, Joan, I think the world of you, but I don't want you to be a captive in your own house."

"What do you mean?" She looked surprised by the comment. "I don't feel that way at all. I enjoy having you around."

"Having me around?"

She looked bewildered. "I like your company."

"Yeah, I guess I'm like a big cocker spaniel." He laughed facetiously.

She tilted her head to the side. "Bill, is there something wrong? I thought everything was going along fine. Just tell me what you're getting at."

It was awkward and he searched for the right words. "What I mean is, you've been real good to me and I value our relationship. I consider you my best friend." As soon as the words left his mouth, he regretted saying "best friend". Considering their relationship, it sounded so impersonal.

"A friend? That's it?"

"No, hell no—more than that. A friend is somebody like Hank. You're a lot more than that. You're special."

"I'm glad to know I'm not like Hank."

"Damn it," he said in frustration, "I can't explain it. I just know how I feel and I want you to know how much I appreciate you. But there's something I need to know." She didn't respond as he paused. "That first night I was here—why did you let me stay?" He sucked in his pride to say what had been understood but not spoken between them. "How did you know I had nowhere to go?"

"Just, uh, woman's intuition I suppose."

"No, you're avoiding something. Men have intuition, too, you know."

She exhaled a deep sigh. "Norma, the waitress at the Travel Depot—we're friends. When she saw us speaking, she called me later and we talked. She said you'd been there a couple of days, sleeping in your truck."

It struck a nerve with Bill and his eyes narrowed. "So you decided you'd rescue me, eh?" His tone was sarcastic.

"No." She scrunched her face, as if offended. "I didn't know that until after we had agreed to meet. Why does all this matter?"

"Because," he sneered, "I'm not some stray cat you can just pick up and call your own."

"This is crazy. What do you mean, call you my own? I've never given you a reason to think that. I don't know what's gotten into you."

"You want somebody who feels obligated to you, don't you? Somebody who won't beat you like that last guy did."

"That's cruel." She looked hurt. "You don't know what I went through."

"What, Joan? Tell me what happened," he pleaded.

She looked down at the table for a long time without speaking. Finally, she said, "He didn't just beat me, he made me lose my child."

He waited for her to spill it out.

"Her name was Melody. She was only three years old and she was beautiful."

He remained silent and kept his eyes focused on hers.

"We took her in as a foster child. I wanted to adopt her, but Eric said to wait. When we had our last blow-up, he told them I was an unfit mother. Lied about me. Hank tried to help, but they took her away." She looked past Bill as if the child were standing behind him. "She loved me more than he did."

Bill squirmed in his chair, put his elbows on the table, and folded his hands together under his chin. "I'm sorry it happened. But, I can't replace her."

She stiffened and looked at him with steely eyes. "So, that's what's bothering you. Poor Miss Victim—that's who you think I am, isn't it?" Her face reddened as she raised her voice. "Well, if you think I'm taking advantage of you, you don't have to stay here. You can leave anytime you want."

Leave. Just like that. He felt caught in a vortex of emotions that seemed to be taking him against his will. But suddenly he didn't feel wanted anymore. "That might be best," he said, raising his voice to meet hers.

"Maybe so." She lowered her voice to a normal tone. "I got along fine before you got here."

That did it. He rose from the chair and walked out of the kitchen. At the front door, he stopped and turned back. "I'll get my stuff tomorrow," he yelled. Then he slammed the door behind him.

He went to his truck and started the engine. With the motor idling, he stared vacantly through the windshield. *What the hell's the matter with me?* He turned off the ignition, pounded the steering wheel a couple of times and sat there for several minutes, knowing what he had to do. He got out of the truck and trudged back to the house. At the front door, he raised his fist to knock, then lowered it. Hoping that she hadn't locked the door behind him, he tried the handle and it turned freely. He went inside and saw her lying face down on the sofa in the living room, sobbing into a pillow.

"I'm an idiot." He said as he knelt beside her. "I'm sorry for starting all this."

She turned her head to face him. "I was a witch," she said. "I didn't want you to go."

"We said things we didn't mean." He kissed her on the cheek and began to massage her back as she closed her eyes.

"Umm," she moaned.

As he continued to rub her back and shoulders, he could feel the softness of her body through her blouse and it aroused a sensual urge in him.

She sat up and looked at him with teary eyes. "Thank you," she whispered. "That felt wonderful." She leaned forward and kissed him.

"So did that," he said, as they parted lips.

"I'm glad you liked it."

"Did I ever tell you what a good looking woman you are?"

"Maybe a couple of times, not that I'm counting. Be careful or I might start believing you." A slight smile curled her mouth.

"I want you to believe it, because I mean it."

He stood and pulled her from the sofa. Gently bringing her body to his, he kissed her as he had not kissed a woman in a long time.

She spoke softly in his ear. "Maybe we need each other."

"I think we do."

She went to her bedroom as he turned off the lights in the house. When he entered her room, she had begun to undress in the dark. Without speaking, he took off his clothes and moved to embrace her. As they came together with their bodies entwined, he kissed her neck and shoulders.

He pulled her to the bed, feeling a surge of pent-up passion, and the slight dampness of her skin smelled fresh and sweet like dew. She yielded to him and, lost in the suspension of time, they lingered in the pleasure of lovemaking.

***

In the early morning, she awoke with her head on his chest. "What time is it?" she mumbled.

He lowered his face to hers. "It's today."

She closed her eyes again. "Don't leave."

The fine texture of her hair felt like silk against his cheek. "I'm not going anywhere."

He pulled up the sheet and it was cool against the warmth of his body wrapped in hers. The world was quiet except for the faint sound of her breathing as he closed his eyes.

He didn't feel homeless anymore.

17

The South had been simmering with racial turmoil for years, and now it was apparent the conflict was about to reach full boil. And nowhere was segregation more fully entrenched or integration more fiercely denied than in Alabama. The state university was a high profile example of an institution of segregation, and Billy was headed directly into the eye of the Civil Rights storm.

There was a sign on the main road leading to the University that read: *Tuscaloosa, Home of Robert Shelton, Grand Wizard, United Klans of America.* It was a bold statement of defiance, and Billy cringed every time he saw it. The vision of a burning cross and men in hoods was as clear as if it had been etched in his consciousness, a scar from many years before.

***

When Billy was nine, his family went to a local park for a picnic on the Fourth of July. The huge park contained wooded areas surrounding expanses of grass, activity areas, and covered pavilions. A shallow creek ran through the woods not far from a public swimming pool and behind that, a large playground. Billy and Jackie swam in the pool for an hour before joining the other kids on the playground. They took their turns on the monkey bars and swings before a lively game of kickball broke out. Afterward, they gathered with their parents to roast wieners on a brick grill, then spread a blanket on the ground to eat hotdogs and drink colas.

As they ate, Billy noticed a large clearing near the center of the park where a stack of logs was setup. He asked his father, "Are we going to have a fire?"

"Maybe so," Jim Burdette answered.

Billy and Jackie finished their meal and headed to the creek to throw rocks at floating sticks. Later they rejoined their parents for a leisurely stroll around the park.

An impromptu baseball game broke out in one corner of the lawn by a group of adults and Jim Burdette was invited to join in. The elder Burdette had been a star athlete in high school and was still in good shape at thirty years old. So he welcomed the invitation, borrowed a glove, and headed for a spot in the outfield. He chased down one ball into a stand of trees and made a powerful throw back to the infield to hold the runner to a triple. When the sides changed, he got a turn at bat and whacked the ball between outfielders and it rolled to the creek. Jim hustled around the bases as the spectators yelled, "Run, run!" Billy and Jackie raised their arms and jumped up as they screamed, "Go Daddy!"

A motley crew of teammates congratulated Jim as he crossed the plate with a home run. The game went on for more than an hour with no more heroics from him, but Jim Burdette left the field with sweat stained clothes and two young boys walking admiringly at his side.

The family returned to their picnic site and when darkness began to set in, the sounds of firecrackers and cherry bombs echoed in the park. Billy and Jackie lit their sparklers and twirled in circles, laughing as they stabbed the air with swirls of mini-explosions.

In the distance, they saw a man approach the stack of logs in the clearing and douse it with gasoline. Three other men arrived and put up a large wooden cross, securing it with posts pounded into the ground with sledgehammers.

"We're going to have a fire," Billy yelled excitedly to his brother. "Let's go."

"Yea!" Jackie yelled.

"Y'all stay here!" Jim Burdette shouted. He grabbed his two sons, one in each arm, clamping his grip with authority.

"Jim, let's leave," said Alice Burdette. "I don't want the boys to see this."

"You take them to the car," Jim said. "I'll be there in a minute."

Several cars drove to the edge of the clearing and formed a circle around the cross and log pile. Men in robes and hoods of different colors got out of the cars, and one of them set the pile of logs ablaze. People from all around the park gathered to observe what was going on.

Alice grabbed her sons by their hands and ushered them to the car.

"What are they going to do, Mom?" Billy asked, frightened by the spectacle. He had heard about these things from his grandfather, even seen long-ago pictures of cross burnings and men in hooded robes. Now the past had suddenly come alive and, sensing an aura of evil all around him, he was terrified.

"Don't pay any attention to them," his mother said.

Despite his mother's plea, Billy couldn't take his eyes off the raging bonfire. Then he saw a black-face dummy hanging by its neck from a tree limb. He could hear chants from the hooded men and shouts of encouragement from the crowd. Turning his eyes from the scene in the distance, Billy looked at Jackie who stared back at him with a scared look.

Billy sat nervously silent in the car with his mother and brother until his father arrived.

"I didn't know Darwin Pritchett was in the Klan," Jim Burdette said, as he got into the car. "He had on a robe and everything."

Billy wondered why the choir director at their church was involved in such a thing. Didn't the preacher say, *Love thy neighbor*?

"He's a sorry thing," Alice said, disgustedly.

"He's alright, he just don't have any use for nigras," Jim replied.

"Hush!" Alice hissed. "I don't want to hear any more about this. I would've never come here if I'd known this was going to happen."

A day that began for young Billy with the innocent joy of playgrounds, hot dogs, and a home run by his daddy, ended in a frightening night with mean-spirited men dressed like the devil.

That's when he realized that evilness sometimes hides behind a mask of innocence.

***

As he grew older, Billy felt like a bystander on the fringe of a mob, not only powerless to do anything about the injustices he witnessed, but guiltily acquiescent. It was just another bit of confusion for him to deal with, like his ill-fated football career and his fall-out with Olivia. Life felt like a jigsaw puzzle with pieces that didn't fit. The confusion became more acute one day in the early spring of his senior year.

It was just past noon and Manuel's Restaurant, only a few blocks from campus, was alive with the lunch crowd. Billy leaned back in his chair and looked at his brother as they waited for the waitress to return with their food.

"So how's it going in Engineering School?" Billy asked.

"It's a matter of survival," Jackie answered. "They don't screw around. If you can't do the work, they'll flunk your ass. More than half of the freshmen don't make it. Chemistry or Physics gets most of them. It would help if the professors could speak English. But the classes are smaller now and things have kind of settled down. I won't be on the Dean's List, but I think I'll survive."

"I'm sure you will. Business School is really not that bad, but some of these bumpkins from the sticks think it is. Accounting is the ball buster. It's not exactly rocket science, but it's more than just adding a bunch of numbers." Billy stopped to reflect on the comparison of curricula. "Hey, it's more than you could do on your stupid slide rule." He laughed at the afterthought.

Jackie grinned, but he seemed preoccupied with other thoughts. "Billy," he said, as the grin disappeared, "I need to talk to you about something."

The conversation stopped briefly as the waitress brought their food.

"You were saying you wanted to talk about something." Billy said, after swallowing a bite. "It wouldn't concern a certain girl would it?"

Jackie arched his brows and nodded in acknowledgement. "You know that Olivia and I have gotten close. I don't date anyone else and she doesn't either."

"Really?" Billy said, sarcastically. "Going steady, eh?"

"That's high school stuff. It's more than that."

"Look, Jackie," Billy said angrily, "I've told you before—that's between you and Olivia. Y'all can do whatever you want to. Don't worry about me. You can marry her for all I care."

"Billy, I wouldn't do anything to hurt you or embarrass you and this is a weird situation. But, I can't help it—I love her and she says she loves me."

As Jackie spoke, Billy was distracted by what he saw through the big plate glass window. Outside the entrance, four black women approached the front door.

"I've decided—" Jackie started.

"Oh hell… shhh," Billy said, raising his hand with his eyes fixed on the front door.

Jackie turned to look as the black women boldly entered the restaurant. Manuel's daughter, acting as hostess, stood speechless as the intruders walked past her.

The four women separated and each found an empty chair at a table otherwise occupied by whites. Some of the diners immediately left their tables and walked out, while others remained in their seats, temporarily stunned by the unexpected guests. Manual's daughter rushed frantically through the kitchen's swinging doors into the back recesses of the restaurant.

One of the black ladies approached the table occupied by Billy and Jackie. A large woman with a pleasant face and pecan-colored skin, she was dressed in her Sunday best. Without a word, she plopped down in an empty chair between the two brothers who sat facing each other across the table.

"Ma'am, we prefer to eat alone," Billy said, calmly. "We're having a personal conversation."

Without a word, the woman got up and sat down at another table.

One of the diners at a table next to the brothers left his seat and started for the door. As he passed by Billy he said defiantly, "Don't ever say ma'am to a nigger." He had obviously overheard Billy's words to the lady.

Billy rose from his chair red-faced and shouted loud enough for everyone in the restaurant to hear. "Don't you tell me what I can't say!"

Jackie grabbed his brother's arm to keep him from going after the man who hurried away without looking back.

Suddenly, Manuel burst through the kitchen doors, his daughter at his heels. He went to each of the black ladies and told them angrily they would have to leave. Manual's daughter and the waitresses went table-to-table telling everyone that the restaurant was closing. The four women joined together and walked out of the restaurant, where they were met by a small group of black men.

Some of the diners attempted to pay their tab, but Manuel waved his hands and ushered everyone out of the restaurant, like a shepherd herding a flock of sheep. The brothers put some money on the table, then hustled out of the restaurant with the others. As soon as everyone was out, Manuel locked the door.

On the sidewalk outside, Jackie said, "That was interesting."

"Yeah, I'm glad it didn't get nasty," Billy responded, ignoring his run-in with the bigoted diner. Then, thinking of the black women, he added, "At least, not for us."

Jackie shook his head, apparently dismayed by the experience.

A pretty coed carrying a couple of books walked by, heading toward the campus. "What happened?" she asked. "Did those colored ladies do something?"

"No, not really," Billy replied.

The coed looked puzzled, but didn't stop. As she walked away, the brothers admired the view from behind. The tight skirt clung to the fullness of her rear-end and her hips swayed in rhythm with each step.

"Hmm," Billy said, keeping his eyes glued to the coed. "They're everywhere, you know. There are more pretty women on this campus than you can shake a stick at. I think I'll give it a try, though. You can have your one course meal—I'm going to try the buffet."

"The frat boys have first dibs," Jackie said, smugly. "Even before mister ex-jock BMOC."

"We'll see," Billy replied. Then, without segue, he suddenly turned serious. "You and Olivia do whatever y'all want. I don't hold anything against either of you. I'll be fine."

Manuel's Restaurant opened the next day with a policeman at the door and everything returned to normal for a while. But nothing seemed normal to Billy anymore. He had denied a seat in a restaurant to a black woman and his brother had declared his love for Olivia.

He felt as if he was standing on the side of the road and the world was passing him by.

***

While he was on the football team, Billy didn't take the maximum course load, so after his senior year, he still needed a couple of classes to graduate. Determined to catch up, he got a part-time job at a local gas station and enrolled in summer school. There was a lot of tension in the air on campus regarding the impending integration of the school, but Billy's desire to get his diploma overruled his fear that violence would break out.

Newspapers and television stations all over the country were filled with stories about the showdown between the federal government and the southern states over the issue of school segregation. Alabama's newly elected governor, George Wallace, vowed to uphold the state law and block the enrollment of two black students, one male and one female, at the flagship state university. President John F. Kennedy and his brother, Attorney General Robert Kennedy, were equally adamant that the law of the land be upheld.

In early June, Billy joined a large group of students at the foot of the steps of Foster Auditorium to register for summer classes. At the entrance, Governor Wallace, surrounded by state troopers, read a speech defying the court order that allowed the black students to register. For Billy, it seemed surreal to be a part of a spectacle that was viewed by the whole world as a stubborn display of ignorance.

He turned to a student next to him and said, "This is ridiculous."

"The Governor's just trying to keep the jigs out," the other student said.

Billy knew that many students felt as he did, but everyone was mixed in the same pot and, at that moment, he felt lonely.

After the Governor's speech, Billy followed the crowd up the steps and headed for the registration tables. Later that day, the campus was placed under martial law and the National Guard was dispatched to enforce the enrollment of the two black students. The Governor once again stood in the way, but stepped aside when ordered to do so by the Guard's commanding general. In the end, the confrontation fizzled out and there was no violence. Yet, the symbolism remained of Alabama defiantly protesting the legal and moral dictates of the nation like an angry child, kicking and screaming at the heels of an adult. It was an indelible image that Billy knew would be hard to erase and a stigma he bitterly resented.

Nothing was more telling of the changing times than the sight of National Guard troops lolling on the quadrangle in summer fatigues. Sent there to quell any attempts at violence, they instead passed their time tossing footballs, smoking, and occasionally drilling. It was a far cry from the patriotic display of the ROTC parade on the same grounds which had so impressed Billy only a few years earlier.

Still, he liked the campus that time of year. The enrollment was less than half its normal size and the class schedule was not as hectic as in the fall or spring. Despite the presence of the Guard, it was a more relaxed environment. The specter of civil turmoil seemed to fade from Billy's mind as he looked forward to graduating in August. But a vivid reminder soon appeared.

One day, as he walked to his class, Billy heard another student say, "There's Vivian Malone". Not far away, he watched a lone black female student stride across the quadrangle. She was accompanied by an obvious escort of plain clothed bodyguards. Other students looked at her with distant curiosity, but no one spoke to her or acknowledged her. An attractive young lady with caramel colored skin and straight black hair, she seemed unfazed by the attention she received. Billy had an impulse to speak to her, or at least wave, but didn't have the nerve.

He watched as Vivian Malone walked toward the Gorgas House, a historic antebellum structure on a corner of the quadrangle and one of the few buildings to survive the burning of the campus by Union Troops during the Civil War. She was led though the gate and, still accompanied by her escorts, up the steps and into the front door. Billy had never been inside the Gorgas House and he wondered what took her there. He surmised that she was a privileged guest and he reflected on the irony.

When he reached his classroom, Billy sat motionless in his desk for a moment and thought about his encounter with his new schoolmate, Vivian Malone. Or rather, his lack of encounter. A coed next to him asked, "Did you see that colored girl?"

"Yeah, she's got a lot of guts."

The coed responded with a curious look.

"More than I've got," he added.

***

Billy graduated in August and got his first real job with a plumbing supply company in Birmingham. He wore a coat and tie at work, had a private office, and shared the use of a secretary. Popular with his co-workers, he felt a sense of importance for the first time since his football glory days. With a salary greater than his father's, he had arrived at a comfortable level of success. But soon the winds of change began to blow in his face.

On a Sunday morning in mid-September, as he listened to a recap of Saturday's football games on the radio, the program was interrupted with a news bulletin. A bomb had been detonated at The Sixteenth Street Baptist Church. It was later reported that four young black girls had died in the explosion. The powder keg of racial unrest exploded around the city and two more black people were dead before the day was gone.

The Civil War had been over for almost a hundred years, but the Civil Rights War was just getting started.

On the way to work the next morning, he drove through a black section of town where signs of rioting from the day before were obvious. When he stopped at a red light, he looked around nervously. There were bricks on the side of the street and, on the sidewalk, an abandoned vehicle with broken windows. A few minutes later, a train blocked traffic at a railroad crossing, and his heart raced as he kept his eye on a few blacks roaming not far away, carrying bricks and baseball bats. The train inched forward, then came to a complete stop. He could see through the gaps in the freight cars a large group of men gathered on the other side in a heated discussion with animated hand gestures.

Realizing he was an easy target, especially in the little Karmann Ghia that had replaced his Chevy, he made a quick U-turn and sped away as fast as he could shift gears. He zipped through side streets until reaching the main avenue leading into town, passing a few police cars stationed along the way. When he pulled into the parking lot at work, he felt a strong sense of relief as if escaping into a safe haven.

Once at his desk, he tried to concentrate on his job, but there was an unsettling atmosphere in the office. The church bombing and violence in the city the day before was on everyone's mind, dominating every conversation. No one knew what would happen next, and some local officials seemed more intent on controlling the backlash from the black community than bringing justice to those who had perpetrated the crime.

After work he went to a nearby bar with a fellow worker.

"This is crazy," Billy said.

"We reap what we sow," his friend Norman replied. "This is what happens when we have evil people in government that condone this sort of crap. It happened to my people in Germany and a lot worse."

He knew Norman was Jewish, but when he said *my people* it became more personal.

"Did you have relatives in Germany during the war?"

"Yes." Norman took a drink and looked at him. "My grandparents. They didn't survive."

"That's tough—I'm sorry." Grainy black and white images of emaciated Jews being led to the gas chambers appeared in Billy's mind.

"I don't feel like I can just stand by and watch it happen to others," Norman continued. "We're just as guilty as the Germans who let the Nazis brainwash them and turn them against some of their own people. Don't you see? History is repeating itself."

"But we're not conducting mass executions," Billy argued. "Yeah, I know it's bad to deny people their rights and I know the government is complicit to a degree in what happened at the church yesterday. Things will settle down."

"We're *letting* it happen. That's just as bad as *making* it happen."

"What can we do? We can't fight George Wallace and Bull Conner and all the crazy Klansmen out there."

Norman stared at Billy with resolve written on his face. "Somebody has to."

Billy realized Norman was not just being idealistic. His friend was serious.

"What are you going to do?" Billy asked.

"I've joined the Freedom Riders."

"Norman, that's dangerous. You can get your ass killed."

"I have to do it, Billy. I have to do it. I couldn't live with myself if I just stood idly by and did nothing." Norman looked Billy straight in the eye and asked, "Do you want to go with me?"

Billy felt as if the eyes of God were looking down on him, waiting for his answer. From his football days he felt he had proven his manhood, but now he contemplated a challenge of real physical danger in a no-win situation.

"Norm, I've just gotten out of school and barely started this job. I can't afford to drop everything and ride in a bus all over the South looking for places to stir up trouble."

"The trouble is already there—it doesn't need stirring up. But that's okay—I didn't expect you would want to do it. I just thought I would ask out of consideration." Norman finished with a mischievous laugh.

"Thanks a hell of a lot. That's real white of you," Billy said, laughing at his own ironic epithet. "When do you start?"

"I turned in my notice today. I'll be around 'til the end of next week and then I'll be off to wherever. It's kind of a moving target right now."

Billy started to make a cute comment about the word "target", but thought better of it. Instead, he said, "Wow, that's quick."

"What happened yesterday was the final straw. It might not make a bit of difference whether I go or not, but I feel like I have to. So, while I'm out *stirring things up*, as you say, you can get started on your way to the top of the corporate world."

Norman made the comment in jest but Billy felt the sting of truth. Conformity—that was what he was heading for. A life as a regular Man in the Gray Flannel Suit. Even as a young man with little business experience, the prospect scared the hell out of him.

"I hate this job," Billy said. "I can't imagine doing this for the next forty years. I'll be a freakin' vegetable." He looked at Norman seriously and his friend stared back with knowing eyes as he drained the last drop of his drink.

"You'll get used to it." Norman shook his head before contradicting himself. "No, actually you won't. You won't get used to it. You'll just give in to it and then you'll be one of them."

"I'll never be *one of them*." Billy's face bore the fierceness of his words. "But I'm no wild-eyed crusader, either." He was resolute in his position, yet trapped by the discomfort of an unclear direction in his life.

Billy couldn't have been more different than Norman on the outside, yet more compatible on the inside. He realized they were both still trying to find their way in the world, just on different paths.

They ordered another round of drinks, and the heavy tone of the conversation lifted as the subject turned to football. Norman was an Auburn grad, an arch-enemy by degree. The two men argued passionately, but good naturedly, about the merits of their alma maters. As they paid the tab and started to leave, they made a bet on the annual rivalry game.

Billy noticed a montage of familiar scenes flashing on the television behind the bar.

The camera focused on Bull Conner saying something, then the scene changed to blacks being doused with high pressure water hoses, beaten with clubs, and attacked by vicious dogs. Billy approached the bar as the image of George Wallace appeared on the screen.

"Segregation now, segregation tomorrow, and segregation forever," Wallace bellowed.

"Tell 'em George," an old man at the bar said. Others nearby expressed agreement.

Billy raised his right arm straight out and yelled, "Sieg heil,"

"Billy!" Norman said, grabbing him by the arm. "Not here."

The old man and several others turned to Billy with stunned looks.

Billy looked at the old man and said, "You know what we ought to do with the niggers?"

"Billy, stop," Norman said.

The old man didn't reply.

"Burn 'em," Billy said. "Gas 'em. Kill all of 'em. That'll get rid of their asses."

"I don't want anybody to get hurt," the old man said. "They just need to stay in their place."

"Yeah," Billy said, "that's what we need to do—keep 'em in their lousy place!"

"Let's go," Norman said.

Billy calmed down, paid his tab, and could almost feel suspicious eyes following him out of the bar.

As they parted outside, Norman reminded him of the bet on the football game. They exchanged barbed insults and he headed for his car, still fuzzy from a few drinks and the scene in the bar.

I'll never get to play in the Auburn game. Olivia quit cheering for me, and Zee can't go to Alabama.

Nothing makes any damn sense.

18

Bill tucked the shirt in his pants, slipped on his loafers, and walked from the bedroom, primed for the Friday night card game with Hank and Lois McElvey. "We've got to leave in a few minutes."

"I need to stick these plates in the dishwasher," said Joan.

When the phone rang, Joan set the dishes down and answered with a lilt in her voice. But her face quickly turned serious as she listened intently to the caller.

Bill noticed the change in Joan's expression and stood by, looking directly at the phone as if he were trying to hear what was being said.

"Of course, we'll go right now. I'll call you back when we get there." She hung up and looked at him with anxious eyes.

"What's going on?"

"That was Lois. She said Hank hasn't picked her up yet. He's thirty minutes late and he doesn't answer his phone. It's not like him and she's worried that something may have happened. We need to go check on him."

"Okay, let's go," Bill said, calmly. "There's probably nothing wrong. Don't assume the worst."

They hurried to Hank's house. As they approached, they saw his big Cadillac in its usual spot in the carport. Everything around it was neatly in place and nothing looked unusual outside the house. Bill walked up the front steps and rang the doorbell before quickly entering the unlocked door. "Hank," he hollered.

Joan followed him inside and they stood in the foyer, listening for a sign of life. The house was ominously silent except for the grandfather clock that ticked away at the foot of the stairway. The light was on in the kitchen, but otherwise the house was unlit and the rooms were shadowy in the faint glow of evening twilight that filtered through the window shears.

"I'll go upstairs," Bill said. "You check down here."

"No, I'll go with you," Joan answered.

Joan stayed close beside Bill as they checked each room upstairs, turning on the lights and peering into the closets. Bill felt it a little melodramatic, as if they were characters in an old horror movie but he didn't voice his amusement. Each room was empty and tidily intact.

Sensing the tension in Joan, he maintained a calm, yet concerned demeanor.

Back downstairs, they quickly went through the bigger, more open rooms. There was no sign of Hank and everything in the house appeared to be in order.

"I don't see anything here," Bill said. "He's probably out for his walk and just lost track of time."

"I'm worried," Joan said. "It's not like him. He looks forward to this night all week. He loves to get together with Lois and us."

"I think it's more about Lois than it is about us," Bill said, fighting a grin.

Joan remained stone-faced. "Where is he?" she said to the empty space around her.

They went into the kitchen and began searching for signs of a note or a clue. The breakfast table was setup for the bridge game with a score pad and glasses on coasters at each chair position. Two decks of cards rested on one corner, a large bowl of chips and a smaller one with dip in the middle.

"I'm going to check his car," Bill said.

Bill stepped from the kitchen into the adjoining carport. When he opened the driver's door to the big sedan, he saw Hank. He was slumped over on his side with his body across the front seat. His head rested on the passenger side as if he were taking a nap. The keys lay on the floorboard next to the gas pedal. Moving to the other side of the vehicle, Bill opened the door and turned Hank's head up. His eyes were open in a blank stare, but he made no effort to speak. Bill bent over and said in a low voice, "Hank, can you hear me?" There was no response, but he could see that Hank was breathing.

"Joan," Bill yelled.

She arrived quickly and ran to the far side of the car. She nudged beside Bill to look at Hank and cried, "Oh, my God!"

"Call nine-one-one," Bill said. "I think he's had a stroke, or maybe a heart attack."

Joan hurried back into the kitchen, leaving the door open. Bill watched with a clear view from the garage as she grabbed the phone on the wall, called the emergency number, and gave them the address. Then, she fumbled with a small notebook on the counter before settling on a page and dialing another number.

He could hear Joan plainly as she spoke on the phone. "Lois, we found Hank in his car." She spoke faster than normal, an urgent tone in her voice. "He's alive, but we think he's had a stroke or a heart attack. An ambulance is on the way....No, please, don't come now. They should be here soon. When we get to the hospital and find out what's going on, we'll give you a call....We will, we'll call you as soon as we know anything...Yes, I know you're fond of him Lois. I'll stay in touch. Bye."

Joan came back into the carport and crouched beside Bill, who had Hank's head cradled in his hands, staring into his blank eyes.

"Hank," Bill said, "if you can hear me, help is on the way. We're with you, buddy."

Joan leaned into Bill and began to sniffle. "Lois was upset. She's very fond of Hank."

"I know she is."

"I love him." She buried her face in Bill's chest and began to sob.

Releasing Hank, he held her tightly and they embraced almost motionless, not knowing if Hank was aware of their presence.

Bill felt relief when he heard the wail of a siren in the distance. The pulsating sound got louder and soon the ambulance pulled into the driveway. Two paramedics rushed to Hank's car and asked Bill what had happened. Then they quickly tended to Hank, checking his vital signs and responses.

"Is it a stroke?" asked Bill.

"Sir, I can't say. But we need to get him to the hospital right now. Do you want to ride with the patient? We can fill out some paperwork on the way."

Bill looked at Joan who appeared still shaken. "I'll go with Hank. Why don't you meet us at the hospital?"

The paramedics lifted Hank onto a gurney and placed him in the back of the ambulance. Bill got in the back and took a seat beside Hank as they drove away with lights flashing.

When they arrived at the hospital, the paramedics rushed Hank through the emergency entrance and into a separate room. Bill was asked to remain in the waiting area and several minutes later, Joan arrived.

A nurse asked them how long it had been since Hank had been stricken.

"We don't know for sure," Bill said. "Based upon where we found him, we think it happened about thirty minutes or so before we called nine-one-one."

"That's good," the nurse said. "In these situations it's important to get the patient to a doctor as soon as possible."

"Did he have a stroke?" Joan asked.

"You'll have to wait and speak to the doctor. I can't confirm anything at this point. Are you the next of kin?"

Joan and Bill looked at each other, as if they had forgotten something.

"Not really," Joan replied. "I'll call his sister."

"Good," Bill said.

"She's his only surviving relative." Joan paused, then added, "Rod's mother."

"Umm," Bill mumbled, remembering Rod Reynolds, the reprobate nephew that Hank had fired from the warehouse.

Joan went to the nurses' station and borrowed a phone book. She called a couple of numbers listed under the name Reynolds before she reached Hank's sister, Betty.

"She said she would be here in thirty minutes," Joan said.

Then she called Lois. "Lois, there's nothing you can do," she pleaded. "There's nothing any of us can do but wait. There's no need for you to come now."

Joan hung up and turned to Bill. "She said her husband of fifty-two years died in this hospital. Isn't it sad she has to come here again under these circumstances?"

"She's coming?"

"Yes, she said it's the least she could do for Hank."

Bill nodded and turned his head away. He knew it was true.

It was the only thing any of them could do.

19

Three carloads of young men left in the early afternoon for the four-hour drive from Branford to the Playboy Club in Atlanta. As honoree of the bachelor party, Jackie Burdette rode in the lead vehicle. Billy rode shotgun in another car, nursing a Coke laced with Jack Daniels. The other guys in the car kept up constant sophomoric chatter and profane jokes as the beer and alcohol fueled the spirit of the occasion.

Billy kept his eyes on the passing scenery and only occasionally joined in the banter. He had an odd feeling, as if he was in a movie and there would be a sudden twist to the plot, a surprise ending to change everything.

By the time they got to the Playboy Club, all the guys had a little alcohol buzz, but not wanting to come across as rubes, their behavior turned sober. They were in the big city now, so they paid for valet parking and straightened their ties before entering. At the door two gorgeous women in bunny costumes with accentuating eye-popping cleavage greeted them. Once inside, it was like a different world. They felt they had entered a realm of decadent sophistication which they had only imagined while peering through the pages of the magazine. Though the nude photographs created the titillation, the ads actually set the tone. The male models in stylish clothes, the expensive watches, and the upscale lines of toiletry were emulated by young men everywhere as iconic images of cool bachelorhood.

The boys from Alabama assumed affected attitudes in an attempt to blend in with the scene around them.

"Hey, Toto, we're not in Kansas anymore," one of them said.

"No, we're not in Ala-damn-bama, either," said another.

Billy bought cigars from one of the bunnies and passed them around among the group. Another bunny came to take their drink orders. He ordered a martini, even though he didn't like the taste.

"Shaken, not stirred," he said to the bunny with a smile.

She smiled back at him and said, "Of course, Mr. Bond." The other guys looked on in envy as she walked away.

When the bunny was out of earshot, Billy said in a voice that sounded like Sean Connery with a Southern drawl, "Ah, Pussy Galore."

"You better believe it," one of the others said. "This place is full of it."

Billy looked at his brother at the end of the table and said, "Enjoy it now, big boy. The ball and chain goes on in a week."

"That's all right," Jackie answered. "I won't have to be sniffing around and playing with myself like all of y'all."

As a bunny walked away after serving a round of drinks, one of the guys said, "Ooh wee! I didn't know that cottontails had such big titties."

Another said, "Yeah, I'll bet she screws like a rabbit, too."

A third chimed in, "Man, that's private stuff. They won't let you touch 'em, much less poke 'em. The only thing you're going to get your load off on is that centerfold in the magazine."

Everybody laughed at the absurdity of it all.

They moved several times to different rooms in the club, the constant banter occasionally interrupted to order more food and drinks. There was a noticeable absence of crude remarks to Jackie about marital sex, apparently in deference to how Billy might take it. But as the night wore on, everyone got oiled up with liquor. It was getting late and they were about to leave when Billy stood from the side of the large table to address the group. He spoke haltingly, with a drunken lisp.

"Here's to my favorite little brother." He lifted his glass toward Jackie at the head of the table and said, "To Jackie."

"To Jackie," one of the other guys said.

There followed a full round of "To Jackie" as everyone around the table raised their glasses.

"And here's to Olivia, the finest piece of...," Billy said before pausing with a big grin on his face.

"Shut up, you drunk bastard," Jackie said, rising from his chair.

"....womanhood in the whole hotdamn state of Alabama," Billy said, as Jackie rushed forward and took a hard swing at him.

Missing with the punch, Jackie lunged at Billy, knocking him against the table. The brothers fell to the floor, rolling and grabbing and cursing. The other guys started pulling them apart when two large men in black suits, apparently club bouncers, rushed over and shouted for everyone to back away.

"It's okay," Joe Mansour said to the bouncers. "We've got it under control."

Big Joe, as they called him, was a heavyweight college wrestler and the biggest guy in the group. He and the others had pulled the brothers apart, lifting them to their feet with their arms pinned to their sides.

The two bouncers were joined by two more, and they stared menacingly at the group of young men gathered around the brothers. Billy and Jackie calmly shrugged from the grasp of their friends and turned their attention from each other to look at the bouncers defiantly. The tension was thick as the two groups appeared ready for action. The other patrons interrupted their conversations to look on as the noise in the room subsided.

Finally, a man in a tuxedo appeared. "You guys pay up and leave, or I'll have to call the cops."

The group stood around their table for several minutes, still watched closely by the bouncers. As the man in the tuxedo watched, each of the celebrants removed their wallets and handed some money to Big Joe. After shoving a wad of bills at the tuxedo man, Big Joe stood beside him, watching closely as he counted out almost five hundred dollars.

The Burdette brothers were sweaty and disheveled, yet calm and half-sobered by the confrontation as the group filed out of the club, closely shadowed by the bouncers. Big Joe carried up the rear, apparently ready for a move by the bouncers.

Billy spoke to one of the bunnies as he staggered out the door. "I'll see you at the Mansion."

The bachelor party was over and the entourage retired to their nearby hotel to sleep off the night. The next morning they drove back to Branford, fortified with coffee and laughter about the night before. The brothers rode in the same car and poked fun at each other, as if it were all a big joke.

"I was about to whip your ass," Jackie said.

"Ha! In your dreams," replied Billy.

Billy wasn't sure how he felt about Olivia, but he always knew that, no matter what, he would stand by his brother in the way blood demands. That is, except for the times he wanted to beat the hell out of him.

The memory of that night stuck with Bill forever. And he never forgot Joe Mansour, especially every year on Memorial Day. Three years after the Playboy escapade, Big Joe returned from Vietnam to his home in Alabama in a flag-draped coffin.

***

As the wedding grew near, Jackie asked his brother to be the best man, but Billy was not enthused with the idea.

"Jackie, you know I want the best for you and for Olivia, too, but I don't want to get in the way of your day. Everybody knows she and I used to go together, and I just don't think it would look right."

"I don't care what it looks like, and neither does Olivia. I have talked to her about it, and she would like for you to be Best Man. It's not like she's the first woman to ever get married who had another boyfriend, and people have to get used to the fact that you'll be her brother-in-law."

"Yeah, but it might be a distraction. We know what the deal is, but it will be an excuse for some people to say crap."

"They'll say it anyhow if they're going to."

"Look, let me stay in the background. It's your day."

"Billy, would it really make you feel out of place?"

He hesitated, then said in an irritated tone, "Yes."

"Then, that's it. I'll get Kenny. Will you at least be a groomsman?"

"Yeah, I think that'll be better."

***

The rehearsal dinner was held at the Riverside Club, an upscale restaurant and lounge on the outskirts of Branford. Jim Burdette acted as host and when he turned to the audience for testimonials, Billy rose from the head table and was the first to speak.

"Well, little brother, we were teammates for a long time and I caught a lot of your passes, but looks like you've found somebody else to hook-up with. And I don't blame you—she's a lot better looking." He looked at Olivia and she smiled. "Besides, I'm an old cripple now and she could probably outrun me." There were a few groans from former Branford players. "Yeah, I think you've scored the winning touchdown this time." Then, he recalled some incidents about growing up with Jackie intended to embarrass him. Jim and Alice Burdette smiled sheepishly as he recounted the time when Jackie conspicuously passed gas in Sunday school. "That's how he earned the name Pepe Lepew or, as we affectionately call him, Peppy." He looked again at Olivia. "I slept in the same room with this guy for many years and I want to warn you about the ghastly body odors that frequently emanate from a certain orifice of your soon-to-be roommate." Billy tried to be upbeat, but his heart wasn't in it and his attempts at humor fell flat. Finally, he raised his glass and toasted the betrothed couple with forced sincerity, then sat down, feeling embarrassed.

On the day of the wedding, he felt totally out of sync and adopted a façade of happiness in keeping with the occasion. In truth, he was neither happy nor sad, but suspended in a state of malaise. For the first time in his life, he felt totally vulnerable and self-conscious. The rented formal wear made him feel uncomfortably conspicuous at a time when his urge was to blend in with the surroundings like a chameleon.

The wedding was held at the First Methodist Church of Branford at five o'clock in the afternoon. The big brick church set on a low hill just off South Main Street. In the bright sunlight, the building was postcard picturesque with massive white columns, a large stained glass window, and a tall steeple that towered above the surrounding area.

Friends of the families and relatives filled the sanctuary with Jack's parents sitting on the front row of one side of the center aisle and Olivia's on the other. When the procession began, Billy assumed a fake smile as he walked down the aisle with the prettiest bridesmaid on his arm. She wore a pink satin dress and smelled like the roses that adorned the chancel. He took his place near the altar and as he looked out at the rows of familiar faces, they all seemed to be staring back at him from the red velvet-lined pews. His brother and the pastor stood together with broad smiles awaiting the bride's entrance and he suddenly felt weak.

"This is really happening," he said, in a voice so low that even those next to him could not hear.

The audience stirred as *The Wedding March* began, and Olivia slowly walked down the aisle with a small girl attending to the flowing train. She was more beautiful than he had ever seen her with the white gown making a striking contrast against her dark skin and hair.

The ceremony was simple and brief. The pastor began the sermon reading from Genesis about God's creation of man and woman. His manner was warm and pleasant, yet his deep voice resonated with veracity as if descending from heaven. Olivia's best friend, Mary Sue Harrison, followed with a scripture reading in a lilting, high-pitched voice. After the soloist sang *Surely the Presence of the Lord is in this Place,* Howard Alexander gave his daughter away. The couple said their vows and kissed as murmurs of excitement floated from the onlookers. They lit the unity candle and presented roses to their mothers. The pastor led the congregation in the Lord's Prayer before giving a benediction. Finally, he announced, "I present to you Mr. and Mrs. Jack Wade Burdette." The couple walked briskly up the aisle as cameras clicked and applause broke out.

Billy stood through the entire ceremony in a dreamlike trance. At the conclusion he dutifully escorted his companion bridesmaid up the aisle, trailing the new bride and groom. Outside, he joined the group gathered at the top of the steps of the main entrance as one of the ushers drove Jackie's car to the front of the church for the ceremonial getaway. The car was decorated with tin cans tied to the exhaust pipe and newlywed words splashed on the windows. Olivia tossed the bouquet over her shoulder and the bridesmaids scrambled for it like a Hail Mary pass into the end zone.

When Jackie opened the door for Olivia, she screamed and turned away, throwing her arms in the air. The crowd burst into laughter.

Jackie looked confused about Olivia's reaction before he reached inside the car and flung something out of the front seat. He looked at Billy at the top of the steps with an accusatory glare. Billy looked down with feigned innocence. Then, he was caught in the moment and a genuine smile spread across his face for the first time all day.

The plastic dog turd looked amazingly real.

The reception was held in the fellowship hall of the church. The large annex adjoined the rear of the main building with a covered walkway and doubled as a gymnasium. Buffet lines were filled with food and drinks to serve guests at tables that filled half the room. At one end of the room, a disc jockey and his equipment were elevated on risers with an area set aside for dancing in front. The crowd drifted in and, by the time the bride and groom entered, the cavernous room buzzed with conversation and laughter.

No alcohol was served, but Billy and some of the other young men in the wedding party had liquor stashed in their cars. They mixed their drinks in the parking lot and congregated outside the building, drinking, smoking, and kidding around. When the DJ started the music, they were pulled inside by their female companions to join the party and dance. Billy connected with the bridesmaid he had escorted, a cute girl two years his junior named Becky Sullivan. She hung around him like a young puppy and, even after she changed clothes, he could smell the scent of roses on her. It aroused him like a sweet pheromone, but didn't totally break his shell reserve.

The bride and groom had the first dance as The Drifters sang *This Magic Moment*. Then Olivia danced with her father, followed by Jackie and his mother. The floor slowly filled as the DJ played songs with progressively faster beats.

Billy couldn't ignore the loud music and the lively atmosphere and felt obligated to take part. He waited for a slow song, then made his way to Olivia's table and led her to the dance floor.

"I was hoping you would dance with me," she said.

"I was hoping that, too."

"I'll be your sister-in-law. We'll be friends, won't we?"

"Of course—I'll always be your friend. You've married a good man, and I'm happy for you." He forced the words, trying to convince himself as much as her.

"I'm happy, too. I'm sorry it didn't work out with us, but I still think the world of you."

"Yeah, I feel the same about you. First loves usually don't last. And we're too much alike. We would've made each other miserable."

"Maybe not." She seemed slightly offended.

"There's one thing you have to promise me," Billy said, turning serious.

"What?"

"That you'll never tell anyone about our secret—especially Jackie. We were crazy, and we didn't know what we were doing."

She stopped dancing and looked at him with narrowed eyes. Then she put her face next to his, angrily speaking in a voice no one else could hear over the music, "It's my wedding day. How dare you bring that up?"

"Because it happened, and you can't pretend it didn't."

"You think I don't know that?" she asked through clenched teeth. "Do you think I would ever tell anybody what a horrible thing I did? And you're just as guilty as I am, so don't worry about me. Just take care of your own big mouth."

"All right, damn it, I'm sorry. I'll never talk about it again."

"Good!"

The music ended and Billy walked behind Olivia as she returned to her table. She never looked back.

He left the building and ambled over to a group of six young men hanging around a picnic table under a stand of pine trees just beyond the parking lot. Each had a cigarette in one hand and a Dixie cup in the other, no doubt filled with beer or something stronger, in the other. The biggest one, James Robinson, was holding court as the others laughed hysterically at whatever he was saying. Robinson stood almost six-three and his lean frame was topped by an outsized head, giving rise to his nickname, Gourdhead, or simply Gourd.

"Come over here, Zooka," Gourd said, as he approached. "We've been thinkin' 'bout some'n."

Billy walked directly to Gourd. "What's that?"

"Well, we been wonderin' how Olivia's gonna feel tonight when Peppy spreads her out. She might be missin' the old Bazooka—what'cha think?"

Billy looked hard at Gourd and, without a word, cold-cocked him with one quick, powerful blow to the jaw. Gourd remained on the ground, holding his jaw with his face planted on a layer of pine needles. The others stood by speechless as Billy walked away.

Returning to his car, Billy swigged down a stiff belt of straight bourbon. The liquor gave him a buzz, and with the adrenaline still pumping from his the encounter with Gourdhead, he totally abandoned his inhibitions. He found Becky and pulled her inside to the dance floor where they gyrated furiously to Chuck Berry's *Johnny B Goode.* When the song was over, they were gleaming with sweat and hyped up on the throbbing beat of the music. They danced two more fast numbers before sitting down. After a short rest, they returned to the dance floor for a slow number. He held her close, and she pressed herself to him without a hint of subtlety.

When the song ended, he led her outside to his car where she poured some bourbon into her Coke. He leaned over and kissed her with a long deep kiss as he stroked her willing body with his hands. As daylight began to slip away, he drove out of the parking lot and the sound of music from the fellowship hall faded in the distance.

By the time he pulled under the big oak tree near the riverbank, they were shrouded in darkness.

They moved to the back seat and began to unfasten each other's clothing.

It was so easy, but something inside of him felt heavy. Despite the primal urge and numbing effect of alcohol, he couldn't forget the beauty of the wedding ceremony or the voice of the preacher describing God's perfect love. Yet, here he was with a heart empty of beauty or love. He was only a stone's throw from the river and, though he couldn't see it in the dark, he knew the secret it held. He saw the vision of the bloody mass he had stuffed in the bag and shivered at the memory of the unclean feeling of his hands. He pulled away.

"What's wrong?"

"Nothing." He exhaled deeply. "I don't want to get you pregnant."

"Do you need a rubber? I have one in my purse."

"It's not just that." He grunted with frustration and said, "I'm messed up in the head right now."

She began to cry.

"Becky, it's not you. You're great looking and really know how to make a guy feel good, but I'm not right for you just now." He knew if he said anything else it would make a bad situation worse.

"I'm not a whore," she said between sobs.

"I know you're not." He kissed her, then placed his cheek on hers and whispered, "I'm sorry, it was my fault." He used his shirt to wipe the tears from her face and she stopped crying. They lay pressed together with their partially clothed bodies moving to the throbbing rhythm of two separate heart beats.

An orchestra of croaking frogs and chirping crickets serenaded through the open windows, a familiar calming sound. The night stood still and timeless. After a good while, they sat up, put their clothes back together and squeezed into the front seats from the rear of the coupe.

"Are you okay," he said.

"Yes, I'm just sleepy." She slouched against the door.

He drove away and they didn't speak for several minutes.

"You still love her, don't you?" she said, breaking the silence.

"What are you talking about?

"Olivia. You know what I mean."

"Are you crazy? She just married my brother. We broke up a long time ago."

"That doesn't matter. You may have some people fooled, but not me. You might as well have it written on your forehead."

"Well, you're wrong, so just stop talking about it."

"You'll find somebody else."

"I *said*, stop talking about it."

She didn't mention it again. He drove her home and gave her a big hug and kiss before she went inside. He walked away feeling like a jerk, but knowing he had done at least one thing right that day. Still, her words echoed in his mind.

You still love her, don't you?

20

Bill left the waiting room and went outside to walk around for a few minutes. When he returned inside, he sat beside Joan and began thumbing through a magazine. Lois and Hank's sister, Betty Reynolds, sat against the opposite wall. Soon, soft footsteps sounded in the hall and a man in a white lab coat entered. Bill set down the magazine and everyone stood up with anxious looks on their faces.

"Hi, I'm Doctor Stephan." A tall, fiftyish man with salt-and-pepper hair and ghost-white complexion, the doctor wore a pleasant face as he introduced himself. "Mr. Stonecypher has had a stroke and he's being well attended to in ICU."

"So, he's okay?" Joan asked. "I mean...he'll live?"

"His condition is stable right now, but it's too early for a complete prognosis. We'll continue to monitor his vital signs, but the residual effects of a stroke are hard to predict. His brain may continue to swell and, if so, we'll have to address that. "

Lois exhaled a long puff of air with her eyes closed as if to cast out her fear of the worst.

"Is he conscious?" asked Bill.

"Yes, he has been at times, but he's not totally aware of what's happening around him. He may not be able to talk or walk for a while. At his age, full recovery could be...a challenge." He looked at the others and seemed to sense their deflation. "But, it's *possible.*

It's fortunate you were able to get him here quickly. That's in our favor." A self-assured demeanor seemed to radiate from the doctor and some of the tension dissipated from the room.

"Thank God," Hank's sister said. She reached to grasp Joan's hand. "And thank both of you," she said, looking at Bill.

"He'll be here for several weeks, maybe longer," the doctor continued. "He'll have to undergo therapy after that. It can be a very slow and tedious process."

"Can we see him?" Joan asked.

"Yes," the doctor replied. "You can go in, but only one at a time. Be aware, though, when he wakes he might not know who you are."

Bill thanked the doctor for his candor and turned to Hank's sister. "Betty, you're his kin, you should go first."

Betty scurried away, leaving the others to await their turn. She returned less than fifteen minutes later.

"How's he doing?" Joan asked.

"I can't tell," Betty replied. "He's asleep and hooked to a machine. A nurse came in for a minute, but she didn't say much." She looked at the others. "Who's going now?"

Lois looked at Joan and Bill. "You two go."

"The doctor said only one at a time," Joan said.

"It'll be okay," Lois insisted. "I've been here before. They're not real strict about that. All they can do is ask one of you to leave."

Bill took Joan by the arm, motioned her forward with his head, and led her out the door.

When they entered Hank's room, he lay with his head propped and his eyes closed. There were tubes in his nose and he appeared colorless and more aged than before. His thin hair was scattered wildly around his mostly bald head. They talked in low voices as the machine hooked to him beeped occasionally and the jagged line on the screen spiked up and down. Fifteen minutes later, Joan reached and gently touched his arm. Then they left.

Afterward, Lois made a brief visit. When she returned to the waiting room, she said, "Looks like he's going to be in here for a while."

"Yes, but he'll recover," Joan said. "I know him, and he's a tough old coot."

"He is, but remember the doctor said this could be a long haul," Bill said. "And you heard what else he said—Hank may never be the same again. This could affect his mind as much as his body."

"Don't give up on him yet," Joan said. She looked at Bill, then to Lois, and suddenly began to cry. She moved to Lois, and the two women hugged.

"I love him," Joan said. She reached into her purse for a tissue and wiped her tears.

"Yes, we all do," said Lois.

Lois put her arm on Joan's shoulder and the two ladies walked out of the hospital with Bill close behind. Outside, Lois turned to hug him, then gave Joan one last embrace before walking away. Bill took Joan by the hand and held it firmly as they made their way to her car.

"You drive," she said, and handed him the keys with a shaky hand.

When they got into the car, Joan leaned back in the seat with her eyes closed.

"Let's go to Mario's," Bill said. "I think you could use some wine and cheese cake." She didn't respond at first, then opened her eyes and turned to him with a weak smile and a wistful look in her eyes. "Yum."

He drove to a small Italian restaurant in a strip mall where they settled into a booth amid the muffled sounds of tinkling silverware and soft accordion music. He ordered a bottle of Zinfandel and, as they chatted, her mood lightened.

"Hank has lived in that house for almost forty years." She held her hand out with a stop sign as Bill started to refill her wineglass. "I've been his neighbor for twelve of those years. His wife died just before I moved in. Her name was Gail. They had a daughter who died of muscular dystrophy as a teenager. He doesn't talk about it much, but a couple of times he has gotten a little tipsy and called me Cindy. That was his daughter's name. He still calls me *his girl* sometimes, and it makes me feel good because he's like a father to me."

"Your father died when you were young, didn't he?"

Joan nodded. "I was eleven. He had a heart attack in his sleep. When Mom woke up beside him, he was dead. It was horrible."

"I can imagine."

"She had a hard time getting over Dad's death and never remarried. Dad didn't leave her a lot, and she had to work hard to support us."

"Didn't you tell me she lives with your sister in Kansas City?"

"Yes. She lived with me for a while, but she wanted to be closer to the grandkids. She kind of gave up on me having kids. And she's better off there."

"That's a good thing for me, too," he said. "Otherwise, I'd still be roaming around looking for some fleabag place to live and I wouldn't know you or Hank."

"That would be terrible."

"It would be for me, that's for sure."

"Me, too," she said, keeping her eyes fixed on his.

They finished their dessert and hardly spoke as he drove home.

When they neared her house, she said, "I'm going back to the hospital."

"Tonight?"

"Yes, I want to stay with Hank."

"His sister is there. Besides, he probably won't know if you're there or not."

"I'll know."

"What about your job?"

"I'll call in the morning. They can do without me."

"I would stay with you, but I need to go to the warehouse in the morning. I'll open up and get Toby started, then come later."

"That's okay—I'll be fine."

They got out of the car and she walked to the driver's side. He kissed her and held her tight, then watched as she drove away.

He thought it would feel strange being in the house by himself. Then he recalled the time when Hank told him, "If you had any sense, you'd just make it a permanent arrangement." Now that he was paying half of the mortgage and sleeping in her bed, he reckoned he'd done just that.

***

Hospitals always made Bill feel uneasy. He didn't like seeing people hooked to beeping machines with tubes in their noses and smelling of sickly body odors. But every day for five weeks he and Joan visited Hank in the hospital. Removed from the ICU, Hank's speech was so slurred they couldn't understand him and they weren't sure how much he understood of what they said. They sensed he recognized them, though, and it made them feel good to see him. The doctors were cautious but candid in their discussions, indicating that Hank would probably never fully recover. Still, they were hopeful he would regain his voice and possibly walk again.

After they returned home from the hospital one evening, Joan seemed pensive, then surprised Bill with a comment in a serious tone. "There's something I need to tell you."

"Hmm, you're kicking me out?"

"No, I'm serious." She seemed conflicted. "Maybe I should have told you before, but Hank told me and Lois not to tell you. I'm afraid he may never totally recover, and there is something you have to know."

"Know about what?"

"About the warehouse. A few weeks before he had his stroke, he asked me to come to his house to witness his will. He had Lois come, too. She's a Notary." She paused, then added, "He's leaving the warehouse to you. The building...the land...the business. Everything."

"To me?" Bill was shocked. "That doesn't make sense. I'm not even kin to him."

"His only next-of-kin is his sister. He's leaving his house and most of his stuff to her. But he knew she wouldn't have any idea what to do with the business."

"I don't know about this. It doesn't seem right."

"Yes, it does. It's nothing but right."

"Why did he think this up now? He didn't know he was going to have a stroke."

"Bill, he's seventy-six years old, and he's had two heart attacks. He's smart enough to know he needs a will that's up-to-date. Once he convinced himself that you could make money operating the warehouse, he decided it made sense for you to have it."

"Well, we'll deal with that in the future. He's not dead, and he's not dying. He could live another twenty years."

"You know better than that. I don't know if he's dying or not. Nobody knows that. All I know is that warehouse will be yours when he passes, and he's not in any condition now to do anything with it. So just go ahead as if it were yours."

"I've always done that. What you've told me won't make any difference in how I manage the warehouse. Of course, I'll think differently about it, knowing this, but..." His voice trailed off as he tried to collect his thoughts. "This is unreal."

"I thought you needed to know."

"Thanks. I won't let Hank know that I do."

"I don't think it matters now."

Joan turned away and, as she headed into the bedroom, Bill followed behind.

"I don't want Hank to die," he said.

"I know you don't." Then she added, "He loves you like the son he never had."

He sighed and stared blankly at her. All he could think of was that afternoon when he got smashed while listening to Jimmy Buffet and drinking margaritas on the front porch.

Maybe he hadn't lost that shaker of salt after all.

21

It had been almost two years since Billy had seen Norman Goldstein, but he recognized him in one of the newspaper photographs of the Bloody Sunday march in Selma. He found Norman's telephone number in the Birmingham directory and they agreed to meet at a sidewalk café located in an affluent part of town.

"I've been working for my father at the clothing store," Norman said. "He doesn't pay me much and he hates it when I go with the Freedom Riders, but Mom sticks up for me."

"I saw you in one of the pictures of that craziness on the bridge in Selma," Billy said.

"That was scary, real scary. I've never been so terrified in my life. I actually thought I might die. People were getting clubbed in the head and attacked by vicious dogs. Then they threw tear gas. I ran like hell. Those mean cowards love to beat the daylights out of a white person. They think we're all a bunch of Yankee rabble-rousers. It's not just the troopers, either. Some of the spectators throw things at us and call us nigger lovers."

"Norm, I know you feel strongly about this, but why do you put yourself in these situations? It's almost as if you're begging to get hurt. You know these things will work themselves out."

"You're wrong. There are too many people who will fight it tooth and nail."

"You guys are just stirring things up and making it harder. Wallace would back off a little if you weren't challenging his authority. The Feds will take care of things like they did at the University."

"That's the way it should be, but it's not the way it is. Things have to be stirred up before the Feds will step in. There has to be a revolt, and there has never been a bloodless revolution. I sure as heck don't want to die, but I can't sit by while young girls are killed by dynamite at church and peaceful citizens are attacked by the people that are supposed to protect them."

"Things will change when the new generation—our generation—is running things," Billy said. "The old ways will begin to fade away."

"No, they won't. There's plenty in our generation that will keep fighting. That's why it will take a revolution, an uprising, to make things happen. It will have to be forced on them. You know I'm right—you just don't want to admit it. It's too easy not to get involved."

Billy knew his friend was right. It *was* easy to simply let things take their own course.

"Norm, I know how you feel, but I'm not sure that marching to Montgomery or holding up protest signs is the best way to go about it."

"I don't know what the best way is. All I know is that the worst way is to do nothing."

Billy painfully realized that was the dividing line between the two men. He didn't see the point in discussing it anymore, so they talked about football and women and the escalating war in Vietnam.

***

A year later Billy received a call from Norman, who had since moved to New York City.

"I'm working as a waiter at night. The tips are good, but some of the customers are real obnoxious. You know how these New York Jews are. Ha!"

"You're a long way from that little cow college in Auburn."

"You better believe it. I've been admitted to Law School at Columbia, and I've already started classes. How about that?"

"That's just great. You'll be in wing tips and suspenders before you know it."

"They're not suspenders, they're braces, you goober." Then Norman's tone turned solemn. "Billy, I want to be a civil rights lawyer."

"Why does that not surprise me?"

"I'm serious. It's what I want to do."

"That's good. And you'll be good at it."

"You think I'm screwed up, don't you? Some bleeding heart liberal."

"Yeah, I think you're a bleeding heart liberal, but I don't think you're screwed up."

"My dad's really happy that I'm going to be a lawyer, and he's helping me out with the money. He doesn't give two cents about civil rights—he hates Dr. King—he just wants me to make some big dough. But that's not why I'm doing it."

"I believe you."

"I've got a big picture of Dr. King on a wall in my apartment. Dad would have a cussing fit if he knew that."

"I'll bet, but doesn't he see the injustice, considering what your family suffered in Germany?"

"It's strange. The way some people think doesn't make any sense. I love my father, but not that part of him."

"I know what you mean."

"So how have you been doing?" Norman asked, changing the subject. "Getting any?"

"Just the leftovers. You know that my brother and Olivia got married. I was one of the groomsmen. That's funny as hell, isn't it?"

"Like a funeral. But you knew it would happen. Besides, there are plenty of women out there and a stud like you has an open field."

"Yeah, it was going to happen and we've been apart for over five years. It just feels a little weird."

"That's what life is Billy—it's weird. You should come to New York sometime and I'll show you weird."

"I'll do that the next time I feel like a freak show."

Billy didn't agree with Norman on some things, but he admired his passion. It was the last time he ever spoke to Norman. He called him the day after Dr. King was assassinated, but there was no answer and no message recorder. The two friends drifted apart, separated by miles and life paths, but he had no doubt that Norman had become a lawyer and was somewhere fighting the fight he believed in.

And, no doubt either, he was wearing wing tips and braces.

***

On New Year's Day Billy groggily rolled out of bed to take a leak and stir himself to consciousness. Bright sunlight squirmed around the edges of the window shade, and the clock on the dresser told him it was almost two o'clock. He grabbed some sweats and quietly closed the door behind him, leaving the young girl to sleep off the hangover from the year-end revelry.

In the kitchen he fumbled through the cabinet, clumsily grabbed the coffee, and filled the pot with water. As he waited for the brew to perk, he pulled the pushpin from the calendar on the wall and tossed 1965 into the trash can. A few minutes later he filled a cup with coffee, grabbed a stale donut from the kitchen counter, and settled onto the sofa in the living room to watch the Orange Bowl.

The game had already started, and he cursed himself for missing not only the kick-off, but also the hour of pre-game hype. As he watched the action, he imagined himself on the field, knowing what a thrill it would have been to play in a bowl game. His years of glory had come and gone, though, with only memories preserved in faded scrapbooks assembled by his mother.

The game was one-sided and, as Alabama scored another touchdown, he rose from the couch, raised a fist in the air, and hollered at the top of his lungs, "Roll Tide."

The noise apparently roused the girl from her stupor, and she emerged from the bedroom, wearing nothing but his shirt with a few buttons fastened.

Through a sleepy yawn, she asked, "What's going on?"

"We're beating the crap out of 'em."

"Good," she said, dismissively. "I'm starving."

"Me, too. How about fixing us something?"

"What do you think, I'm your wife?"

"Just for a day, baby, just for a day." Then he added smugly, "And a night."

"Oh, God, I don't remember a thing."

Bull, he thought; she remembered. It's just a woman's way of excusing a healthy appetite for sex. He remembered, too; remembered to be safe.

She prepared an afternoon breakfast, and they ate eggs and toast and grits and washed it down with lots of black coffee while watching the game. Billy focused on the smallest details of the action, alternately cheering or cursing each play. On every down he yelled out the formation, play call, and nicknames of the players involved. He knew all the upperclassmen on his team personally, and most of the younger players by name, number, and position.

The girl paid little attention, snuggling up to him on the couch. Finally, she went into the bathroom to shower. During a commercial he rounded up some clean sweats and tossed them into the bathroom for her. After a lengthy bout at the vanity with her face and hair, she rejoined him on the sofa. By then it was halftime.

"Why didn't you go to the game?" she asked.

"And miss being with you?" he said facetiously. He grinned as she stuck out her tongue at him. "I don't know, I guess I'm trying to get on with my life. Maybe I'm like an addict and I'm trying to stop, but I'm going through withdrawals."

"You're just like all these crazy guys. You think if you lose a stupid football game the world's coming to an end."

"You're right. A lot of us act like complete idiots about this stuff. It's kind of a macho thing, I guess. And, yeah, it's stupid and childish. But we can't help it. It's in our genes, like whiskers and sex."

"Whiskers and sex?"

"Yeah, that's quite a metaphor, isn't it?"

"I don't know about whiskers, but girls have sex in their genes, too. Shopping and sex."

"I've noticed. Not so much the shopping part."

"Oh, shut up, you pervert. You're so full of it."

"I'll drink to that."

He went into the kitchen, opened the refrigerator, and called back to her, "Want a beer?"

"Are you crazy? My mouth still tastes like the bottom of a birdcage."

When he returned to the sofa and took a swig from the can, she changed her tune.

"Oh, what the crap, maybe I can wash out the bird droppings with Budweiser." As she headed for the kitchen, she added, "I can start those stupid resolutions tomorrow."

Once the game was over, he quickly switched channels to watch the Rose Bowl.

"I want you to see this one guy. He plays for Michigan State, and he's from Branford. His name is Zee Willingham."

When State's defensive team took the field, Billy put his finger directly on the television screen, pointing to Zee.

"There he is—number twenty-two. I knew him when he was a kid growing up. That was my number, too"

"He's colored."

"No kidding," he said, sarcastically. "Otherwise, he'd be playing for Bama. He's a helluva player."

He told her about how he met Zee and how Zee helped his brother rescue him from the quarry when he injured himself.

"After that, I couldn't play anymore. At least not well enough for that level. See, I really get into these games because I played with a lot of those guys. And before I got hurt, I could hold my own. I don't blame anyone for what happened to me, but I'd give my left arm to be in their shoes. Like I said, I'm still going through withdrawal pains."

Billy kept his eyes on Zee whenever Michigan State was on defense. On one play Zee intercepted a pass and made a spectacular return, darting around lunging opponents for more than fifty yards.

"Go, Zee, go!" he shouted. "Look at that. Did you see that son-of-a-gun run?"

"Yeah, he's good," she said.

Zee played a terrific game, though his team lost. The announcers repeated several times that pro scouts rated him as one of the top players in the country at his position.

When the Rose Bowl was over, Billy took the girl home. They kissed good-bye to two days of no boundaries. He never saw her again, but there were others to take her place.

***

The next day was Sunday, a day Billy normally devoted to watching pro football. Instead, he went to the gym and worked out. Afterwards he went to the stadium of a nearby high school where he saw a group of young boys tossing around a football. He casually acknowledged them and began jogging on the asphalt track that circled the field. After a few laps, his left ankle began to throb and he was reduced to a slow, limping walk. When he stopped to sit down on an aluminum bench, he watched the young boys running around on the dormant brown turf. In the distance he could see a blocking sled behind one of the goal posts. He always hated that drill.

One of the young boys threw a long spiral toward another streaking downfield. The ball sailed beyond the outstretched arms of the intended receiver and rolled onto the track. Billy walked over to toss the ball back to the nearest one. Instead, the boy started running away at full speed.

"Hit me," the boy said.

Billy flung the ball as hard as he could but, with no warm-up, his arm was stiff and the ball fell short. Slightly embarrassed, he jogged over to retrieve the ball when some of those among the group motioned with their arms and called for him to join them.

He introduced himself as Bill, and they told him their first names. If he had told them he was Billy Burdette, they would have known who he was. But he was no longer the Branford Bazooka. He was just another guy off the street they had met by accident on a Sunday afternoon.

The boys divided up to begin a game of touch, and they needed him to even the sides. On one play he positioned himself as a defensive back and broke up the pass. The next time the receiver caught the ball in front of him and sprinted past him with ease. The speed and quickness which he possessed at one time had abandoned him, and he was no match for the young teenagers. After about thirty minutes he thanked them for letting him play with them and left the field.

It was a mild winter day and he had worked up a sweat. The feeling of exertion was exhilarating, and he felt good. It didn't bother him that he couldn't run with the youngsters or that they didn't know who he was. Driving back to his apartment, the memories of the bowl games the day before were still fresh in his mind. Alabama had won the Orange Bowl, and Zee had played well in the Rose Bowl. But the best part was seeing Zee wear his number and knowing that it wasn't a coincidence.

Later he watched the local sports on television and a recap of the Orange Bowl celebration. The Alabama players were greeted home by a throng of cheering fans on a sunny day in January. Then the announcer mentioned a note of local interest.

"Zee Willingham of Michigan State and Nash High School in Branford was named the Most Outstanding Defensive Player in the Rose Bowl. Unfortunately, the Spartans went down in defeat and are now stranded in Los Angeles due to a heavy snow storm in the Midwest."

Billy thought about the irony of it. He lived his dream of going to Alabama but couldn't play football while Zee only dreamed of going to Alabama, but lived to play football. There seemed to be a lesson there.

Maybe life is what happens when a dream dies.

22

Billy walked into his office and set the legal pad on his desk. He ripped the notes from another mind-numbing hour-long meeting and stuck them in a manila folder labeled CRP. The Cost Reduction Program, facetiously referred to by the junior managers as the Crap plan, would now go to the top of his to-do list. He scanned three memos from the IN tray on the edge of his desk, then added them to the pile in the FILE tray. More bullshit. He closed the door, then sat down and rested his chin in one hand, propped by an elbow on the arm of his chair. Oblivious to the bustle throughout the building as five o'clock approached, he gazed at the clutter on his desk as if it would tell him where his life was headed.

Soon, the office drones would begin evacuating their hives and, after a little more busy work, he would follow them out into the real world. He knew what awaited him there. Beyond the façade of normalcy, the flames of a world in chaos surged all around. The civil rights rebellion was in full swing, and Alabama was in the white-hot eye of the fire. While most people took it in stride as if it were something apart from their lives—a political battle to be fought out in the courts—Billy saw it differently. He could see the country would be changed forever. The inevitability of it was obvious, and it amazed him how bitter and shortsighted the resistance was. He knew Norman Goldstein was right. Why so many others couldn't see it was just one of the things that made no sense to him.

What happened with Olivia didn't make sense, either. He couldn't come to grips with what went wrong between them, and he would always blame himself. Stuck in his memory was a conversation they had one afternoon while sitting on a bench on the edge of the quad.

***

"We should have gotten married," Billy said.

"I would have," she responded, "but I didn't think you wanted to. I was scared and confused."

"So was I."

"We should have thought it over more," she insisted.

"Sure, but we didn't. We can't change what happened."

"I wouldn't blame you for hating me for doing something so horrible," she continued.

"No, I don't hate you. I'm the one to blame."

She looked down and said sadly, "I don't know what love means anymore."

He didn't know either. He just didn't want to be the first to say it.

***

Billy's feelings for Olivia had cooled, and he knew that night in Peavy had changed her as well. He never blamed her for getting on with her life, but when she married his brother, he felt betrayed. How could she put the darkness of their sin behind when she remained attached to a link that led straight to the past?

It was all tearing him apart—the racial turmoil, an athletic career that died on the vine, a corporate career with a promise of emptiness, and most depressing, a constant reminder of the fickleness of love.

Billy's father once told him that they lived in Alabama because that's where God wanted them to be. But now, after spending his whole life in Branford, he realized it was time to make a change. He took a pen and began scribbling notes on the legal pad.

He felt a surge of motivation as he drafted an outline for his resume.

***

Billy had his resume professionally printed and sent it to companies all over the country. Cities where he had never been—New York, Chicago, San Francisco, St. Louis—and towns he had never heard of. Places where he knew no one. Places far away from Branford and Peavy and familiar football fields and church bombings.

A letter came back from Mathews Chemical Company in Cheyenne, Wyoming, offering an interview. It was further from Alabama than he had ever been. He had driven to Dallas once, and it seemed that the forests and hills gave out somewhere on the other side of the Mississippi River. The flatland and scrub brush of Texas offended his sense of the landscape. But he knew the Rocky Mountains ran through Wyoming and he imagined the landscape there would look something like he had seen in the cowboy movies.

After a trip to the library, he learned that Cheyenne was not a big city, not like Birmingham, and certainly not like New York or Chicago. Although there was nothing about horses or cattle or ranches that appealed to him, he thought he might like the people. He figured they wouldn't look down on somebody from Alabama like the Yankees up north would.

Wyoming was a long way from the places and people that haunted him. It seemed like the kind of place where God wanted him to be. So, he placed a call to the personnel manager at Mathews Chemical to schedule the interview and asked the man if he could receive mileage reimbursement and drive his car instead of flying. That would give him a chance to see parts of the country he had never seen and give him a feel for the place that might become his new home. Plus, it would actually save the company some money. He didn't mention that he was scared to death of flying.

The personnel manager agreed, and Billy scheduled a week of vacation for the interview trip.

***

On his way to Wyoming, Billy stopped for gas at a roadside stop near Memphis. Sitting idly in his car as the attendant filled the tank, he peered into the restaurant through a big plate-glass window. The sight of people eating in the booths next to the window gave him an urge for a snack and he could almost taste a slice of pecan pie.

He went inside and took a seat on a stool at the counter.

"Do you have any pecan pie?" he asked the waitress.

"Darlin', I sure do. Florine just made a pie this mornin' and it's so good it'll make you think you've died and gone to Graceland."

"Well then, I'll have a slice and a cup of coffee."

As Billy sipped his coffee, he noticed an eighteen-wheeler pull into the gravel parking lot and a heavyset driver step down from the cab. In short order, the truck driver walked into the restaurant and sat down on the stool beside him.

"What'll you have, Jaybird?" the waitress asked, with obvious familiarity.

"I'll have a sheepherder special," the trucker responded.

"Now, what on earth might that be?"

"That's a piece of ewe," he said with a satisfied grin.

The waitress looked at him with fake contempt and said, "You couldn't handle it."

"But I could die tryin'."

"Well, that would be the only good thing to come of it—you dying."

The trucker laughed and placed his order. As the waitress walked away, the trucker struck up a conversation with Billy.

"Where you headed to?" the trucker asked.

"Wyoming."

"That's a long-ass way. You from out there?"

"No, I'm from Alabama. I'm moving there." That was getting ahead of the game, but it gave Billy a feeling of confidence to state the possibility as a fact.

"What kind of work you do?"

"I don't know if you'd call it work. I mostly go to meetings and talk on the phone."

The trucker gave him a perplexed look and tugged at his cap, which was adorned with a Confederate flag.

The two men continued the conversation between bites as they ate their food. The trucker spoke loudly, with a Southern accent so exaggerated it could have only been achieved through inheritance.

"Ain't many niggers in Wyomin', are they?"

"There aren't many people at all. It's the least populous state in the country," Billy said, ignoring the crux of the trucker's comment.

"That so? Never been there, but I been to California and there's sure lots of people there. I went to Bakersfield, and them people there are kinda like people here in Miss'sippy. 'Cept ere's too many wetbacks. I seen L.A., too, and it's a big shit hole. Kinda like New York fuckin' City."

Billy finished his pie, listening patiently as the trucker continued to talk about the places he had been and the people he'd met.

"You know, the problem with this country is the goddamn Yankees," the trucker continued. "If they would keep their ass outta our business and quit stirring up the niggers, everthin' would be a lot better for everbody."

This was the only thing that Billy hated about the South. It was as if the land, the food, the past were all tainted by the acrid smell of bigotry. There were too many people like the trucker, too many George Wallaces and Bull Conners, to forgive as benign distractions.

"I guess they ain't Yankees in Wyomin, just good ole' cowboys. Still, it ain't the South. Not like Alabama, where you're from."

"I know," Billy said. "But that's not all bad. I've lived in Alabama all my life, and I love it, but I'm ready for a change. I don't like all this fighting about civil rights and integration. I know it's going to happen, but I don't like all of the crap that's going on. It's too much bullshit to worry about."

"Don't let the niggers run you off," the trucker said.

"It's not them that bothers me," he responded. "It's the ignorant rednecks I can't stand."

The trucker looked hard at him. Billy steeled himself, ready for an angry response or even a punch, but the satisfaction he felt for saying the words was worth the risk. The trucker just stared at him, red-faced. Billy wasn't sure if it was from contempt or shock, or both.

Billy turned away and, without saying another word, laid his money on the counter. Remembering the waitress's claim about the pecan pie, he turned to her and said, "Gotta go to Graceland now."

She laughed and said, "See what I mean?"

"Yes, ma'am." Then, in his best Elvis voice, he added, " Thankya, thankyaverymuch."

Billy stopped in the restroom on his way out, checking behind to make sure the trucker didn't follow him. When he went outside to get in his car, the trucker stood in the parking lot talking to two other men. Three semis were parked nearby, two of which had arrived while he was in the restroom. The trio eyed him suspiciously.

As Billy approached within a few feet of the truckers, he looked at the one called Jaybird and said, with a smile, "Have a good trip."

The trucker responded with a grunt and a steely glare.

In his car, Billy turned on the eight-track and the nasal twang of Bob Dylan singing *The Times They Are a Changing* began. With the windows rolled down and the music blasting at full volume, he drove slowly past the truckers. They returned his possum-like grin with scowls.

Billy pulled onto the highway and headed west, laughing like a fiend—high on pecan pie and tomorrow's sunrise.

23

Bill stomped the snow from his shoes and walked into the house. "I guess winter is here."

"I think so," Joan replied. "You have a message on the phone from your brother."

He replayed the message and Jack's voice sounded ominous. "Bill, call me back as soon as you can. I'll be home all night."

When he called, Jack answered on the first ring and skipped the usual how's-it-going talk. "Bill, Dad hasn't been feeling well, so we took him to the hospital last week. We just got the results back today. It's not good news."

"What is it?"

"He has pancreatic cancer."

"Uhhh, damn." Bill grimaced and exhaled a deep breath to gather himself.

"It's the worst kind," Jack said. "The survival rate is almost zero, and it usually works fast."

"How long has he been sick?"

"Nobody knows. You know he'd be the last person to complain, but Mom says he has been real tired for a couple of weeks and hasn't had much of an appetite."

"How is he handling it?"

"He's down. In fact, he's pretty depressed and you really can't blame him. It's hard to sugarcoat it. The doctor has been up front with us. At Dad's age, the outlook is pretty grim. Most people don't last a year with this stuff. This is a terrible way to spend his retirement. It's only been a little over a year since he hung it up."

"What kind of treatment can they do?"

"Chemo, maybe radiation. The doctor wants us to come back tomorrow with Dad and discuss the options."

"Jack, tell me the truth. How much time did the doctor say he has?"

"He said, realistically, probably anywhere from a few weeks to a few months. Our main concern at this point is to try to control the pain as much as possible."

"Ah, geez," Bill sighed. "I'll make arrangements to come down. It may take a couple of days to get things lined up, but I'll get there as quick as I can."

"Mom and I can handle it. You don't have to drop everything right now."

"Don't give me that crap. I've been gone a long time, but I'm not going to abandon my own father. Or Mom, either. This has to be really tough on her, too."

"Sure, it is, but she's holding up. You know how strong-willed she is."

"Yeah, but she's always had Dad to fall back on for support. It's hard to imagine her without him. It'll be fifty years next July, won't it?"

"Uh-huh. I'm not sure he'll make it 'til then."

"What a pile of horse shit!" Bill groaned. "Anyhow, I'll be there in a couple of days."

Before Jack could reply, another thought hit Bill. "Hey, by the way, while I'm down there maybe I can come by and check out the new Taj Mahal I've heard about."

"Hell, yeah. We'll drink beer and eat peanuts and throw the shells on the floor."

"I'll bet. I'm sure Olivia would love that."

"Oh...I thought you knew."

"Knew what?"

"Olivia moved out. We're separated."

"Separated?" Stunned by the news, Bill raised his voice. "When did *that* happen?"

"About three months ago. You haven't talked to Mom since then?"

"I guess not."

"Well, don't worry about it. It's been a long time coming. I'm just concerned with taking care of Dad now. And Mom."

"Yeah, me too. I'll see what kind of arrangements I can make, and I'll call you back tomorrow."

"Okay. Hey, Bill, I'm looking forward to seeing you again. It's been too long, you sorry sack. What the heck have you been up to?"

"No good, just fartin' around. I'll tell you about it when I get there. See ya, man"

Bill turned to Joan, whose face was solemn. "It's bad news. My dad has cancer."

"That's terrible." She looked at him with a pained expression. "I'm sorry."

"It's the worst kind—pancreatic cancer." He paused, then added, "I'll have to go to Alabama as soon as I can. I may have to stay a while. I'm not sure what I can do with the warehouse."

"What can I do to help?"

"You don't need to do anything. Just keep helping Hank with his rehab."

She moved closer and hugged him. "I'll pray for your dad—and for you."

"Thanks. I'm not very good at that, but I appreciate it."

He squeezed her tightly before releasing her to walk away. So many thoughts were going through his mind that he had to privately sort things out. As much as he tried not to, he couldn't quit thinking about Olivia and the knowledge of her separation from Jack. It was a trivial detail in light of the news about his father, and he felt guilty for the thought, but he couldn't deny it.

After dinner, he checked the airline schedules. The flights were expensive and he hated to fly, but he booked a trip to Birmingham for three days later. Then he sat down and started making a list of things to tell Toby about running the warehouse. After a while, he lost concentration. He went to the pantry, removed a bottle of scotch, and poured himself a stiff drink.

When he entered the living room, Joan turned off the television. He sat in the recliner across from her and spoke softly. "My dad's a good man."

"I'm sure he is."

"I wouldn't say otherwise, but he really is. He's always worked hard, and he gets along with everybody."

She remained silent.

"Nobody deserves this," he continued. He took a swig of scotch and stared at a distant wall. Turning back, his eyes seemed to look straight through her and into the past. "I haven't been close to him in a long time. I haven't been close to anybody in my family. My brother's wife left him and I didn't even know it. I haven't forgotten them, I just haven't been around, and I haven't stayed in touch. Now I guess I'll have to return as the prodigal son."

"I'm glad you're going—you need to. I just hope you come back."

Her comment jolted him. "Why do you say that?"

"Because it's your home."

"My dad once told me your home is where God wants you to be."

"Where does God want *you* to be?"

"I've never figured that out. Somewhere, I guess."

Bill finished his drink and went to the bedroom. Joan turned the television back on to watch the news, leaving him to his private thoughts.

Alone in the bedroom, he pulled the picture of Olivia from his wallet before peeling to his shorts. He gazed at the photo briefly before turning out the light. Joan soon joined him in the darkness, and they fell asleep as gusts of winter wind whistled outside the window.

***

Bill would be gone for a week so he had to give Toby a crash course on running the warehouse. It wasn't that the place would fall apart, and he planned to stay in touch by phone, but he wanted to make sure the young man wouldn't panic or feel overwhelmed.

For the next two days he worked closely with Toby, teaching him the computer system and the customer files. He found the young man to be bright and quick to learn, but some things that came up during the course of a business day required a sense of judgment that was impossible to anticipate. There was no choice except to teach Toby as much as possible in the short time available and hope for the best.

He taped a small sheet of paper on the base of the office phone with his parents' number.

"Call me if you have a question about anything," he said. "If I'm not there, leave a message."

"I will. But I can handle it, sir."

"I know you can, but some people will want to talk to me. Tell them you'll have me call them back. Don't give anyone my number."

"I won't, sir."

"You've got the cheat sheet for the computer system and the card file with all of the contact numbers. At the end of each day make a list of things that happened, so we can talk about them when I get back. This is a list of all the things you need to do every day."

He handed Toby a one page sheet of typed instructions and sat patiently as the young man read a list of things he had been taught. "You have any questions?" he asked, as Toby looked up from the sheet.

"No, sir. You can count on me."

"I know I can. I trust you. You'll be fine. Just remember, don't worry about doing something wrong. There's nothing that can't be fixed. We're not dealing with nuclear weapons."

"Yes, sir, I understand. I'll try not to make any mistakes."

"That's not what I just said. You'll make mistakes—just like I would if I were here. But don't let that keep you from getting things done."

"Yes, sir."

"You remember our rules, don't you?"

"Yes, sir. Come to work on time. Always be polite to people, even if they are not polite to you. And don't get hurt or hurt anyone else."

"You forgot one."

Toby stared at him with a blank look.

"Rule Three A — have fun," Bill said.

Toby smiled. "I can do that. I really can."

"Okay, here's the keys. It's all yours for a week. I'll stay in touch."

He watched as Toby secured the office door, the alarm system, and the door to the warehouse. As they parted outside to go to their vehicles, they shook hands and Toby said, "Have a good trip, sir."

"Thanks, I will. See you in a week."

***

Joan arose the next morning in the pre-dawn darkness to drive Bill to the airport for his red-eye flight. He retrieved his bag from the back seat and they hustled to the terminal in the frosty morning air. She waited as he checked his bag at the counter, and then walked with him to the gate. When they kissed and embraced before he boarded, she felt as if she were a military wife sending her lover off for a tour of duty.

As she drove home afterward, Joan thought about how different it would be without Bill around. She had almost forgotten that feeling. Yet, she knew he was bound for a place where he needed to be. It was sad about his father, but she was glad he was reconnecting with his family.

Still, she couldn't deny a selfish thought.

She had cringed when Bill told her his brother's wife had left him. And now she felt completely at the mercy of the beautiful woman whose memory lived in Bill's wallet.

24

A warm feeling came over Bill as the plane pulled to the gate and the flight attendant announced, "Welcome to Birmingham." A few minutes later, he walked into the terminal and saw his brother in the crowd just beyond the counter at the gate.

Wearing a big smile, Jack thrust his right hand out and grasped Bill's for a shake. "How are you, you old son-of-a-biscuit-eater?"

"I'm still kicking," Bill said, an equally bright smile on his face. "Looks like you haven't been passing up many biscuits yourself."

"Hell no, brother. And you know how those biscuits are—they make your damn pants shrink." Jack patted his stomach, which bulged from his V-neck sweater.

"I'm a little over my playing weight myself."

"Ah, you look good. How was the flight?"

"You mean flights. And a three hour layover in Denver." Bill arched his back slightly and exhaled. "I left at six-ten this morning."

"Well, let's grab your bags and head out."

They walked the concourse and down to the baggage claim area, talking away like a couple of brothers who hadn't seen each other in years. The terminal was spacious and modern, but Bill was struck by the absence of the bustling crowds he had experienced in the Denver airport and years before in Atlanta. They passed a souvenir shop with racks full of merchandise displaying *Alabama 1992 National Champions.*

"Roll Tide," Bill said.

"They could do it again this year," Jack said. "Last year was a bummer with that NCAA crap, but we're seven and oh right now. Two years out of three's not bad."

"Yeah, they're looking great," said Bill.

After retrieving his luggage, Bill followed Jack to his car in the parking lot and stuck his bag in the trunk. He strapped himself into the passenger seat of the BMW. "Nice wheels, Peppy."

"Oh, jeez, I haven't been called that in a hundred years." Jack turned the ignition and started from the lot.

"I guess you think your farts don't stink anymore."

"Yeah, they do. I just don't have a jerk of a brother around to tell the whole world about it." He stopped at the gate and paid the ticket.

Bill laughed, recalling memories of him and Jack bedeviling each other. Then he noticed a bulky piece of equipment between the seats with a cord plugged into the cigarette lighter. "What's that?"

"It's a phone." Jack made a frown and quickly dismissed it, as if slightly disgusted. "It won't be long before we wear 'em on our wrist like Dick Tracy."

Bill didn't respond but he felt the gap of worldliness between him and his brother.

"How about going through town?" he asked Jack. "I'd like to see how things have changed."

Jack kept his eyes on the traffic ahead. "You'll see."

Bill looked out the window intently as Jack maneuvered through the main streets. He was shocked at what he saw. Birmingham looked like a shell of the vibrant city he remembered. He passed buildings that once housed thriving businesses, now abandoned and decaying like a forgotten cemetery. They stopped for a red light at the intersection of Second Avenue and Nineteenth Street and it appeared eerily calm.

"This is sad," Bill said. "I used to think this was the center of the universe."

Jack glanced at his brother. "You've been gone a long time. Everything's south of town now."

"South of town" meant over the mountain, or the south side of Red Mountain. "*That's where the rich people live*," Bill's father had told him as a youngster.

Bill vividly recalled the bustling heyday of Birmingham in his youth—the self-proclaimed "Magic City"—fueled by coal and forged with iron and steel. But those times were followed with the dark days clouded by racism, hardened politicians, and the decline of the industrial economy. Now, the signs of magic in the city were as dormant as the empty vats in the steel mills.

Still, there was an attraction to Bill for the city and the surrounding region, an affinity that went beyond nostalgia. For the first time, he realized that no matter how long ago he had left this area, it had never left him. He still felt a part of the place that had formed him, just as surely as if he were die-cast from one of the foundries which once glowed with life.

Beyond the city, Jack followed a route that Bill recalled traveling many times as they approached Branford, his old hometown.

"Look familiar?" Jack asked.

"Yeah, it really does."

Unlike the main city, Branford did not appear to have been discarded. He passed through older neighborhoods that once had seemed idyllic to him, but now appeared less inviting, and the aging homes were actually much smaller than they had appeared in the eyes of a young boy. In other places, new communities had sprouted up with treeless streets and larger homes, straight from the developer's cookie cutter.

Branford, it appeared, was on its way to becoming Everytown, USA.

When they reached the house where he was raised, Bill walked to the front stoop and rang the doorbell as if he were a stranger.

His mother opened the door and let out a joyous scream as she nestled into his hug with the biggest smile he had ever seen on her.

He stepped inside with his mother under his arm. Jack followed right behind.

"I waited a long time for this day," she said through tears Bill had seldom seen.

"Me too, Mom. You look fantastic. Where's Dad?"

"He dozed off. He'll wake up in a little while." She patted him on the back and added, "You look good, too. Nice and trim."

"I've put on a few pounds."

"You don't look like you've gained any weight."

"You just don't remember how skinny we were when we were kids."

"And that's a good thing," Jack said, grinning.

"I remember everything," his mother said, with a hint of incrimination. "A lot more than you two will ever know."

Bill got his bag from Jack's car and placed it in the bedroom they had once shared. The room had been updated, their twin beds replaced by a double bed and a small desk. The original stain on the pine-paneled walls was now covered with pale green paint, coordinated with the bed linens. The paint and pictures on the walls failed to completely cover all the nail holes left by the posters and pennants with which the two boys had virtually plastered the room.

He thought that somehow the house must have gotten smaller over the years, yet was otherwise much as he remembered it. There was a bigger television in the spot where the family had once gathered every Sunday to watch *The Ed Sullivan Show* and he noticed a couple of unfamiliar pieces of furniture. But there was a feeling of unpretentious simplicity about the surroundings as if lost in a time warp of yesterdays. Reminders of the days when he had lived there were displayed in framed photographs on the walls and souvenirs of long-ago family vacations filled an étagère.

In the kitchen, he looked down and said, "When did you get the hardwood floor?"

"About three or four years ago," his mother replied. "Jim installed it."

Bill looked closer, inspecting the molding and doorways with the eyes of a professional installer. "He did a good job."

"You know Dad," Jack said. "He doesn't do things half-assed."

His mother looked at the floor as if she could see her husband's image. "It's beautiful."

The look on her face said everything about his parents. Bill stepped to her and they hugged. It was so good to hold her that he felt unsteady on his feet. "I miss you so much. I love you, Mom." The words erupted from his heart.

"I love you, too." She buried her face in his chest and patted his back.

He had never heard those words before nor held her so closely. The years melted away and he was once again her Billy. He wanted to hold her forever but finally released her and wiped a tear with his shirt sleeve. He turned to see Jack give a nod and a smile.

They moved into the living room as the door of the master bedroom opened. His father walked slowly down the hall and joined the family. Looking older and thinner than Bill expected, his father's appearance was unsettling. He reached to grab an outstretched hand and was surprised by the limp grip. It was far from what he recalled of the calloused hands and once firm grip of his father, formed by youthful days on a farm and years of blue-collar labor.

"Hey, Billy," his father said.

"Hi, Dad." Overlooking his father's frailty and use of his boyhood name, Bill managed a broad smile.

"Welcome home, son." His father's voice was hoarse. "It's good to see you. It's been a long time."

"Yeah, I know. I'm glad to be home." He looked his father over and asked, "How are you feeling?"

"I'm fine. That's not what the doctor says, but what the heck does he know?" His father forced a smile. "This chemo is hellacious. Makes everything I eat taste like tinfoil. It seems like the cure's worse than the symptom. If I gotta feel like this, I might as well go ahead and die."

"Jim, don't talk like that," his mother said, frowning.

"Dad, sit over here with Mom," Jack said, taking his father's arm. "Bill's going to tell us about living in Wyoming. We want to hear about him chasing dogies and fighting off wild Indians. Ha!"

"Yeah, let's hear it, son." His father exhaled deeply as he sat down beside his wife on the sofa. "I don't know beans about Wyoming. Never been there, never will."

"Jim, I told you not to talk that way."

"Oh hell, Alice, you know I'm never going to Wyoming. I don't want to go anywhere unless it's back to Branson."

"Mom, Dad," Jack said, stepping in to settle down his parents.

"Okay, Bill, tell us about Wyoming," his mother said.

He shrugged. "It's a nice place and really beautiful. Kinda out of the mainstream. There's lots of open spaces and, once you get out of the city, not a lot of people."

"Not a lot of blacks, are there?" asked his father.

"No, not many." Bill turned his eyes to Jack, then back to his father. "Dad, you'd like all the outdoor sports they have—lots of deer and some big game like elk and antelope. Good fishing, too—all kinds of trout and bass and...." His father looked at him glassy-eyed and his mother squinted her eyes and shook her head. He realized he was speaking of things his father might never enjoy again so he quickly switched subjects and told them a little about the city of Cheyenne.

But he didn't tell them anything about himself except that he managed a warehouse and lived in a rental unit.

When Jack went into the kitchen to get a soft drink, Bill followed him.

"What's with Dad?" Bill asked. "How did he get sick so fast?"

"It's in his head. He knows the odds. The chemo takes something out of him, too, and just seems to delay the inevitable." He handed Bill a soft drink.

Bill popped the tab on the can and took a swig. He thought of his father and the drink tasted like tinfoil.

***

Bill spoke to his mother as she set down a bowl of mashed potatoes on the table in the formal dining area.

"Mom, you don't have to do this for me. We can just eat in the kitchen."

"No. We're going to eat in here."

Bill and Jack pitched in as their mother filled the table with a feast of fried chicken, biscuits, gravy, mashed potatoes, fried okra, creamed corn, and ice tea. Their father joined them and they enjoyed a family meal for the first in years. Too many years. Bill felt guilty for causing the separation, but the feeling was overshadowed by the overpowering warmth of being with his family.

"This is the best meal I've had since the last time I was home," Bill said.

"You shouldn't stay away so long," his mother said.

Bill's mother was not a woman to lavish words of affection on her family, but when he ate her food, he could taste the love. "Wow, I'm stuffed," he said, as he finished off a dish of bread pudding. "Mom, you're still the world's best cook."

"I'm glad you enjoyed it. I don't get a chance to cook a big meal much anymore."

"Yeah," his father added, "I eat like a damn bird these days." In front of him was a plate less than half-eaten.

"I eat like a bird, too," said Jack. "A vulture."

"You know what I meant," Alice said, looking at her husband. "A meal for more than the two of us."

"I know, babe—Billy's right. You *are* the best cook in the world. The best wife, too."

Alice leaned to Jim and kissed him on the cheek. "Love you," she whispered.

Bill looked at Jack and they exchanged knowing looks as they witnessed the display of affection by their parents, something they had never seen as young boys. A tranquil aura seemed to fill the room like the calmness of an autumn sunset when the world is bathed in an amber glow. He felt an overwhelming attachment to everything in his presence—his parents, his brother, the house—as if it were a part of him, inseparable by time and distance.

He was home.

***

After dinner, Bill went for a drive around Branford with his brother.

As Jack chauffeured him around the small town, he stopped at several familiar places.

"That's where the Spinning Wheel used to be," Jack said, slowing down as he drove by a car wash.

Bill looked at the site where a drive-in restaurant once stood. "I remember cruising through there many times in Mom's car. They had great milk shakes. Remember the car hops on roller skates?"

"Yeah, I'd forgotten about that," Jack said. "Let's go out to the school. They've fixed up the football field pretty good, but the main building is looking a little worse for wear."

They arrived at Warrior County High as daylight began to give way. Jack parked in front of the school, and they walked around the grounds. It was Saturday and all the doors were locked. There was a new gym adjoining the main building, connected by a covered walkway. At least twenty trailers were placed between the school and the football field behind. New metal bleachers had been added to the visitors' side of the field, along with new sod and a giant scoreboard.

"This place has really changed," Bill said as they began to leave.

"A lot of blacks go here now," said Jack. "Many of the white kids go to the private school, BCA. That's Branford Christian Academy."

Bill didn't say anything, but he thought about how idealistic he'd been in his youth and how simplistic his views were. He had believed everything would be better if they would just change the stupid laws. It was clear to him now that he hadn't been nearly as smart as he thought and it would take more than new laws to change some things.

Jack drove away from the school, and soon they were in a familiar neighborhood. Neither brother spoke as they passed several blocks of modest homes set back from tree-lined streets. He saw only blacks in a neighborhood that had once been a white sanctuary. The destination was obvious, and Bill wondered why his brother was going there. Then Jack stopped in front of a yellow brick house.

"It hasn't changed a whole lot, has it?" Jack asked.

"No, not a lot. The yard's not as nice as Mr. Alexander used to keep it, and they cut down that big oak tree where the swing used to be."

As Bill stared at the house where Olivia once lived, his mind was filled with a cascading rush of bittersweet memories. "Jack, why did you come here?"

"I thought you might want to see it."

"Are y'all on good terms?"

"Yeah. She doesn't hate me, and I don't hate her. We just kind of drifted apart, as they say. But this house has some fond memories for me, and I'm sure for you as well. It's okay to have good memories."

Bill wondered if his brother was thinking straight. Maybe the strain of the divorce was getting to him.

"It's funny, isn't it?" Jack continued. "We each had our chances and she dumped both of us. I guess she's not a Burdette kind of woman. Ha!"

For the first time, Bill detected a feeling of rejection in his brother. "She didn't dump me, and I doubt she dumped you."

"Sure she did. She's found a new sugar-daddy. Screw her." An angry look grew on Jack's face and his voice turned bitter. "I don't need that crap. You were lucky, brother."

Jack's composure seemed to vacillate from one moment to the next. *He still loves Olivia*, Bill thought. *He's just angry about losing her.* He wondered if it was him or his brother that was having the most trouble coming to grips with their feelings for the same woman.

They drove back in silence to their parents' house. The family gathered in the living room and revisited stories they had shared many times before. Each time the stories came alive again as they thumbed through scrapbooks and photograph albums.

One small black-and-white photo showed Jim, Alice, and the boys posed in their bathing suits on a beach. Small print in the white margin read Daytona Beach 7/29/54.

"I remember when that picture was taken," his mother said. "That was the day a big wave came along and knocked Jim's bathing suit to his ankles." She chuckled. "I can still see him bending over to pull it back up with people all around. They got a good look at more than his bare fanny."

"It happened pretty fast." His father had a look of childlike embarrassment.

"That was so funny," said Jack.

Bill grinned then exploded into laughter.

His father joined in as everyone had a good laugh about the story they had relived for years. Bill was heartened when he saw the spark of joy in his father, a man whom he respected and loved more than he had ever realized.

For more than an hour Bill was absorbed in reverie as he and his family stoked the coals of memories that would never turn to ash. Afterward, Jack invited him to his house the next day, then excused himself to go home.

Bill stayed up to watch television with his mother after his father went to bed. When she retired, he stayed up with the volume turned down to watch a local program featuring Alabama football. Finally, as midnight approached, he went to bed in his old room.

It was strange how everything appeared to be so different,

yet so familiar. The town, his family, his boyhood home. Even a yellow brick house that once had an oak tree with a swing in the side yard.

Maybe Dad was right. Maybe this is where God wants me to be.

25

Bill felt out of place in Jack's house. Located in an upscale suburb of Birmingham, it was enormous and looked like a home you might see featured in *Southern Living*. Every room was decorated with expensive furnishings. At least, everything looked expensive to Bill. He had no clue how much things like that cost, but he was pretty sure it was a lot.

"Why don't you stay here tonight?" Jack asked toward the end of the day. "I've got plenty of room, as you can see."

"I'd rather stay with Mom and Dad. I'll only be here for a few days, and I need to spend most of my time with them."

He didn't admit to his brother that he was uncomfortable in the mini-mansion. It felt more like a museum than a house. Besides, it was a little spooky knowing it was where Jack and Olivia had shared a bed.

"How about another drink before we leave?" Jack said.

"Sounds good, but don't forget, you have to drive me home."

"That's no problem. I've been pickled over the years. A little more brine won't hurt. How about a snort of brandy?"

"I haven't had that in a long time. I've been on more of a beer and scotch diet."

"You'll like this."

Jack went to the bar and poured two glasses of cognac from a triangular-shaped bottle with a Hennessy label.

"This looks like the good stuff," Bill said.

"It's pretty decent. Nothing but the best for my big brother." Jack raised his glass.

"Cheers!"

Bill returned the toast and they sipped their brandies, nodding to each other in agreement.

Suddenly, out of the blue, Jack said, "You're the one she loved."

Bill's whole body tensed, frozen in a state of shock. Had his brother gone mad? He stared back at him and took another sip of brandy to gather his thoughts.

"Jack, you're letting this divorce get to you. It's too emotional right now. Let's not talk about it."

"No, it's about time we talked about it." Jack took a sip of brandy. Then, he raised his voice a notch and bellowed, "I said it's you, damn it!" Smothering his words in sarcasm, he continued, "You, the All-American boy. Mr. Football Hero. The one-and-only Branford Bazooka."

Stunned by the outburst, Bill set down his drink, stammered and stretched his arms out in a questioning gesture. "Jack … what …?"

As Bill lowered his arms, Jack moved forward and put his face within inches of his brother's. At fifty pounds heavier and three inches taller, Jack hovered over Bill as the two men locked eyes.

"I'm not good enough for her," Jack said through his teeth. The veins bulged in his neck. "And, she's not good enough for me either. She's just sloppy seconds." Jack unclenched his teeth and snarled, "To hell with her. You can have her, every damn bit of her. But, that would be nothing new for you, would it? She's been in the pasture a few years, but aged tenderloin is the best, they say."

"That's enough!" Bill shouted as he shoved Jack hard in the chest. Staggering back, Jack held onto his glass as the brandy flew into the air. Bill shoved him again, hard enough to cause Jack to stumble halfway across the room and fall upright into a high-back chair.

Bill stood facing his brother, prepared for a confrontation he was hoping against. Jack rose from the chair and threw his empty glass against the wall, shattering it into pieces. He tightened his fists and bowed his neck as if coiled for a strike. "I could beat you to a pulp," he said. Anxious seconds passed before he calmly relaxed. "But it wouldn't solve anything anymore than if I beat her."

Bill was sure he could still whip his brother, but he knew Jack wasn't thinking straight. "Why would you want to beat me or her?"

"For screwing around on me," Jack shouted. "I know what happened a couple of years ago out in Yellowstone. You think I'm a fool?"

"Yellowstone?" Bill sighed, recalling the near tryst with Olivia. "That was nothing. We had dinner for Christ's sake. Nothing else." It was a half-truth but the essence of the deceit was honorable.

"It's funny she acted differently after that. Are you sure she didn't talk you into bed? Just for old time's sake, I mean."

"Jack, I swear we didn't do anything." Bill felt justified for shading the truth, but it didn't erase the guilt of lying. Sure, he had slept with Olivia in Yellowstone but he hadn't *slept* with her.

"We had dinner," Bill added. "A couple of drinks. We talked." He paused and looked at Jack with a serious look, feeling the burden of proving his innocence. "Jack, I've done a lot of things I'm not proud of and I'm no saint, but I would *never* do anything to violate your trust. We're bound by blood and that means more to me than anything in the world."

Jack stared back at his brother blankly. Then, he slumped down in the chair. With his head hanging sadly from drooped shoulders, he looked defeated, like a boxer in the dressing room after a knockout.

Bill returned the stare, wondering what was going through his brother's mind. It felt like he was in a dream and had flashed back more than twenty-five years into the past. He and Jack and Olivia. Déjà vu.

Finally, Jack raised his head. "Ah hell, I'm messed up," he said, in a low voice. "Don't pay any attention to what I say. My mind is going around in circles." The sadness in his face slowly disappeared and his voice returned to normal. "I believe you," he said.

Relieved, Bill felt a sudden surge of compassion for his brother. His eyes glazed with moisture. He stepped to Jack and put a hand on his shoulder.

Jack stood and patted Bill on the arm. "I believe you," he repeated. "You mean more to me than anything else, too. I just say dumb things sometime. I'm not angry at you. It's not your fault and I'm not angry at you or Olivia. You'll be leaving in a few days, and you need to see her before then." Jack was perfectly lucid, with no trace remaining of the angry outburst.

"Why did you take me by her house yesterday?" Jack had no answer for the same question the day before.

"I don't know—just an impulsive thing. Maybe a farewell and a reconnection all in one."

"What do you mean? I never once mentioned her name. She and I were over years ago. I came home to be with Dad. When you told me you were separated, I never had any intentions of seeing her. Besides, you're still married." Again, he spoke words that he wanted to believe, but fell short of total honesty.

"Just a legality. We have to work out a few things. Or rather, our lawyers do. The house goes up for sale next week." Jack took another glass from the bar and poured himself a new shot of brandy.

Bill stepped away and looked out the bay window at the perfectly groomed yard and the picture-book flower beds of pansies, colors aglow in the late afternoon. So many thoughts were buzzing around in his head that he couldn't concentrate on one before another popped up. It was all surreal. He had carried a picture in his wallet for more than twenty-five years, and now the picture was trying to come to life.

"What about this other guy? The sugar-daddy you talked about."

"I'm not sure about it. That was bullshit frustration talking. I think she's been fooling around, but that's not what tore us apart. In fact, I don't blame her, really. I haven't been a great husband to her or a great father to Brooke. I haven't been unfaithful, but I haven't been faithful either. I've been too self-absorbed to be concerned about anyone else."

"I've been pretty much into myself for a long time, too," Bill said. "Must be a hereditary thing."

"Must be."

"I live with someone now that I can talk to."

"Is it the woman named Joan on the answering machine where you live?"

"Yeah."

"Are you serious about her?"

"I don't know, Jack. I'm just trying to put my life back together. She's a good woman and she deserves a good man."

Jack looked at his brother as if he were looking into Bill's soul. He drained the last drop of his brandy and set the glass on the counter. Then abruptly, he said, "Let's go."

On the way to his parents' house, Bill gazed out the side window without really seeing anything. He and his brother hardly spoke until they approached a large cemetery.

"Do you want to see Mom and Dad's plot?" Jack asked. "We've got a little time before they close the gates."

"Yeah, I think so."

"We'll stop at Coach's grave on the way. There are stripes on the road that lead right to it—a red one that goes one direction and a white one going another. They meet at the bottom of the hill where he's buried. Mom and Dad's plot is not far away."

Jack drove past the iron gates of the huge cemetery. He followed the red stripe, passing by thousands of graves before he stopped at the foot of the hill near the headstone of The Coach. They walked to the gravesite and stopped to stare at the marker.

"I remember when he came to our house," Jack said. "Everybody in town knew he was there. That was the most excitement Branford ever saw."

"That was something, wasn't it?" Bill said, a tingle of reverie in his voice. "I was so pumped up I didn't know what to do or say. I was scared to death, too. He was so intimidating."

"I would have given anything to be as good as you," Jack said.

"That would have been something, wouldn't it? Coach coming to our house twice."

"Yeah, that would've been great." Then Bill's expression changed and he spoke somberly, "That was the best day of my life. I wish I could have played for him." He thought about the tragic day at the quarry and knew his sadness was obvious to Jack. As he followed his brother back to the car, Bill could still hear the sound of The Coach's gravelly voice echoing in his mind. *Nice run, Burdette. Way to stick your bonnet in there.* It was funny, he thought, how The Coach always called a helmet a bonnet.

A short drive later, they made another stop in the cemetery and walked to a spot near a dogwood tree. A few brown leaves fluttered in an October breeze before falling onto the patchy green grass.

"It's a good place," Jack said.

"Yes, it is," Bill agreed.

It was a good place to lay his father and someday his mother, too. He knew it was where God wanted them to be.

"When I'm gone, I want to be right here," Bill said.

"There're no more plots available in this section," Jack replied.

"I don't need one. They can just toss my ashes right here with Mom and Dad."

Jack nodded.

They had barely left the cemetery when Jack began singing. "*Just a bowl of Butterbeans. I don't want no collard greens.*"

Bill interrupted. "I remember that song. I know every verse."

"I know you do."

Bill sensed Jack was probing; his choice of song was too obscure to be an accident. What else did he know? "Did Olivia tell you we sang it in the hotel bar in Yellowstone?"

"Yeah, she told me. She said y'all had a great time. That kind of bothered me, but she swore nothing happened. I lied to you about her acting differently after that. It's just part of my paranoia. Sometimes things get screwed up for no apparent reason. You know—life's a bitch."

"Yeah," Bill said. "Yeah, it is."

Jack began to laugh. Mildly at first, then louder and more animated. Bill picked it up and soon they were both laughing uncontrollably, neither having any real reason to laugh except that it felt good. Each time one would stop, the other would start again.

"Oh crap," Bill said, wiping tears of laughter from his eyes. "Life's a *big* bitch."

He laughed a little more.

"B-I-T-C-H," Jack said with a big grin.

They were kids again. Buddies being buddies.

Jack pulled a cassette from a pocket on the sun visor, slid it into the slot on the dash, and the driving sound of Lynyrd Skynyrd filled the car. When the chorus came, the brothers' voices rang out in unison, "Sweet home Alabama."

Bill closed his eyes and thought how, despite their differences, he and his brother were so much alike.

When Jack stopped the car in the driveway of their childhood home, he looked at Bill and sat still in his seat for a moment. Then he took a pen from the glove box and swiped a small sheet from a note pad on the dash. "Here's her address and number. You need to see her before you leave."

Bill took the sheet, folded it neatly, and stuffed it in his pocket. "Jack, I'll never speak badly of you. I never have and I never will."

"I know that. I feel the same way."

Bill hesitated before saying what he was thinking. "I guess that's what you call brotherly love." The words tumbled painfully from his mouth, and his voice broke with emotion as he spoke.

"Yeah, I think that's what it's called," Jack said. "Maybe that's the best kind."

They shook hands with a grasp that lingered. Bill got out of the car and headed toward the house that held so many memories. Then he turned to watch his brother drive away into the gray light of early evening.

Reaching into his pocket he felt the sheet of paper to make sure he still had her telephone number.

26

Bill didn't call Toby the first day, hoping to develop the young man's sense of responsibility. But he wasn't about to let anything go wrong with Hank's warehouse. Besides, he knew that someday the whole thing would be his, and he felt the weight of ownership on his shoulders. So, he called in mid-morning of the second day.

"Toby, it's Bill. How are things going?"

"Everything is okay now."

"What do you mean—now?"

"Well, when I got here this morning—I was on time—there was a truck driver waiting to get unloaded. When he backed up to the door, his truck got away from him—I guess his brakes failed—and he hit one of the racks pretty hard."

Bill felt a sudden rush of anxiety. "Did it damage the rack?" he asked, sensing his worst fears unfolding as he spoke.

"A little bit, but it didn't fall down." Toby spoke progressively faster as he continued. "But a fifty-five gallon drum of that solvent on tier three fell off and broke open—don't worry, nobody got hurt—and stuff spilled all over the floor. I called the fire department and the HazMat team came and cleaned it up. Everything is back to normal."

"What do you mean, everything is back to normal?" he shouted angrily into the phone. "Why didn't you call me?"

"W-e-l-l..." Toby dragged the word out slowly like a scolded child. Then his voice changed. "Hey, boss, I'm just kidding. You know—having fun like you told me to. Nothing's happened that I couldn't handle."

Bill pulled the phone away from his ear to collect himself.

"Boss, are you there?"

"Yes, Toby, I'm here," he said calmly, but still shaken. "Damn, don't do that to me, son. I just about had a heart attack."

"I'm sorry, sir. I didn't think you would believe me."

"Well, I might not the next time, even if you want me to."

Bill asked more pointed questions, reading from a copy of the checklist he had given Toby. After a thorough grilling, the young man's answers calmed his fears. Everything seemed to be under control.

"All right, I've got to go," Bill said. "I'll call you again tomorrow."

"Yes, sir."

"And, Toby—no more kidding around, okay?"

"Yes, sir. I'm sorry."

"No, don't be sorry. I told you to have fun, and I told you not to worry about making a mistake. Let's just forget about Rule Three A for the time being. I think we've had enough fun for a while."

"Yes, sir."

Bill shook his head and set the phone into the cradle on the kitchen counter.

Nearby, his mother was preparing lunch. "I know it's none of my business," she said, without looking up from her chore, "but may I ask what Rule Three A is?"

Bill grinned and shook his head in disbelief. "Rule Three A says to pull the boss's chain."

Alice raised an eyebrow and continued peeling a head of lettuce.

***

Bill left his parents sitting in the back yard and excused himself to go inside and make a telephone call. He dialed the number Jack had given him, halfway hoping Olivia wouldn't answer. When she did, the sound of her voice made him feel unsure, like the first time he had asked her for a date thirty-five years earlier.

"Olivia, this is Bill."

There was no response at first. The silence made him want to hang up before she finally replied.

"Hi. It's so good to hear from you. I'm glad you called."

With no suggestion of emotion in her voice and, without seeing her face, he couldn't judge her reaction.

"I guess you know about my dad. I came down to be with him for a few days."

"Yes, Jack told me. How is he doing?"

"He gets around okay, but his spirits are down. His chances aren't good, and it's tough on Mom. There's nothing anybody can do, including the doctors."

"That's so sad. I pray for him."

"I appreciate that."

"You know about me and Jack, of course."

"Yeah, that was a shock. I hated to hear that."

"It happens. And it's been coming. It's pretty amazing that we lasted this long. But, I'm glad we stuck together—for Brooke's sake. She's old enough to deal with it now."

"That's good."

"I'm glad you called." Quickly, she added, "I've already said that haven't I?"

It sounded to him like she felt as awkward as he did. Gathering his nerve, he said, "I was wondering if I could see you before I left."

"I've been wondering the same thing. That's why I'm glad you called. *Oh,* there I go again. Have I mentioned that I'm glad you called?"

The hint of laughter in her voice relaxed the tension.

"I'm glad, too. What's convenient for you? Can we meet somewhere?"

"I'm free just about any time. I'm in a condo right now, but it's still a mess from the move. We haven't figured out everything about the houses and all this other stuff. I stayed in Destin for a month, but I needed a place here where all my friends are."

He knew about *the houses*—the one Jack was occupying for the moment, and the beach home in Florida.

"We can have dinner somewhere," he said, "but I don't know my way around here anymore."

"No. Come to my place. It's not that bad. We'll have more privacy. I can throw something together. How about tonight—is that too soon?"

"Uh, no, that will work if you don't mind making it a little later. And don't bother with dinner—I'll eat with Mom and Dad. My mother puts together a special meal for me every night. Dad usually doesn't eat much, but he likes to sit with us. It makes him feel kind of...normal, I guess."

"Of course. Spend as much time as you can with your mother and father. You have such a nice family. I know they're glad to have you here."

"It's a good thing. Not about Dad, but just being together after so many years. Anyhow, how about eight o'clock tonight? Jack gave me your address, and I think it will take me about thirty or forty minutes to get there from here. I'm not used to all of this traffic."

"It's not bad that time of night. Eight o'clock is fine, or whenever you get here."

***

Before dinner, Bill called Joan.

She sounded winded when she answered. "I just walked in."

"Sorry, I wanted to catch you before we ate. I forgot we're an hour ahead of you."

"That's okay. I've got some exciting news. Hank started talking last night. Can you believe it?"

"That's *great!* I knew the old geezer would come around."

"He still can't walk, and he has a long way to go with his therapy, but his spirits are good. So, how are things down there?"

"It's strange being back. It's not the same place I remember. And it's sad to see what Dad is going through. His chances are a lot worse than Hank's."

"I'm sorry to hear that. How's your mother?"

"She's handling it well. I'm real proud of her. And I've spent a lot of time with my brother. On top of what's happening with Dad, he's pretty down with this divorce hanging over him."

"His wife is that pretty woman who was your high school sweetheart, isn't she? The one you met in Yellowstone."

He wished he had not mentioned it. Joan knew about his past with Olivia and the fourteen-hundred miles separating them no doubt magnified her imagination.

"Yes," he said after a slight hesitation.

He detected a hint of suspicion in Joan's voice but tried to convince himself there was nothing to feel guilty about. Yes, he had arranged to meet Olivia, but it had been at the urging of his brother. And yes, she was an old flame, but her marriage to Jack had dimmed that flame many years ago. And finally, yes, they had foolishly rekindled the flame in Yellowstone, but the Devil had been denied on that one.

It didn't work. He couldn't fool himself and knew he couldn't fool her so he abruptly shifted his direction. "You won't believe the call I had with Toby today."

When he told her the story, she said, "That's hilarious."

"Yeah, he's got more nerve than I thought to do something like that. I could do without the practical joke, but I think he'll handle it okay without me." He took a deep breath. "I'm glad I came. I feel badly for being away so long."

"I'm sure your family would like for you to stay longer."

He sensed insecurity in her voice. "Don't worry—I'll see you Sunday night. But, I've promised Mom and Dad that I'll come back soon."

"I'll be here."

Afterward, he sat on the edge of the bed in his old room. Thinking about the call from Toby, a grin spread across his face. He recognized the potential in the young man and had developed a real fondness for him. Almost like a son. Then he remembered Joan's last words. *I'll be here.* And his heart swelled with feelings he had never shared with her.

But first he had to see Olivia.

27

Bill used Olivia's directions to find the upscale development. At the gated entrance he punched the code she had given him, then followed the main street past large, imposing homes built around a golf course. A turn just beyond a lake led him to a section with clusters of condos. Each unit had two stories, a two-car covered garage, a small patch of yard, and a private entrance.

When he parked his mother's Monte Carlo in front of the unit with Olivia's address, the reality of seeing her face-to-face suddenly hit him and he began to feel apprehensive. Questions darted through his mind like shooting stars. How would she act toward him? What would he say to her? What was in the future for either of them? Most of all, though, his anxiety was heightened by the fact that he had never come to grips with his feelings about her. He wasn't sure he was ready, but he had to make that decision now. He took a deep breath and gathered his nerve.

Before getting out of the car, he checked himself in the mirror and ran a comb through his hair one more time. Outside, he straightened the folds in his shirt, and carefully tucked it back into his pants. Then he strode to Olivia's front door with his cup of confidence only half full.

When she opened the door, he smiled and his eyes widened at the sight of her. She looked radiant, with a casual elegance, in gray slacks and a scarlet top that perfectly matched her lipstick and fingernails. Her hair was clipped short, accentuating her prominent cheekbones, and her dark complexion showed few signs of the years. The lines of her clothes followed the contours of her still youthful body in a modest, yet alluring, fashion.

"Hello, beautiful," he said.

"Hello, handsome." She opened her arms.

He walked into a hug and inhaled her scent; fresh and natural, like a gardenia. Then he forced himself to step away. "It's good to see you."

"And you, too. I'm so glad you could make it. Come in." She closed the door behind him.

"This is a nice place," he said, looking around.

"Thank you. It'll do for now. Have a seat." She led him to a thickly cushioned beige sofa and set herself in a matching side chair. "Would you like something to drink? Wine, coffee, Coke?"

"No, thanks. I'm fine." He crossed his legs and rested his elbow on the heavily padded arm of the sofa. The relaxed pose didn't match the uncomfortable feeling that he didn't belong there.

"I won't be here too long," she said. "But once everything is settled between Jack and me, it might take me a while to find a new place just like I want."

Without replying, he stood and walked to a window overlooking the golf course. It was well after dark, but the lights from the back of a sprawling house on the other side of the fairway gave a glimpse of the lush landscape. "You play?" he asked.

"A little." She rose and walked to stand beside him, looking out the window. "Do you?"

"No." An indulgence for the idle rich, he thought. Not that it mattered; they were just warming up, trying to find the right pitch. He needed to move around, work off some of the uneasiness. "You want to show me the rest of the place?"

"Sure."

Olivia babbled away as she walked with him through the two bedroom townhouse, but he wasn't focused on anything she said. He noticed a couple of unopened boxes in one room when she explained her decorating plans, but he only pretended to pay attention. His mind was suspended in a dreamlike state with an uncertain grasp of time and place, and he could have been in the Palace of Versailles or a mud hut for all he was aware.

After touring upstairs, they moved back to the main floor.

"How about something to drink now?" she asked.

"Okay, whatever you're having."

She went into the kitchen and returned with two glasses of white wine. "You need to visit more often," she said, as they resumed their seats in the living room.

"This is a long way from where I live," he replied. "In more ways than one."

"How so?"

"It's a different place now. And I've changed, too."

"Everyone changes. I sure have."

"Maybe so, but you're still the prettiest girl in the Heart of Dixie. The years have been good to you."

"Still the same old Billy—always full of bull. But you know a woman never gets tired of flattery. And look at you—you look great. The world must be treating you right, too."

"I wouldn't go that far, but I can't complain."

She took a sip of wine and a smile grew on her face. "You remember when you came to my sixteenth birthday party dressed as Popeye?"

He laughed. "Yeah, I remember, Olive." The memory popped into his mind and he felt the frosty uneasiness melt away.

For almost an hour they relived their youth. It wasn't what he came to talk about, but they both got caught up in the moment and for a while the years that separated them disappeared. He was Popeye once again, and she was Olive Oyl. He was Bogart and she was Bergman. He was Zooka and she wore his letter sweater. She laughed at his stories and he remembered how it was to feel like the most important person in the world.

Then the memories wound down and they just looked at each other. The smile on her face slowly disappeared.

"I always dreamed of being Mrs. Burdette. And the dream came true, but now I'm waking up and the dream is over." Her voice had a melancholy flavor.

"I lost some dreams along the way myself."

"It broke my heart when you got hurt. You were such a good player. It seemed that it injured more than just your leg. You weren't the same person after that."

"I guess I was hard to live with, eh?"

"Not really. I still loved you."

"I loved you, too. But things changed after we went to Peavy."

"Only for you. I got over it."

He had promised himself not to get angry, but his feelings spewed out like a ruptured boiler. "That is so callous!" he shouted with a disgusted look. "How could you get over something like that? It was murder, damn it!"

She flinched and a startled look popped on her face. "Why are you bringing this up after all these years? Bill, don't let it destroy you."

"It's what I deserve." He calmed but the anger remained on his face. "I destroyed that child of ours, and you did, too."

"So, that's what you want—for it to destroy me like it has you?" She raised her voice and spoke of "it" as if referring to an incident instead of a life. "Well I won't let it. I'm going to live my life, and you can wallow in self-hatred if you want."

She didn't understand him, couldn't fathom the way he felt. "No, Olivia, I don't want anything to destroy you. I think too much of you for that."

"How comforting—you *think too much of me for that.*"

"No, I didn't mean to say it that way."

"How did you mean to say it—that you loved me too much? Is that the way you meant to say it? Because you know I've always loved you. I married Jack because I couldn't have you." She stared at him and the words hung in the air. "There, I've said it. I'm sorry, but it's true." Her voice weakened and tears rolled down her cheeks.

She finally admitted what he always knew but wouldn't admit to himself; she always made choices that were best for *her*. "Don't say that. We would have never made it together." He gritted his teeth in anguish. "We can't talk like this."

"Is it too hard for you to say you love me?" She raised a hand to brush the tears from her cheeks.

"You're still married to my brother. I can't betray him."

"Is that the reason you can't say it? Or is it because you don't love me?"

"I love that you're a part of me. I love that you made me feel like the most important person in the world. I'll always love you for that."

"But you're not *in love* with me, are you?"

"I've carried your picture in my wallet for more than thirty years."

"That's not an answer. Maybe you're just in love with a picture."

"So what if I said I was in love with you? Would that make you happy? Would it make things right? Then what would we do?"

"We would know. That's all I need."

He couldn't say it. For all those years he had waited to say it, and now he couldn't. The words were stuck in his head, but he couldn't pull them out of his heart. At that instant everything became clear to him and he knew exactly what he had to do.

"I have to go," he said, rising from the sofa.

She exhaled a deep sigh, and a pained look slowly spread across her face.

He sat down again and said, "But first I have to ask you something."

"What?" she said sullenly.

"Have you ever told anyone about Peavy?"

"No. You asked me that once before. In Yellowstone—remember?" She sipped the last drop from her glass of wine.

Bill looked at her knowingly. "Like I said before, things change."

"Have you told anyone?" she asked.

"Not anyone you know," he answered.

Their eyes met, and they stared at each other intensely.

"I told Jack," she finally confessed.

He nodded, acknowledging his suspicion.

"Did he tell you?" she asked.

"No." The intensity melted from his face, and his anger turned to sadness. "It was cruel to tell him."

"We argued. He accused me of being unfaithful. It's not true. We both had too much to drink, and it spilled out of me like a volcano that had been waiting to erupt all these years." She burst into tears, buried her face in her hands, and put her head on her knees.

He pulled her up and held her tight as she wept into his chest. "It's okay," he whispered. "It's okay."

They held a silent embrace for a long time. Then he kissed her on the cheek and let her go. From a nearby table, she grabbed a tissue and wiped her tears, then stuffed it in her pocket. He grabbed her limp hands and placed them together in his.

"Here's looking at you kid," he said.

Her eyes narrowed as a half-smile froze on her face.

Then he turned and walked out the door into a drizzling rain.

28

As he left the development, Bill looked again at the mini-mansions with cobblestone driveways and chandeliers glistening through glassed archways spanning ornate front doors. They were impressive but none were as pretty, he thought, as a certain little house in Wyoming.

A couple of miles past the exit gate, he stopped at a convenience store and went inside where he grabbed a beer from the cooler. Handing the clerk the money, he asked, "Do you have any scissors I can borrow? I'll give them right back."

The clerk looked at him suspiciously and answered "No", without bothering to look around her workstation.

After a minute of browsing the store, he found a small pair of scissors and returned to the counter. He paid for the scissors and dashed through the rain to his car under the canopy that covered the gas pumps. Sitting in the driver's seat, the beer fizzed as he snapped the ring tab and took a deep swig. The cold liquid tingled as it flowed through his bloodstream, yet had an oddly warming effect in his head. Then he lifted his wallet from his back pocket and took out the picture he had carried for so long. Grabbing the scissors, he went to work on the picture as the pieces fell into a small pile in the passenger seat. When the job was finished, he scooped up the laminated bits of yesterday and tossed them into the trashcan between the pumps.

Across the street he saw a church with no signs of life. He drove there and parked under a portico at a side door. Away from the busyness of the convenience store and shielded from the noise of the heavy rain beating down on the car, he took another big gulp of beer to calm his nerves. Realizing he was on church grounds, he felt a little heathen, but he figured he would make up for it with what he was about to do.

He reached for the phone his brother had loaned him, and called Joan.

"I didn't expect to hear from you again tonight," she said. "Is everything okay?"

He sensed the concern in her voice. "Yeah, everything is fine. I'm drinking a beer at church."

"Bill, are you drunk?"

"No, I'm sober as a Baptist in the front pew. I called because I really need to tell you something."

"What is it?" she replied, a tone of concern in her voice.

"I love you."

The phone went silent.

"Can you hear me?" he asked.

"Yes, I hear you. Please don't joke about this."

"I'm not joking and I'm not drunk. I love you and I can't hold it in any longer. I wish I could reach all the way to Wyoming and kiss you."

"I wish you could too."

He could hear the faint sound of crying and waited patiently for her to speak again. "I'm still here," she said.

"Good. I need to know if you feel the same way."

"You know I love you." The words didn't drown out her sniffles. "If you told me I would have to walk all the way to Alabama to ever see you again, I would start out the front door right now."

"That won't be necessary," he said. "But now I have to ask you something else."

"What?" There was apprehension in her voice.

"Will you marry me?"

He heard her begin to cry again. Finally, she said, "Bill, you're not supposed to propose to a lady over the telephone."

"Well, I figured if you said no, I could save the money of a flight back." He suppressed a grin as if she could see him from halfway across the country.

"You better come back," she said, "because I was lying when I said I would walk to Alabama."

In a serious tone he said, "I've known for a long time that I love you. I don't have much, you know, but I'm working on it."

"There's nothing you don't have that I need."

"That's good, because the only thing I don't have that I need is you. So?"

"So, yes, I'll marry you. Of course, I'll marry you, you...crazy... goofball, you."

"Good. I'll go to bed a happy man now."

"You won't be nearly as happy as I am. But I'll be happier when you get back."

"Yeah, then we can get in bed and really work up a happy time."

"You're such a rounder," she said through a laugh. He could almost see the smile on her face.

"I'll take that as a compliment from a Wyoming cowgirl. Well, anyway, I guess that's enough excitement for one night."

"Well, there's something..." Her voice trailed off.

"What?"

"Nothing," she said. "It can wait. I'll tell you when you get home."

"This is not a trick like that joker Toby pulled on me, is it?"

"No," she said in a whimsical voice. Then in a more sober tone, she said, "Don't hate me for asking this, but what about the pretty woman in that picture you showed me—Olivia? She's divorcing your brother, isn't she?"

"Yes. You know about her and me. I haven't kept anything from you. But I realize now why I carried that picture around with me all these years. It wasn't about her—it was about me. It was about remembering how things used to be and how they might have been. It caused me to lose a lot of years of my life. I can't get them back, but I don't want to lose any more. I think a lot of Olivia and I always will, but she's not you. That picture is gone, and I would rather have you in flesh and blood than any picture in the world."

The sound of joyful tears started again. "I love you," Joan said.

"I love you, too. I'll call tomorrow. Goodnight."

"Goodnight."

Bill put the receiver in its cradle and finished off the beer, feeling better than he had in more years than he could recall. The visit with Olivia and the emotional conversation with Joan had put his mind into overdrive. He dashed through the rain into the chilly night air and tossed the beer can in a dumpster behind the church. Then he pulled onto the road to go somewhere he hadn't been in more than thirty years.

He would only be in town for two more days, and there was a mission left undone. As he neared Branford, he saw the sign marking the road to Peavy, eighteen miles away. An irresistible attraction tugged at him as he made the turn onto the road as if caught in the force field of a giant magnet.

The dark, two-lane road wound through terrain of alternating wooded hillsides and flat fields. Houses were scattered sparsely along the way, and the road was all but deserted. He remembered how the little town of Peavy looked and wondered if any of it still remained. Especially, the low L-shaped building where he had paid the devil five-hundred dollars to fix his mistake.

The rain soon picked up again and big drops came down with a thudding noise against the car. With the wind slanting directly into the windshield, the visibility of the road almost disappeared. The edge of the blacktop blended into the narrow shoulder then dropped off sharply, so he kept his eyes focused on the white stripe of the centerline. Torrents of water ran in the ditches on both sides of the road, emptying into a creek heading toward the river.

Thunder boomed in the distance and bolts of lightning exploded nearby with the sudden fierceness of an artillery attack. It made no sense to keep going. He should stop and turn around, away from the driving force of the rain. But he had come this far, and the urge was too strong to stop now. He looked into the windshield with squinted eyes as the wipers fought against the sheets of water with a furious swoosh-swoosh beat.

In the distance he could barely see the Black Warrior River through a clearing in the trees to his left. Then rounding a curve, he saw a bridge. It was newer and bigger than the one he remembered. The rain let up slightly, and as the road straightened out, he could see the other side of the bridge which now covered the area where he had once parked at the base of the old bridge.

He pulled the car onto the shoulder of the road and could almost see a bag lying on the floorboard beside him. Stepping into the rainy darkness, he headed for the bridge as if he had no choice. No one was in sight but he knew he was being watched from above. Halfway across the span he stopped at the edge of the concrete wall. The Black Warrior River roiled over its banks and rushed furiously downstream.

He stood there for a long time, looking down and listening to the river roar past him like the last thirty years of his life. His mind turned back in time and even now he could see the blood stained sheet beneath Olivia and the bloody mass that the charlatan doctor left behind. It was a night that would always be a part of him. Yet some things have to be buried, he thought, just like loved ones who pass from the present but are never forgotten. And the living must go on.

Bill moved back a step and said, "God, forgive me."

At that moment, the cold rain felt cleansing, as if sent from heaven to wash away the blood. And he knew the river would carry away anything that was caught in its current.

Returning to the car, he quickened his pace until he was running as fast as he could. He felt lighter, freer than he had just minutes before. He sat in the car for several minutes, panting for breath. Though he was soaking wet and numb from the frigid air, he felt perfectly content. He closed his eyes and saw a crowd cheering wildly and a band playing at full blast as he scored a touchdown for the Warrior County Choctaws. Then he recalled the lean figure of a wise old man in Wyoming who believed in him. And, finally, he saw the glowing face of a woman who had saved him. A woman who loved him.

The rain stopped and he started the car, turned around and headed back to Branford. A minute later he looked in the rearview mirror and the bridge had disappeared completely. The old bridge no longer existed and maybe Peavy didn't either. He didn't care.

29

Joan walked into the break room and sat down beside her co-worker, Doris. She removed a sandwich and an apple from a paper bag. "I'm famished," she said, pouring hot tea from a small thermos into a cup.

Doris lifted a spoonful of fried rice to her mouth. "How's it going with your boyfriend? Is he still in Alabama?"

"Yeah, he'll be back Sunday." Joan grinned with a sly look as if holding back a secret.

Doris swallowed her food. "I haven't seen that look on your face in a while. In fact, I'm not sure I've ever seen that look. Things are heating up between you two, aren't they?"

Joan kept grinning. "Well, kind of. We enjoy each other's company."

"That's a cop-out if I ever heard one. A cat is something you have around for company. I think you have more feelings than that about Bill. And he does for you, too, or he wouldn't have hung around so long."

Joan took a bite of her sandwich and a gulp of tea as Doris ate another spoonful of rice.

"You're a different person since you met this guy. More outgoing. More...perky. I'm happy for you. "

"Thanks. But perky?"

"You know, like a woman in love. Any day, I expect you to come in here and tell me he's made an honest woman out of you."

"Honest?" The word stung and Joan was offended.

"Oh, don't give me that holier than thou stuff. He needs to marry you. You're too much a prize for him to pass up."

Joan started to tell her friend the news, then hesitated with her mouth frozen open. She was dying to tell her about the phone call last night but was determined to wait until Bill returned to make any marriage announcements. Instead she changed the subject "How did your review with Harold go?"

"It went well. He said I was good with the customers but I need to talk less and listen more." Both women laughed.

I'll tell her Monday morning and there will be plenty to talk about. The smile lingered on Joan's face and then she had another thought. *Joan Burdette—that sounds nice.* The name stuck in her mind and, like a favorite song that keeps repeating in your head, wouldn't go away.

Joan went straight to Hank's assisted living home after work. The parking lot had been cleared and only a few inches of snow lined the perimeter. Inside, the air was warm and fresh with a scent of pine. After checking in, she made her way down a quiet hall to Hank's room.

"Hi," she said, as she saw him sitting in a padded chair next to a window.

He labored with a guttural response of "Hi."

Joan pulled a side chair next to Hank, turned it to face him and spoke slowly. His eyes were bright and, although he had a hard time speaking, she knew he understood what she was saying.

"Bill's in Alabama," she said.

Hank nodded a little and slowly said the word "Alabama" with a deep slur.

Joan touched his arm. "You don't have to talk." I know it's not easy. I just wanted to see you and tell you something.

Hank looked out the window and pointed.

"Yes, it snowed," she said. "It's cold outside but it feels so fresh. I don't think it snows much in Alabama."

Hank put a hand up and turned his head aside as if to agree that snow wasn't common in the south. Joan remembered that he was a Navy vet and surely knew more than she did about the rest of the world.

"Hank, there's something I want tell you because if I don't tell someone, I might burst wide open."

He opened his eyes wide.

"Bill asked me to marry him."

Hank beamed with a smile.

She stood and leaned down to give him a hug. "Of course, I said yes and I'm thrilled." Then she walked to the window and stared at the sun glistening off the snow. Turning to him, she said, "I've always wanted a child."

He nodded and she hugged him again, holding the embrace until her runaway heartbeat slowed down. Then she kissed him on the cheek. "Love you," she said.

"Wuv vou," Hank said, the words forced from deep inside.

The words stirred in her head just as they had when Bill said them the night before. It was a good feeling and she cherished saying them as much as hearing them. She sensed that Hank felt the same way.

When she left the building, Joan hesitated before starting the car. Bill would be home the next day and she couldn't wait. *He'll be happy about it,* she thought. *I know he will be.* She put her hand on her stomach and could almost feel something growing inside.

30

Four months later, Bill returned to Alabama to be with his father in his last days. This time he didn't travel alone. Instead, he was accompanied by his new bride, Joan, who had never met any of his family.

"I'm so glad to have you in our family," Alice said, warmly embracing her new daughter-in-law just inside the doorway.

"And so am I," Jack said, stepping forward to give Joan a quick hug.

Bill walked in, hugged his mother and shook hands with Jack.

"Bill tells me how sweet you are and, coming from him, that's quite a mouthful." Alice smiled at her son, who rolled his eyes.

Bill looked at Joan. "I didn't say *sweet*. However, in Alabama, that's a good thing."

"Yeah, real good," Jack echoed.

Joan laughed. "Thank you, Mrs. Burdette. But I know I could never live up to what Bill thinks of *you*."

"Okay," Bill said, "That's enough of that."

"Sit down," Alice said. "I know you must be tired."

"That's all we've done all day." Bill said. "Drive, fly, sit. But somehow, I'm worn out and I know she is."

"Oh, yes!" Alice said with her eyes lit up. "How do you feel?"

"I'm fine," Joan said.

Bill and Joan settled on the couch, Alice in a wingback chair, and Jack took a seat in his father's favorite recliner.

"When's the big day?" asked Jack.

Joan smiled and said, "November eighteenth."

After several minutes of get-acquainted talk, Bill asked, "Is Dad awake?"

"No," Alice replied, "but you can look in. The medicine keeps him asleep most of the time."

"It's good," Jack added. "He's not in pain."

"I'll be right back," Bill said to Joan. As he stepped away, he heard his mother renew the conversation with Joan in an animated voice as if her spirits had been lifted.

Bill cracked the door to the second bedroom, the room he shared with Jack as a boy, and saw his father lying in bed on his back with his eyes closed. A lamp on a side table provided the only light. He walked in and stood looking down at his father for a moment. Then he sat in a familiar swivel rocker that had been relocated from the master bedroom.

The room was quiet and Bill could barely hear his father breathe. He sat motionless and lost track of time, oblivious to the small clock beside the bed. Then his father rolled onto his side and opened his eyes halfway. "Billy," he said weakly.

"Hi, Dad."

"You get married?"

"Yeah."

Jim moved a thin arm toward Bill. "Gimme a shake."

Bill stood, gently took his father's limp hand, and moved it up and down a couple of inches.

Jim's eyes rolled back and his lids closed. "I'm proud of you, son," he whispered.

A tear streamed down Bill's face and he felt like his heart might explode. "I'm proud of you, too, Dad. I'll try to be half as good a father as you are." He didn't know if his father heard him or understood. He only knew that he had been given a second chance and he would never forget that promise to his father.

Bill and Joan stayed with Jack for the next week before

returning to Cheyenne. On the flight home, Bill looked out the window and said, "I don't think I'll ever see Dad alive again."

He turned and put his hand in hers. "He's lived a good life. It's time."

***

Two weeks later, Bill held Joan's hand as his father's casket was lowered into the ground near the big dogwood tree. Adjacent was the spot where his mother would someday join him. Nearby, The Coach rested in peace at the spot where the red line meets the white line. A gray cloud covered the sky and a shroud of finality hung in the air. Three days had passed and the tears had turned to sorrow buried deep inside but now they began to flow again. When Bill finished saying a few words to his father's soul, he hugged his mother, then his brother.

Afterward, her sons helped Alice into Jack's car. Bill turned and took Joan's hand and Olivia stepped to Jack to place her arm in his. Bill thought it was strange considering their still-impending divorce.

Jack spoke to Olivia in a quiet voice and then she walked away to her car. "Olivia and I are working on things," he said, as he got into his car.

Bill was shocked. "That's great," he replied, almost by sheer reflex.

Bill felt the promise of renewed devotion mixed with the pall of death, all wrapped together in a giant ball of emotion. It's amazing, he thought, how confusing love can be sometimes.

The next day, Bill followed Jack's directions to the old high school in Branford. He and Joan found the school empty during the summer break, but were able to get in a side door. The building was badly in need of repairs and Jack had told them it was to be demolished and replaced by a new school the following year. They walked down the corridor, which was well lit by daylight pouring through the large windows in front of the building. In the center of the main hall facing the entrance was a large glass case filled with trophies and surrounded by a hundred or more framed pictures and memorabilia. A large red and blue banner spread overhead: *RIVERVIEW RAIDERS.*

They had just begun looking at the pictures and trophies when they were approached by a gray-haired black man who appeared from an office down the hall. As he approached, Bill gave a prearranged silent sign with an inconspicuous finger to his mouth.

"Hello. May I help you?" the man said. He looked to be about fifty.

"I hope we're not trespassing," Bill replied. "We just wanted to look around before they tear the building down."

"That'll be a while—next year some time. But you're welcome to look around."

"This used to be called Warrior County High School," Bill said.

"Yes, for a long time it was. But a few years ago the county combined two schools—Warrior County and J.W. Nash—into one community school. They wanted to create a sense of unity among all of the students, so they changed the name to Riverview."

"That's interesting," Joan said.

"I'm the Athletic Director. Football coach, too. That means I get to explain to whiny parents why their precious little boy doesn't get to play in every game. Or why I had to kick him off the team because he was being a knucklehead." He caught himself in a rant. "I'm sorry. I was just on the phone with one of those whiny parents."

"I hope we didn't bother you," Joan said.

"No, no, it's no bother. You're welcomed here." He glanced at Bill before asking Joan, "Are y'all from around here?"

"We're from Wyoming," Joan said. "Bill went to school here."

"Wyoming?" The man looked at Bill and said, "What took you way out there?

Bill smiled. "It's a long story. Real long." He started to say something else but Joan cut him off.

"Bill played football here." She paused and grinned at Bill. "In the fifties, I think."

The comment brought a feigned grimace to Bill's face. "Late fifties," he said.

"What's your full name?" the man asked, a studied look on his face.

"Bill Burdette." The hint of a smile creased his face.

"Billy Burdette? He sure as heck did play football here," the man said, looking at Joan. "The old Branford Bazooka. He was terrific, probably the best player ever to come out of this school. Look over here," he said, pointing to a trophy.

Joan moved closer to read the inscription:

Billy Burdett
1959 Most Valuable Player
First Team All-State

"Now look over here." He showed her a team picture labeled *1959 Alabama State Champions.* "That's him in the middle, holding the ball—number twenty-two."

She studied the picture and smiled, recalling the man's description. "The Branford Bazooka—that's funny."

He then showed her the other pictures on the wall arranged by year. In the earlier years, pictures of the all-white Warrior County Choctaws in red and white uniforms were lined up beside the all-black Nash Wildcats in blue and white uniforms. As the years progressed, the colors on the faces of the players in red and white uniforms grew darker. In 1980, the colors of all the uniforms changed to blue and red as if they had been blended together and the team identified as the Riverview Raiders.

"I'm going to move all of this stuff to the new school in a couple of weeks," the man said. "That's another fringe benefit of being the head jock around here. Ha!"

"Hey Joan, look at this," Bill said. "That's Zippy Willingham. He's the best player that ever came out of Branford." He pointed to a picture of a black player, wearing number twenty-two on his Pittsburgh Steelers uniform. The picture was labeled:

Zee "Zippy" Willingham
J. W. Nash High School 1959-1962
Michigan State, All American 1966
Pittsburgh Steelers 1969—1981
NFL First Team All Pro

"Zee," Joan said, recognizing the name below the picture. "I know that name. Bill has talked a lot about Zee. He loved him to death. Do you know him?"

The man fiddled with his white goatee. "Yes ma'am...uh...that's me."

Her mouth dropped, and she looked at him oddly, then back to Bill who had a grin plastered all over his face.

The two men burst out in hysterical laughter, shook hands, and continued to laugh like school kids.

"Bill! You set me up, darn your hide."

Bill stopped laughing but couldn't keep the smile off his face. He put his arm around Joan and pulled her tight. "Oh, I love you." He kissed her on the cheek. "You're a good sport."

She sighed and then grinned. "The things I have to put up with," she said, looking at Zee.

"I'll bet." He shook his head and then turned aside. "There's a picture of my team over there." He pointed to the cluster of pictures of Nash High teams. "Billy was older than me, and we couldn't have played together if we wanted to in those days. But I saw him play many times, and he was very good. He could've played at Alabama if he hadn't gotten hurt."

"Remember," Bill interrupted, "I told you Zee was there at the quarry. He and Jack saved my life."

"I don't know about saving anybody's life but, yes, I was there when he got hurt," Zee said, looking at Joan.

She put her arms around Zee. "Thank you." Then she walked back to the picture with young Billy Burdette in the middle.

"Bill was a really good player, wasn't he?"

"Oh, come on," Bill said, faking embarrassment.

"Yes, he was very good."

"Well, you know what?" Bill asked rhetorically. "That was a long time ago. What matters now is I'm going to be a daddy." He patted Joan's stomach.

"Well congratulations." Zee seemed to pick-up on Bill's exuberance, typical of a new father. "Is this your first?"

A sobering thought hit Bill but he responded quickly. "Yeah."

"Well, three more and you'll catch up with me."

Joan spoke up. "I don't think so."

"No, we got a late start," Bill said. He moved to Zee and gave him a man hug. "Great to see you again, Zip. Good luck you old river rat."

"Same to you, Zooka." Zee gazed at Bill for a second with a glint in his eye and then headed back to his office.

Bill and Joan joined hands and walked out of the building to the car.

"I'm glad you brought me here," she said, as they drove away.

"So am I." A moment later he added, "I think the world of Zee."

"I can tell he feels the same way about you." She put a hand out and patted his knee. "And so do I—daddy."

He exhaled a deep breath of air. *Daddy—that sounds good*, he thought. *That sounds very good.*

In November, William James Burdette, Jr., was born. They call him Billy.

POSTSCRIPT

I was born in Alabama and lived the first twenty-two years of my life in the state. For most of that time, I lived in Birmingham, which in my youth was a bustling industrial city forged by coal, iron, and steelworks. The "Pittsburg of the South," it was called. I have many fond memories of growing up there and still call it my hometown. Later, I moved to Tuscaloosa to attend the state University, from which I received two degrees and spent one year as a full time Instructor.

Segregation was the law of the land in the South during those years and, even as a young boy, I wondered how that could still be possible so long after the Civil War. When the Civil Rights movement heated up in the early 1960's, I found myself caught in a conflict of historic racial animosity. That conflict has been well documented over the years and I could not write this book without recognizing the times in which much of it is set. Some scenes in the book are taken from personal experience.

I say all of this in an effort to put things in perspective. The resistance to fully recognize the human rights of all citizens in the South was a tragic mistake and doomed to failure. Blame for that can be placed in many hands, the most guilt belonging to those in powerful public offices. But that time has passed. Today Birmingham struggles to revive its economy like many cities that once relied on an engine of heavy industry which now sits idle.

But the people survive, even thrive, and live among themselves, free from the yoke of institutional separation. And the University of Alabama remains a stalwart institution of higher learning of which I am a proud alumnus. In the novel, "Branford wasn't just a place to Billy; it was as much a part of him as the blue in his eyes." And so it is with me and Alabama; it's in my DNA. My family tree is firmly rooted there and, like any loyal son, I will always be true to my family.

Although I have attempted to keep the setting as authentic as possible, it is a work of fiction. The towns of Branford and Peavy as well as Warrior County exist only in my imagination. But the Black Warrior River definitely does exist, as anyone who lives in the area can attest. A cemetery is also mentioned in the book and refers to Elmwood, a large public cemetery in Birmingham. The legendary Alabama football coach, Paul "Bear" Bryant, is buried there. At the entrance of the cemetery, the road is marked with a red line and a white line, each following a different route until they converge at the foot of Coach Bryant's gravesite. My parents are buried nearby.

As for Wyoming, I have been a visitor to the state but have never lived there. I've always admired the beautiful rugged scenery of that part of our country and it's like being in a different world from Alabama. But I have found that people are much the same across the United States, regardless of accents and backgrounds. And, while I have stated my pride in my native state, I'm even prouder to be an American.

In writing this book, I had no political or social agenda. It is not intended to be rigidly anti-abortion with disregard to circumstance, though I do not judge those who take such a position. That is a question I leave to the conscience and belief of the individual. Rather, it is a story of the power of redemption. And I believe the road to redemption begins with faith in God's grace that leads to a path of self-forgiveness.

ABOUT THE AUTHOR

Michael K. Brown, known to friends simply as Mike, was born in Alabama and grew up in Birmingham. A graduate of the University of Alabama, he has lived in the Atlanta area for most of his adult life. He held management positions for three major companies before leaving the corporate world. *Somewhere a River* is his second novel to be published. His first novel, *Promise of Silver,* was released in May, 2014, by Ingalls Publishing Company. Presently, Mike lives in Loganville, Georgia, where he and his wife, Judy, own and operate a flooring business. They have three sons and three grandchildren.

www.ingramcontent.com/pod-product-compliance
Lightning Source LLC
Chambersburg PA
CBHW061530210726
48287CB00006B/1902